Robin—

ILLUSTRIOUS

QUANTUM SERIES, BOOK 9

Enjoy Max & Stella!

MARIE FORCE

Illustrious
Quantum Series, Book 9

By: Marie Force
Published by HTJB, Inc.
Copyright 2025. HTJB, Inc.
Cover Design by Ashley Lopez
Layout: E-book Formatting Fairies
ISBN: 978-1966871019

Cover Models: Bob and Arlene Bouley on the eve of their 1958 wedding, used with the permission of the Bouley family.

HTJB, Inc.
PO Box 370
Portsmouth, RI 02871 USA
marie@marieforce.com

The Quantum Series

Book 1: Virtuous *(Flynn & Natalie)*
Book 2: Valorous *(Flynn & Natalie)*
Book 3: Victorious *(Flynn & Natalie)*
Book 4: Rapturous *(Addie & Hayden)*
Book 5: Ravenous *(Jasper & Ellie)*
Book 6: Delirious *(Kristian & Aileen)*
Book 7: Outrageous *(Emmett & Leah)*
Book 8: Famous *(Marlowe & Sebastian)*
Book 9: Illustrious *(Max & Stella)*
Book 10: Momentous *(Olivia's story, coming 2026)*

With much love and so many happy memories, this book is dedicated to my parents' best friends and my cover models, Arlene and Bob Bouley, a love story for the ages.

A NOTE FROM MARIE

I took a few liberties with the timeline in this book, including moving Max and Stella's anniversary from January to December, so I could write this story the way I envisioned it. I hope you enjoy this visit with the Quantum family, which has exploded in numbers since we last saw them. xo Marie

CHAPTER 1

Max

I start the day before my fiftieth wedding anniversary the same way I've begun my days for most of my adult life—with the industry trades that keep me up to date on the latest Hollywood news and gossip. I've never outgrown my desire to know everything that goes on in this town. *Variety* and *The Hollywood Reporter* are the two weeklies I never miss in print. My tech-savvy kids make fun of me for preferring print, but I'm old-school that way. I like the feel of paper in my hands as I enjoy my morning coffee. I'm not a complete dinosaur, however, as I also subscribe to the online versions, mostly to get the daily updates and alerts when something big happens.

Show business has two speeds: molasses when you're trying to get a project green-lighted and lightning when the shit hits the fan. I'm perusing the latest issue of *Variety* when I see it, a small piece about Vivian Stevens publishing a memoir in which she'll share her "deepest, darkest secrets."

My heartbeat slows to a crawl, and I nearly choke on my coffee.

At least one of her deepest, darkest secrets is also mine.

She wouldn't dare write about me, would she?

As if a trapdoor has opened under me, I'm hurled fifty-three years into a past I buried so deeply, even my beloved wife knows nothing about it.

Dear Christ in heaven...

This weekend, Stella and I will celebrate our golden anniversary, first with a family dinner tomorrow night, and then with five hundred of our family and friends on Saturday. Then we're headed to St. George, Utah, for Christmas with the family I value beyond all the professional accolades, above the fame, the fortune and the many perks of celebrity. My wife, children, grandchildren and our tight-knit group of friends are my whole world. The possibility of anything threatening my marriage or family is a nuclear-level concern to me.

After Christmas, we're spending ten days in Mexico with the family and the huge posse of friends who are like family. We've been looking forward to these next few weeks for months, and the thought of none of it happening because of me and my fifty-three-year-old secret is unbearable.

I'm as rattled as I've been in years when I pick up the phone to call my son, Flynn, who's also my closest friend. His celebrity has eclipsed mine and his mother's many times over, and not only am I incredibly proud of him, but I also I love him deeply and respect his opinion. He's street-smart and savvy in a way I'll never be, which is what I need right now.

After three rings, the call goes to voicemail.

"Flynn, it's Dad. I need to see you. Immediately. Call me."

I can't believe the way my hands tremble as I set down the phone. While I wait for him to call me back, I force myself to read the item about Vivian's upcoming memoir.

STAR OF SCREEN AND STAGE VIVIAN STEVENS TO 'SPILL THE TEA' ON COSTARS, HUSBANDS AND LOVERS IN HIGHLY ANTICIPATED MEMOIR

Superstar Vivian Stevens will soon publish a memoir spanning her more than fifty-year career in movies and television. Known for her sultry beauty as much as her many husbands, Stevens won her first Oscar, for Best Actress, in 1983 for her performance in the revival of Funny Girl. *She*

*went on to win a Best Supporting Actress Oscar ten years later in Marlon
Jacobs's tour-de-force film* Santana, *which swept awards season that year.*

*She's also a three-time Emmy Award winner for her longtime role as
the formidable matriarch Tess Lawson on* Collaboration, *and a Tony
winner for the 2005 revival of* My Fair Lady.

*Despite her many professional accomplishments, Stevens is perhaps
best known for her messy personal life, which has included six husbands,
one child, four divorces and the suspicious death of her third husband,
stuntman Brock Lawton, whose murder remains unsolved thirty years
later.*

*"I've worked with everyone who's anyone," Stevens said in a release
issued by her publisher ahead of the book's late January release. "I've kept a
few secrets that'll shock the world, and I'm ready to tell the true story
behind the glitz and glamour. And* what *a story it is."*

*A bidding war is on behind the scenes to secure the rights to the book's
first excerpt, due to be released in early January.*

I'm going to be sick. Vivian had *seven* husbands. I was the first, but
no one knows that. It was over before it began, forgotten almost as
fast as it happened.

The one person who doesn't know, who can't *ever* know, is my
beloved wife, Stella, who hates Vivian Stevens with the heat of a
thousand suns.

That thought registers one second before the scone I had for
breakfast erupts onto my copy of *Variety* along with two cups of coffee
and whatever was left from last night.

I roll up the mess and drop it in the trash before I go into the
bathroom that adjoins my office to splash cold water on my face and
brush my teeth. My stomach roils with more bile that I spit into the
sink.

This secret has the potential to blow up my entire life and everything I hold dear.

I'll have to tell Stella—and the kids—about Vivian before they
hear it from someone else.

They'll hate me for this.

I hate myself for it.

Our golden anniversary celebration, Christmas, the trip to Mexico... Hell, the rest of my life with Stella is suddenly at risk, which is something I never would've thought possible before this morning.

Another surge of nausea has me hanging over the toilet with the dry heaves.

My cell rings in the other room. I grab a hand towel and hurry to answer it, hoping it's Flynn. I'm relieved to see the name he gave himself in my phone, No. 1 Son, on the caller ID. Our only son is the youngest of our four children.

"Hey."

"What's up, Dad? You sounded weird on that message."

"Can you come over? Now?"

"As in today?"

"Flynn... Please."

"Are you sick? Is Mom?"

"Nothing like that, but it's *urgent.*"

"Let me move some stuff around. I'll be there as soon as I can."

"Thank you."

I hit the red button to end the call and put the phone on my desk as I drop into my chair, turning to face the garden. I need something to stare at while I wait for Flynn. He'll know what to do. He gets shit done in this town. He knows everyone, and everyone knows him. His Oscar-winning career is among the proudest things in my life.

Will a massive scandal that involves me ruin everything for him? For his partners and closest friends at Quantum Productions? They're like extra children to Stella and me. Are they successful enough in their own right that something blowing up for me can't touch them?

The possibility that a mistake I made years ago could come back to haunt my wife, our family, Flynn and his partners is the most terrifying thing that's ever happened to me.

I've rarely experienced this level of fear. My life has been blessed beyond all measure with true love, family, friends, success, money... I have it all, which means I also have everything to lose.

Flynn

"Something's up with my dad," I tell my wife, Natalie, when she emerges from the bathroom after a shower. I'm holding our youngest son, Bennett, who's three months old today and not interested in his morning nap.

I watch as she rubs lotion on her arms, which drives me wild, but then everything she does turns me on as much as it did more than six years ago when we first met. "What do you mean?"

"He left a frantic-sounding message that he needs to see me right away, and when I talked to him, he said it was urgent but not a health issue for him or Mom."

"Well, that's a relief." She runs a brush through her long, dark, wet hair. That, too, is sexy. Hell, she's sexy when she breathes. As much as I've loved her from the start, seeing her as a mother to our four children has made me adore her more than I ever thought possible. "I'll take Ben. You need to get over there."

"Is it weird that I'm afraid of whatever he's going to tell me? I've never heard him sound like he did on that message."

"Play it for me."

While juggling Ben, I find the message on my phone, put it on speaker and press Play, adding volume so she can hear it.

She listens intently. "He does sound strange." She takes Ben from me. "I've got things covered here."

"We've got the foundation meeting this afternoon."

"I'll handle it. Take care of your dad."

I stand to kiss her and Ben. "I'll do my best to make the school pickup." Our oldest, Cecelia, known as Cece, is almost six and in kindergarten at the same school where her two younger siblings, Scarlett and Rowen, attend preschool. They love the school and can't wait to get there every day.

"Text me if you need me to do it."

"In case I forget to tell you later, you're the glue that holds this whole thing together."

"Duh, I know."

Smiling, I kiss her a second time because I can never resist her. That's been the case from the first day we met, when her crazy dog, Fluff, bit me in a Greenwich Village park. Best thing to ever happen to me.

Fluff, a fifteen-pound ball of fur who's now at least a hundred and twenty in dog years, lifts her head off her bed to give me a suspicious look. She's probably remembering the time she bit my ass when I was face-first in my beloved. I'm sure that's one of her favorite memories.

"Let me know what's up with your dad."

"I will, and I'll be home as soon as I can."

"We'll be here."

As I collect my wallet and keys, I don't want to go. I don't want to hear whatever he has to say. I don't want anything about my blessed life to change. I'm the luckiest son of a bitch on the face of the earth, and I know it. I have the best wife, children, parents, sisters, nieces, nephews, friends and partners. My career is on fire, and I'm still madly in love with my wife after all these years together.

Before Nat, I would've told you I already had it all, but that wasn't even close to true. I needed her and our four incredible kids to show me what truly matters in this life.

I drive an SUV full of child seats these days, albeit a black Mercedes GLS 450 AMG. My days of being a car slut are mostly in the past, even if I keep my collection in climate-controlled buildings that're my son Rowan's favorite places to visit. We had his second birthday party there a few weeks ago.

On the way down the hill that leads into town, I dictate a text to my dad. *On the way.*

At the next light, I see that he read it, but he doesn't reply.

I want to call my sisters to ask if they know what's going on, but my dad sounded so strange that I decide to keep this situation to myself until after I see him. If needed, I'll call the girls then.

The "girls" are the three older sisters who treated me like a baby until I was thirty and begged them to knock it off. Most of the time, they treat me like a grown-up, but they still backslide every now and then.

I take a call from Hayden Roth, my best friend and business partner. "What's up?"

"Hey, so Cammy Smith is in town and wants a meeting with us."

A meeting with one of the hottest young actresses in the business would be a top priority at any other time.

"Can you set it up for tomorrow?"

"She was hoping for this afternoon."

"I can't today. I've got some family stuff to deal with."

"Everything okay?"

"I hope so. How are Addie and the girls feeling?" Hayden's entire family has been down hard with the stomach flu for the last two weeks. He's the only one who's escaped the plague.

"Better, thankfully. We're good to go for the party and vacation."

"I'm glad they rallied in time."

"Me, too. I would've hated to leave them at home alone for Christmas."

I laugh, because Hayden hates to go anywhere without his four baby girls.

"I'll get with Cammy's team and set something up for tomorrow. I'll text you the details."

"Thanks."

After I end the call, I change lanes twice in rapid succession, wanting to get to my parents' house in Beverly Hills, handle whatever's happening with my dad and get to the kids' school in time for pickup so Nat will have one less thing to do this afternoon. I've got an hour to give my dad before I'll have to leave to get there in time.

Cece gets nervous if we're late, so we try not to be, although we've reminded her that LA traffic sometimes results in snafus. We also had to tell her what a snafu is without fully explaining the acronym. Thinking about that makes me smile as I recall Nat and me fumbling our way through it the way we do most things with our sharp-as-a-tack five-year-old. She keeps us on our game, and we wouldn't have it any other way.

Let me tell you... Having four kids in six years isn't for the faint of heart, but as I'm about to turn forty on Christmas Day, we moved quickly to have the big family we both wanted. Luckily, my bride is ten years younger than me, which comes in handy, especially after a sleepless night with a fussy baby. Nothing fazes her when it comes to our kids. She was born to be a mother. Whereas a night without sleep wrecks their old man.

I pull into the driveway at my parents' palatial home and park behind my dad's black Escalade. He's remained true to the Cadillac brand even as foreign cars became all the rage. It's one of many things I tease him about.

I enter the house through the breezeway door that connects the kitchen to the three-car garage. I'm surprised to find my dad standing by the massive kitchen island, looking as shell-shocked as he sounded on the phone. "What's wrong?"

He brightens slightly at the sight of me and gestures for me to follow him down the hallway to his office.

I go in ahead of him, and he closes a door that's almost always left open. Max Godfrey doesn't like being sealed off from his family. "You're scaring me."

He sits behind the desk where he's held court, as my sisters and I call it, since we were little kids. My earliest memories occurred in this room as I watched in awe while my dad talked business with some of the biggest stars in the world, helping to put together projects that would go on to be monster hits. He's as successful a producer as he is an actor and has the awards on the shelf to prove it.

"Did you see the news this morning about Vivian Stevens writing a memoir?"

"I haven't seen any news today. What about it?"

"It was in *Variety*. Talked about how she's spilling her deepest, darkest secrets."

"So what?"

He looks agonized as he says, "I'm probably her deepest, darkest secret, and when the book is released next month, my life—and my marriage to your mother—will be ruined."

CHAPTER 2

Flynn

My dad has been an actor his entire adult life, but he's never been a drama queen, nor does he exaggerate. To hear him speak in such dire terms makes my knees weak as I drop into one of the plush chairs in front of his desk. The most serious conversations of childhood took place there, covering every topic from grades to girls to sports to the right thing to do in any situation.

"What're you talking about, Dad? What does Vivian Stevens have on you, and what's it got to do with Mom?"

He leans forward, resting his chin on his hands. "A couple of years before I met your mother, I was... I was *involved* with Vivian."

"Okay..."

"Your mother hates her guts."

"What? Mom doesn't hate anyone."

"She *hates* Vivian. She stole your mother's first fiancé right out from under her nose, as your mom puts it, while pretending to be her friend."

"Wait. Mom was *engaged* before you?"

"Yes, to Jonah Street."

"*What?*" Nothing has ever shocked me more. My mom and *Jonah Street*? What the actual hell? He was the star of *Thunder Row*, the first film I was in as a green twenty-two-year-old, determined to make my way in the business that'd made my parents famous.

"They'd been engaged for a very short time while they shot *London Town* with Vivian. According to your mother, Jonah was all about her until Vivian swooped in with no respect whatsoever for their existing relationship. Mom said Vivian made it her goal in life to land that man, no matter who she had to steamroll to get him."

"Damn. And he went for it?"

"Men were positively dazzled by Vivian in her heyday. She was incredibly beautiful and absolute magic on film. Not that your mother wasn't a stunner, too, because she was—and is. But Vivian had this fearless sexiness to her that made men nearly feral for her. It's hard to explain what I mean because everything is so different now. Most women are fearless in their sexuality and in command of their own lives and destinies. It wasn't like that back then, except if you were Vivian Stevens. I learned later that much of her moxie was a façade, but it worked for her. She had the attention of the whole world."

I'm still stuck on the fact that my mother was engaged to Jonah Street—and that she, who banned the word *hate* in our home while we were growing up, hates Vivian Stevens.

"Mom was humiliated by him leaving her for Vivian. There was a nasty screaming match on the *London Town* set that derailed her career for a time. It was ugly, and she's never forgiven either of them."

"Is this why she was so opposed to me doing *Thunder Row*?"

He nods. "She was outraged that Jonah had advocated for you to be cast. She felt like he was screwing with her by working with you. But she didn't want to do anything to mess up the opportunity for you, so she gritted her teeth and kept her mouth shut."

"Wow, the stuff that goes on that you never know about."

"Yes, exactly, and that's how I find myself in a terrible spot. This thing with Vivian and Jonah happened before I met Mom. It blew up into a massive story after Mom lost her shit with Vivian on the set and called her a whore. The whole town was still talking about the showdown between them when I met Mom."

"So you've never told her you were with Vivian?"

He shakes his head.

"Dad. Seriously? In more than fifty years together, that's never come up?"

"I would've been afraid to mention her name around your mother. That's how much she loathes her. Mom believes that Vivian didn't just steal her fiancé, but she also made sure she was blacklisted in the business. Mom couldn't get an acting job after that to save her life."

"Is that why she shifted her focus to music?"

"That's exactly why. She blames Vivian for ruining her acting career. Believe it or not, that was her first love."

"I can't picture her as anything other than a singer."

"She came to love it, but she never got over the way she lost control of her career or who caused that to happen."

"I'm sure if you tell her the truth after all this time, she'll understand why you didn't tell her then."

"There's more."

I'm afraid to ask what he means.

"I wasn't just involved with Vivian."

I've gone from afraid to terrified in the span of one sentence. "What do you mean?"

"I was married to her for eight months."

This must be what it feels like to have a potential scandal threaten the foundation upon which entire lives, including mine, have been built. "*What?*" That's all I can manage to say. "You're telling me Mom doesn't know that, and now Vivian is poised to publish a book that could blow the lid off that secret?" My voice gets higher and shriller as that sentence unfolds.

"Yes."

"*Oh my God*, Dad. How did you keep a marriage between two stars a secret?"

"Our manager at the time, Bobby Scott, was livid that we'd gotten married. He insisted we keep it secret, or he'd drop us. We were fine with that. Vivian feared losing her sexy edge if people found out she was married. I had similar concerns. You may find it hard to believe that your dear old dad was ever a sex symbol, but it would've hurt my career, too. It wasn't like it is now, when you couldn't possibly keep something like that private. No one ever knew except Bobby and the lawyers who negotiated the divorce."

Normally, I'd curl my lip up at the reminder that Bobby Scott, who later turned out to be a scumbag, managed my dad's career for a time. I'd also have something to say about him referring to himself as a sex symbol, but the only response I have to this information is, "Holy shit."

"I don't know what to do."

I've never once heard my father say those words. He *always* knows what to do.

As I withdraw my phone from my pocket, I realize shock and fear have me truly shaken, which is something else that almost never happens. I send a text to Natalie. *My dad needs me. Can you do the school pickup?* I hate to ask her, because she'll have to take the baby, which is a lot for one person to manage, but I can't leave now.

While I wait for her to reply, I text my friend Emmett Burke, the chief counsel at our company, Quantum Productions. *I need you to come to my parents' house right away. 911-level legal emergency.*

Nat replies first. *No problem. Is everything ok?*

Yeah, but he needs me. I'll explain when I get home.

Take your time. I've got the kids and will do the foundation meeting by Zoom. No worries.

Thank you. Love you.

Love you, too. Call if you need me.

I will.

"I've asked Emmett to come here," I tell my dad.

"What're you thinking?"

"I don't even know yet. I'm still processing the last fifteen minutes."

"I'm so afraid your mother will leave me."

The thought of my parents as anything other than blissfully happy together strikes fear in my heart. "She won't, Dad. She loves you."

"She'll say she never knew me at all."

"She'll understand why you didn't tell her."

"Will she? Would you? If Natalie didn't tell you she was married before she met you, would you forgive her for keeping that secret for years?"

"If she'd done it to protect my feelings, I suppose I'd try to understand."

"Your mother, who's the most reasonable person any of us has ever met, is positively *un*reasonable when it comes to Vivian Stevens. She's like a bull seeing red when the woman's name is mentioned. She won't be able to get past this."

All I can think of is the massive party my sisters and I have planned for this weekend to celebrate their fiftieth anniversary. Everyone who's anyone in our lives will be there, a total of more than five hundred guests coming to Hayden and Addie's home, where a tent is being erected in anticipation of the big event.

We told them it's a birthday party for Hayden and Addie's daughter Lily, but they know the truth. My mother despises surprises. We learned that lesson the hard way when she turned fifty, and we threw a party she wasn't properly turned out for—in her opinion, anyway. We've never made that mistake again. "I can't believe you didn't tell her you had a first wife."

"To be honest, I'd mostly forgotten about it. It's not like we talk about Vivian or what went on all those years ago. I never give that woman a thought until someone mentions her name, or she's on *Extra* or *Access Hollywood* or something, which doesn't happen much these days. Otherwise, she's not part of our lives."

My phone buzzes with a text from Emmett. *I'm on my way.*

Let me know when you're here. I'll let you in.

"Emmett's coming."

"Will I have to tell him this?"

I stare at Dad, incredulous. "If you want his help in figuring out what to do about it, then yes, you have to tell him. And I hate to say it, but you have to tell Mom, too."

He's shaking his head before I finish the sentence. "I can't."

"Dad... You're sitting on a live grenade. If the woman has written a book, people already know about you and her. There're editors and marketing people reading it, not to mention excerpts probably going live at any minute if the book is out in January."

He goes pale. "The people working on it must be under NDAs."

"Probably, but my point is people already know. You have to tell Mom before she hears it from someone else."

"I can't tell her this. I simply cannot."

"You have no choice, unless you want to wait around for the grenade to explode in her face with no warning."

He drops his head into his hands and moans. "She'll never forgive me."

"You two have had a wonderful run together. Surely she'll understand why you kept this from her back in the day."

"Will she? I'm not at all certain of that."

"She loves you. I'm sure of that. You've built an amazing family and life for yourselves. I can't imagine one of you without the other. You have to tell her, Dad. You absolutely must."

He rubs his chest as he grimaces. "I might be having a heart attack."

I sit up straighter in my chair. "For real?"

"I don't know. My chest feels tight all of a sudden."

"Should I call the paramedics?"

"No. Don't do that. I'm sure it'll pass." He continues to rub his chest. "I can't... I can't lose her, Flynn. She's my whole world."

"And you're hers. Don't forget that." Even as I reassure my father, I'm terrified of how my mother might react to learning her husband kept this massive secret from her for decades.

"You don't understand how she gets on the topic of that woman. To this day, after fifty years in a happy marriage and family, hearing Vivian's name sets her off like nothing else ever has."

I've never known my mother to behave about anyone the way he's describing. She's a make-love-not-war kind of gal, always encouraging us to see the good in others and to steer clear of unnecessary drama and strife. Maybe she hammered that home with us, wanting better for her children, because of what she went through.

"It reminds me of how angry she was after Julian dumped Aimee."

Dad nods. "That's one of the few other times I've seen her so angry with someone."

Julian Remington's parents, Corbin and Kate, were close couple friends with my parents. My sister was crushed by Julian's sudden decision to end their years-long relationship, and it took a long time for her to bounce back from that disappointment. Mom and Dad were outraged by the way Julian treated their daughter.

"Mom will hire Kate Remington to represent her when she hears about this," Dad says, his expression as glum as I've ever seen it.

The Remingtons are legendary Hollywood divorce attorneys and weathered one of the most epic splits this town has ever witnessed about twenty-five years ago. It went on for close to a decade as they battled over the firm they'd run together and custody of their six sons and three daughters, most of whom have since gone into the family businesses or are on their way there after law school. Mom has stayed close with Kate, who runs her own boutique firm with her daughters and nieces, while Dad kept in touch with Corbin, who works with their sons. He's the senior partner at the firm his father founded.

My parents went out of their way to remain neutral amid the ugly battle that provided endless headlines, but they strongly disapproved of the ordeal their friends put their children through. They say it's not for nothing that none of the nine Remington kids has ever married.

"Mom isn't going to hire Kate or any other divorce attorney."

"I wouldn't be so certain, son. This'll be bad—as bad as it gets." He looks up, brightening ever so slightly when he seems to have a thought. "How can we find out whether Vivian mentions me in the book? I mean, it'd be a shame to bring this up to Mom if there's no need for it."

I grimace. "What reason would she have *not* to mention it? And I hate to say that our family's profile has never been higher than it is these days."

"Thanks to your incredible success."

"And yours—and Mom's."

"But mostly you."

I hate that he's right. If there's a bombshell related to our family in Vivian's past, she'd be crazy not to include it if she wants to sell as many books as possible.

"We'll see what Emmett has to say and go from there." My phone buzzes with a text from him. "He's here. Be right back." I walk out to let my friend in through the breezeway door. He wears an exhausted but happy look about him, three months after he and his wife, Leah, welcomed their first child, a son named Holt in homage to his wife Leah's former last name. He was born six days after Benny. "Thanks for coming, man."

"Of course. What's wrong?"

"I'll let my dad fill you in."

I lead him through the kitchen, down the hallway to Dad's office, bringing a surreal feeling with me. It'll take a minute to fully process the things I've learned about my parents today. Right when you think you know the people closest to you as well as you possibly can, you find out otherwise.

Dad stands and leans across the desk to shake Emmett's hand. "Thanks for coming, Emmett."

"Anything for you, Max. You know that."

Dad sighs as he returns to his seat, seeming diminished by the shock of the day's events. That scares the shit out of me. My dad is never diminished by anything, but the thought of real trouble with his adored wife has him terrified. I know how that feels after coming all too close to losing my own beloved once upon a time, after I kept something important from her.

Fortunately, we were apart for only a short time and were able to work it out. I learned my lesson early on, and my only goal in life is to make her blissfully happy so she'll never have reason to leave me again. There're no secrets in our marriage, and there never will be.

Apparently, Emmett is also unsettled by my dad's uncharacteristic aura of defeat. "You're not sick or anything, are you?"

"No, nothing like that." Dad continues to rub his chest.

If that keeps up for much longer, I'm calling the paramedics. Maybe if he's in the hospital when he tells Mom this news, it'll go over better. I'd find that thought funny if I wasn't so rattled and scared.

"I learned something today that has the potential to rock my marriage and, well... my entire life."

As Dad lays out the details of the story, I can tell Emmett is almost as stunned as I was to learn these things about my parents. They're extra parents to all my friends, many of whom had difficult or nonexistent relationships with their own parents. Mom and Dad are a huge part of our close group. We look up to them in every possible way.

In our found family, what happens to one of us happens to all of us, and I'm sure Emmett is already twelve steps ahead of us, thinking about the potential fallout. That's his forte in situations like this.

"Dad's wondering if there's any way to get an advance copy of Vivian's book so he can see what's said about him. It may be possible to spare my mother from this information if he's not mentioned."

"I can reach out to some of our contacts in New York to see if they know anyone at the publisher who might be able to help us out, but we'd need to be careful. It wouldn't take much to bring the trail right back to Quantum and to you, Max."

"We can't let that happen," Dad says. "My goal is to keep this under wraps by any means necessary."

"Are you willing to sue to stop the publication?" Emmett asks, sounding hesitant.

"Wouldn't that mean he has something to hide?" I ask.

"There might be a way to protect your identity, but I can't promise that."

"Let's try to find out what's in it before we discuss legal action," Dad says.

"Max, you know how much we all love you and Stella, right?" Emmett asks tentatively.

"I do, and we love you all like our own."

"Family takes care of family, and I'll do my very best to protect you in this, but…" He leans forward. "You *must* tell Stella about this if there's any chance of it leaking and becoming public ahead of publication."

"That's what I said, too. Because of who we are in this town… you, Mom, me… a lot of people would take great pleasure in this story, especially if it caused obvious trouble in a marriage that's long been considered a rare Hollywood success story."

"Yes," Emmett says. "Exactly that."

"I'll talk to her." Dad looks tenser than I've ever seen him. He's still rubbing his chest, which adds to my considerable anxiety. As far as I know, in fifty years there's never been a serious threat to their marriage.

Until now.

CHAPTER 3

Flynn

$\mathcal{I}$ drive home in a state of shock and disbelief, tinged with a considerable amount of fear. For the life of me, I can't picture my parents as anything other than happily married and showing the rest of us what a successful marriage looks like. If you'd asked me if I thought I knew them, truly *knew them* and all their secrets, I would've said yes, of course I do, and so do my sisters.

None of us could've guessed there were skeletons in their past the likes of which I heard about today. My dad was *married* to Vivian Stevens, and my mother doesn't know that. My mother was *engaged* to Jonah Street before Vivian stole him from her, resulting in Mom having to change career paths and hating Vivian ever since.

And now, Vivian is poised to publish a memoir that could possibly blow the lid off decades-old Hollywood drama that'll still captivate the world all these years later. That's how big Vivian, Max and Stella are in this community and around the world.

All of them have enjoyed monster careers. While my parents are still in the spotlight well into their late seventies, Vivian has dropped out of sight recently. I haven't thought of her or heard anything about her in years, whereas Mom won a Grammy for her duets album three years ago. Dad is an executive producer on a film that's generating significant Oscar buzz for everyone involved.

This story going public would be explosive and deeply damaging to my parents' marriage and everything we all hold dear—especially if my mother were to hear about it from anyone other than my dad. Even if he tells her himself, we might be looking at a marital disaster.

My stomach is in knots as I park in the garage and go into the house through the room that Natalie has organized with cute old-school lockers for each child's belongings. I take a second there, soaking in the familiar comfort of the lockers that bear the kids' names and thinking about how she's converted every corner of my former bachelor pad into a home for our family.

No matter what happens between my parents, I've got her and our kids and the rest of our family and friends. We'll get through this the same way we get through everything—together. But even knowing that, I still feel blindsided by a crisis I never saw coming, especially at a time when I expected to be celebrating my parents, not fearing for their future.

I'm still there, leaning against Cece's locker, when Natalie comes looking for me. "Hey, I heard the garage. Are you okay?"

"I... I don't know."

She comes to me like the dream come true she's been for me since the day we met and wraps her arms around my waist. "I'm here. What can I do?"

Steeped in the scent of my love, I hold her close and breathe in the reassurance that comes with her. There's never been another human being who could calm and center me just by breathing the same air the way she can. "This helps, love. Thanks."

"Do you want to talk about it?"

I want to forget this day ever happened, but I don't keep things from her. "After I see the kids. I missed them this afternoon." When I'm not working, I try to spend as much time at home with my family as I possibly can to make up for when I'm away. Not that I work out of town much these days, but every new film comes with premieres and press tours that take me away from the only place I want to be.

"They missed you, too. Rowan was very sad that Daddy didn't pick him up."

"Aw, poor guy. I promised him I'd be there after school when I dropped him off." Our older son is all about Daddy, which I love. "I'll make it up to him."

"He'll forgive you the minute you walk into the room."

"Let me go spend some time with them, and then I'll fill you in."

"I've had a pit in my stomach since you texted earlier."

I pull back from her to kiss her forehead and lips. "I'm sorry. Didn't mean to be secretive. It was just a lot."

"Whatever's going on, we'll figure out what to do the way we always do."

"I'm counting on that."

She takes my hand to lead me into the family room, where the kids are watching a movie before bed. They've all had baths, and Cece has a towel clipped around her neck so her long dark hair won't get her nightgown wet. She hates when that happens. Fluff is curled up in her lap, where she is any time Cece is around. Natalie's beloved dog shows no sign of slowing down with four little ones to supervise.

"Daddy!" Rowan lets out a scream when he sees me, launches off the sofa and runs to me on chubby little legs that I'm obsessed with.

Fluff lifts her head to see what caused the annoying outburst, sees it's me, grunts and goes back to sleep. Business as usual.

I scoop up Rowan and swing him around, making him delirious with laughter.

All our kids have dark hair, brown or hazel eyes and rosy cheeks. I think they're the most beautiful people on the planet, after their gorgeous mother, of course. I keep Rowan on my lap when I sit on the sofa to kiss Cece and Scarlett, who's four. Bennett is snoozing in the carriage that we use as a bassinet. We joke that he can sleep through anything, but we're thankful that such an easygoing baby is bringing up the rear of this squad.

We intentionally had our kids close together for three reasons.

One, we wanted to get through the baby years (and the teen years) all at once. Two, we hoped if they were close in age, they'd grow up to be best friends. And finally, I'm getting old, and as I've discovered, fatherhood is a game best played by the young and energetic. Natalie says I'm ageless, but she has to say that.

The girls are tranquilized by *Frozen*, as usual, so I give Rowan my full attention with the tickles that make him belly laugh. I love to make him laugh like that.

"Don't get him wound up at bedtime," Natalie says as she folds the endless laundry four little beings generate in a day.

I've suggested getting a housekeeper or nanny—or both—but she's not having it. She wants to take care of her family herself while also doing an amazing job running our childhood hunger foundation.

I smile at my own personal Wonder Woman, who makes my world and that of our children go round smoothly and efficiently.

"Ten more minutes, people," Natalie says.

"Daddy just got home," Scarlett replies.

"Oh, so you did notice me, huh?"

She gives me the shy smile that makes me swoon and snuggles up to me.

I raise an arm to put around her while holding Rowan with the other one.

For a second, they make me forget the worries I brought home. But then it all comes rushing back to me in a flood of dread and anxiety. It's been a long time since anything has thrown me the way this has. I'm eager to talk it out with Nat, who always makes me feel better about whatever has me upset. Usually, it's something happening at work, with some egotistical celebrity causing us grief. I much prefer that to potential trouble between my parents.

I help Nat get the kids to bed and read two stories to Rowan while Nat reads to the girls. We dole out kisses to everyone and tell them we'll see them in the morning. Rowan has yet to sleep past six a.m. since he's been in his big-boy bed, but we keep hoping the day will come when he does. The girls were always great sleepers, so he's been a shock to our system in more ways than one.

Whereas our girls are sweet and gentle, he's rough and tumble. He drives them crazy with his desire to smash things while making as much noise as possible at all times.

I think he's hilarious, but the girls don't agree.

With the older three settled, Natalie rolls the carriage into our room to nurse Ben in the hope that he—and we—might sleep through the night.

"Talk to me." She's settled against a pile of pillows with the baby in her arms. "What's going on?"

Normally, the sight of her feeding one of our babies distracts the fuck out of me, but tonight, even that doesn't take my attention off the dread. That would concern me at any other time, because there's almost never an instance when I don't look at her and forget anything and everything that isn't her.

I change into a T-shirt and shorts and then stretch out next to her on the bed. "My dad called me after he read that Vivian Stevens has written a memoir."

"Because your mom hates her?"

Startled, I look up at her. "How do you know that?"

"She told me about what happened with Jonah Street."

"Wait. She told *you* that? I'd never heard about her and Jonah until today."

"Really? I assumed you knew."

"No, none of us knew about that or that my dad was married to Vivian Stevens for eight months before he met my mom."

She startles so hard that Ben releases her breast and lets out a squeak of annoyance. "*What?*" Smooth as can be, she resituates the baby as she continues to stare at me.

"My mother doesn't know."

Her mouth falls open with the same shock I felt when I heard about this earlier. "Come on. No way."

"Apparently, the blowup with Vivian was still fresh when he met her, so he kept that tidbit to himself so he wouldn't upset her—and possibly ruin his chances with her."

"He never told her he was *married* before her?"

"No, and now he's panicked because Vivian is publishing a tell-all memoir next month that promises to reveal her deepest, darkest secrets. He says he's probably the juiciest secret of all."

"He has to tell your mom this. Right now."

"That's what Emmett and I told him."

"Oh my God, their anniversary, th-the p-party. It's all this weekend!"

Hearing my calm, cool, collected wife stuttering spikes my already-considerable anxiety. "Believe me. I know. I'm already wondering if the happy couple will be speaking at their big cele-bration."

"I'm sure they'll work this out. They're rock solid and always have been."

"I don't know, hon. He's kept something *huge* from her for more than fifty fucking years. And the thing he kept from her involves the only enemy she's ever had. Something tells me that's not gonna go over well."

Max

I'M WORRIED THAT I'VE BEEN HAVING A HEART ATTACK FOR HOURS NOW as I wait for Stella to get home. Our devoted housekeeper, Ada, left dinner I couldn't eat because my whole body is in an uproar. I sit in the dark, waiting for Stella to return from rehearsal for her upcoming show at the Hollywood Bowl, which is set to be broadcast on NBC. She's been equal parts excited and nervous about the opportunity to introduce her music to a whole new generation. If we're mired in a massive scandal, will the show she's put so much time and effort into be canceled?

God, I can't even think about it getting that bad.

With the show in final production, our fiftieth anniversary this weekend, the upcoming trip, the holidays, Flynn's fortieth birthday—this is the worst possible time to drop a bomb on her. But Flynn and Emmett were adamant that she be told right away lest the news reach her through someone other than me.

The possibility of that happening is so horrifying as to be nearly paralyzing. I can barely breathe as I contemplate the many ways this situation could blow up my beautiful life and marriage to the woman I love with my whole heart and soul.

She knows that.

I hope that'll matter to her.

What if it doesn't? What if she hears the name *Vivian Stevens* and *married to me* and forgets she ever loved me at all? If there's one thing my Stella is unreasonable about, it's her loathing for "that woman," as she refers to her whenever her name is mentioned.

A less secure man would've worried that Jonah Street had been Stella's true love. Otherwise, why would she have hung on to the enmity for Vivian for decades after the incident that caused her to despise Vivian in the first place? But Jonah was the least of it. Stella believes Vivian was also behind the sudden end to her acting career, and nothing can convince her otherwise.

I have no doubt at all that *I* am the love of her life, not Jonah Street. I'm the one who's stood by her side for all these years, raised four children with her and adored twelve precious grandchildren—so far. We've survived career highs and lows, the loss of our parents, health challenges and everything else that's come our way without so much as a single night in which we went to bed angry with each other.

My father used to say that Stella and I are two of a kind, and that's the truth. The thought of any threat to us and our marriage is simply unbearable.

By the time I hear the garage door open to indicate her arrival, I've worked myself into a nervous breakdown to go with the ongoing heart attack. She'll take one look at me and fear something terrible has happened to one of our precious kids or grandkids. I force myself to pull it together, so I won't terrify her.

I'm standing in the kitchen, drink in hand, when she comes in, all smiles after a long day apart. "Hey! I'm sorry I'm so late. We had the *best* dress rehearsal. I didn't want it to end!"

She's still so freaking gorgeous, even in her mid-seventies. Every one of her blonde hairs is perfectly done, as is her makeup from rehearsal. It's a little heavier than what she wears on a regular day, but it's so artfully done that it shaves twenty years off. Not that she needs that, because she doesn't. She's aged as beautifully as anyone ever could without a lick of plastic surgery or fillers. She says those things are for people in denial, even if she indulges in a bit of Botox here and there.

I look at her and see everything I ever wanted in the world. If I lose her... or, God forbid, disappoint her so profoundly she can't forgive me...

I can't. I wouldn't survive it.

"Did you eat?"

"No, I waited for you."

That stops her short as she takes a good look at me. "You must be starving."

"Not really. I didn't mind waiting."

"Is everything all right? You never wait this late to eat. What's that you say about dying in your sleep from heartburn?" She continues to study me as if she can see the torment that has to be showing itself despite my desire to play it cool. "What's wrong, Max? And don't say nothing. I can see it's something."

"Let's eat, and then we'll talk."

"Is it one of the kids?"

"No, they're all fine." For now, anyway. If there's trouble between Stella and me, none of them will be fine for long.

"Tell me what's going on. You're scaring me."

"I never want to do that. You know that, don't you?"

"Of course I do."

"I have something I need to tell you, something I should've told you years ago..."

She stares at me as if I'm someone she's never met, which is probably how it feels to hear I've kept something from her for years. *Decades.* "What is it?"

"Did you hear that Vivian has written a book?"

The look that crosses her face is full of disgust. "Why *in the world* would I care about a book by that woman? Why do *you* care?"

"I... I don't care, but the writeup I saw in *Variety*... It said she's going to spill all her deepest, darkest secrets."

"You're worried she's going to talk about stealing Jonah? Good. Let her. Then everyone else can see what I've known about her for ages. She's a lying, sneaky, nasty bitch."

"It's just that I... Before I knew you, I, um... Well, you dislike her so intensely, and when we met, you and Jonah had recently split, you'd told off Vivian, and the wound was still fresh."

She stares at me without blinking, without seeming to breathe. "What happened before you knew me?"

"I knew her."

"You knew her. What does that mean?"

"I... ah..." I look up at her, at the blue eyes that've held me captive since the day we met, right after the whole world found out how much she hates Vivian Stevens. I kept my mouth shut that first day, afraid she might never give me a chance if she knew the truth about me and Vivian. I've kept it shut every day since then because I told myself it didn't matter. Stella and I were happy and madly in love. Who cared what—or who—had preceded her and us?

She comes to me, places her hands on my chest and gazes up at me, looking at me the way she always does, as if I hung the moon just for her. How will she look at me after she hears what I need to tell her? "Max, darling, whatever is causing you to stutter? You never stutter."

I cover her hands with mine.

"And why are your hands freezing? What the heck is wrong?"

"I don't know how to say something that's going to upset you deeply, which is the last thing I ever want to do. You know that, right?"

"Of course I do, but you're scaring me. Whatever it is, just say it so we can get on with it."

Will it be that simple? With anything else? Absolutely. With this? No chance.

"I... ah... Before I knew you, well before... I was..."

She doesn't blink or breathe or move a muscle as she waits to hear what I've got to say.

I want to freeze time permanently in the era before she knows about me and Vivian. I fear the after will look nothing like the before.

"You were what?"

I force myself to look her dead in the eyes when I say the words that'll change everything. "I was married to her."

For a second, her expression doesn't change. Her head tilts. "You were *what*?"

"I was briefly married to her. When you and I met, the situation with her was still... raw, and I decided not to mention it because I figured it would ruin any chance I had to get to know you."

Her hands drop from my chest as she takes a step back. "You decided not to mention it." The words are said in a tone I've rarely ever heard from her, especially directed toward me.

"I didn't want to upset you, and it was long over with her. We were married for, like, ten minutes."

"How long?"

"Eight months in total, but we only lived together for six of them, and I was away on location for much of that time."

She sucks in a sharp deep breath full of shock and hurt that lacerates me.

"Stell..."

"No." She holds up a hand to keep me away from her, which in fifty-two years together has never happened. I'm far more accustomed to her pulling me toward her than pushing me away. "No."

"Please try to remember what it was like then. She'd hurt you so badly, ruined your career and forced you to start over. The last thing I wanted was to bring her into the beautiful thing we were building together."

Tears fill her eyes as she shakes her head. "We'll be married *fifty years*. *Tomorrow*... it'll be *fifty* years, and for all this time..."

I'm gutted by her tears. My Stella rarely cries, and when she does, it's only because she's heartbroken over something major.

"You lied to me. All this time... We've been living a gigantic lie."

The words hit like poison arrows to my heart. "*No*. We've been living a dream come true that never would've happened if I'd stopped everything to tell you this. You would've walked away from me and never looked back—and think about what we would've missed if that'd happened. Please, Stella... I never wanted to hurt you—not then or now."

"Well, you have. You've hurt me more than anything or anyone ever has."

A sense of desperation unlike anything I've ever known fills me with panic. "Sweetheart... Remember how you felt about her back then? You wouldn't have given me the time of day if you'd known I'd been with her, and all I wanted was a chance with you. From the first second I ever saw you in Merv's Green Room, you're all I wanted."

Tears stream down her face, every one of them a knife to my heart. "You lied to me. Our entire life together is a lie."

"No, Stella, no, it isn't. I love you more than my own life, more than anything in this world, and you *know* that. You know it."

She shakes her head. "I don't know anything. I want you to leave."

"What?"

Saying it slower this time, as if I'm not capable of understanding, she says, "I want you to leave this house. Right now. Get *out*."

I'm shocked to the core of my being. She's kicking me out? No, she wouldn't do that.

But she doesn't yield as we stare each other down, both of us blinded by tears. Fear blots out everything else, like the moon covering the sun in a solar eclipse.

"Stell..."

"If you love me at all, please go. I don't want you here."

I can't move or think or even breathe. She's really kicking me out. It's unbelievable and unbearable at the same time. Other than when one of us was working out of town, we haven't spent a night apart in so long, I can't recall the last time, since we stick close to home these days, wanting to be near our children and grandchildren.

God, the kids... What will they say when they hear I upset their mother so badly—the night before our fiftieth anniversary—that she kicked me out?

Somehow, I get my legs to move, to propel me upstairs to pack a bag, going through the rote steps I've followed before trips and work commitments, but never for a reason like this. Never because my wife told me to go.

I sit on the bench at the foot of our California king and wipe the tears from my face. If you'd told me when I woke up this morning that Stella would kick me out of our house because of Vivian Stevens, I would've been amused by your imagination.

Nothing about this is amusing.

It's terrifying and devastating.

The foundation under me has cracked wide open, letting in a flood that threatens to take down everything I've worked so hard for all my life. The successful career means nothing compared to the family Stella and I raised under this roof. We've been a team for so long, I can't imagine being without her for a night, let alone the rest of my life.

Just this morning, we woke early, cuddled in bed, discussing the big celebration weekend ahead, and then had coffee together before she left for rehearsal. How could everything have been perfect twelve hours ago only to blow up like this in the same day?

My phone buzzes with a text from Flynn. *How are you? Did you talk to Mom?* I decide to call him. My hands are shaking so hard, I can barely hold the phone.

"Hey," he says. "What's up?"

The sound of my son's voice brings a flood of new tears to my eyes. I'm one big raw emotion right now.

"Dad? Are you there?"

"I'm here. I told her."

"And?"

"She asked me to leave."

"No." That single word is full of devastation that ricochets through the phone to stab me in the heart. My chest aches fiercely. "She wouldn't do that."

"She did. I'm packing a bag."

"Come to my house."

"I don't want to disturb you guys."

"I'll come get you."

"No. No, son. That's not necessary. I'll check into the Beverly Hills Hotel or something."

"If you do that, it'll be online by morning, if it takes that long. Please come here."

He's right. Of course he is. "I'll be there shortly."

"You're sure you're okay to drive?"

I'm not sure of anything anymore. "Yeah."

"Be careful."

"I will."

"See you soon, and, Dad?"

"Yes?"

"She loves you. Please remember that."

Does that even matter anymore? "I'll try."

I end the call and go into the bathroom that adjoins our bedroom to pack my shaving bag. A glance in the mirror reveals the dreadful toll this day has taken on me. My face looks haggard. My eyes are red and swollen. For the first time, I look every minute of my seventy-eight years.

I put the shaving bag in my suitcase and zip the case closed, pulling it behind me as I head for the stairs. I realize halfway down that I forgot my phone charger, but I'll borrow Flynn's. The first floor is dark when I land at the bottom of the stairs, leaving my bag by the breezeway door as I go to get my keys and wallet.

Stella is nowhere to be found as I walk through the kitchen, feeling as if I've been set adrift on a raft in the ocean or something equally dramatic. As I take my bag to the Escalade and settle in the driver's seat, hoping I can drive safely, I've never felt despair quite like this. I sit for a long moment, taking in the beautiful house that's been our sanctuary for decades. I can't believe this is happening, especially on the eve of our golden anniversary.

A light goes on upstairs, and I'm transfixed, hoping for a glimpse of my love. But I see no sign of her after several breathless minutes. I shift into Reverse, back out of the driveway, press the button on the remote to close the security gates and drive off in total disbelief.

CHAPTER 4

Flynn

"My mom asked him to leave."

Natalie's expression conveys the same distress I'm feeling. "Oh my God. I don't believe it."

"From the way he sounded, he doesn't believe it either. He's coming here."

"I changed the sheets in the guest room last week after Olivia slept over, and there're clean towels in the linen closet."

"Thanks, hon." I kiss her forehead and leave her to finish the nightly skincare routine that's one of her few indulgences at the end of long days with four young kids.

Thinking about my beautiful wife helps to keep the panic from overtaking me.

My parents have split.

Hopefully, it's temporary. But what if it isn't?

I can't even go there. After I grab the towels from the linen closet in the hallway, I put them in the bathroom that adjoins the guest room. Then I sit on the bed and compose a text to my sisters.

I can't believe I'm saying this... But there's trouble between Mom and Dad.

I give them the highlights—or lowlights—of what happened today and apologize for dropping this on them out of the blue and in a text.

Mom asked him to leave. Dad is on the way over here.

Ellie initiates a four-way FaceTime call.

"Are you fucking kidding me?" she asks when her face appears on my screen.

"I wish I was."

"Dad was *married* to Vivian Stevens? The same Vivian Stevens that Mom hates?"

"How does everyone know that but me?"

"It's a girl thing," Annie says when she joins the call. "You wouldn't understand. I can't believe this."

"You guys," Ellie says, "the party is in *two* days."

The party has been ruthlessly planned by my sisters as well as my assistant (and Hayden's wife) Addie, with some help from me when they allowed my input. It's out of our hands now. "What the hell do we do about that?"

"Worst case," Annie says, "they put on the performances of their lifetimes, unless they want everyone speculating about trouble in paradise."

Aimee joins the call. *"Dad was married to Vivian Stevens and Mom didn't know that?"*

The high-pitched tone of her voice is wildly out of character. Aimee is the calm one, or so she likes to say.

"I can't wrap my head around this," Ellie says tearfully. "Mom must be devastated."

"I'll go check on her," Annie says. "She shouldn't be alone right now."

I'm relieved Mom won't be alone tonight. "That's a good idea."

"What're we going to *do*?" Aimee asks. "Like, what in the hell do we do?"

Natalie comes in and sits next to me on the bed. "We give them space to work this out."

"We don't have time for space with the party in two days," Ellie reminds her.

"They'll be fine at the party," Natalie says. "They're accomplished actors."

"That's true." I put my arm around Nat, needing her close to me now more than ever.

Annie's phone shifts over to her Bluetooth as she pulls out of her driveway and heads for Beverly Hills, wiping away tears that won't quit. She lives the closest to Mom and Dad and can be there in about fifteen minutes.

"Are you okay to drive?" I ask her.

"I'm fine. Just stunned like the rest of you are."

"Be careful, Annie," Aimee says.

"I will."

"I can't believe Mom told him to leave," Ellie says.

"I can," Annie replies. "Mom sees red when that woman's name is mentioned. It happened recently when we were at lunch with Kate Remington, and she made a joke about how Vivian hasn't gotten divorced in a while, which isn't good for her business. Mom shut that right down."

"You had lunch with Kate?" Aimee asks tentatively.

The subject of Julian and the Remingtons is a source of pain to Aimee, who once hoped to marry Julian.

"We ran into her when we were shopping," Annie says. "It was spontaneous, but the point is Mom's entire disposition changed at the mention of Vivian's name. Can you imagine what she must be feeling after finding out Dad was once *married* to her? My God. She has to be out of her mind."

"How could he have kept such a thing from her for all this time?" Ellie asks.

"Mom loses it at the mention of the woman's name," Annie says. "Imagine what it was like back then, not that long after Vivian swooped in and stole Mom's fiancé, and they had that huge fight on the set of their film. They were big enough by then that everyone must've known about it. Dad would've been afraid to say the woman's name around Mom."

"That's what he said earlier when he told me," I tell them. "The nasty exchange between Mom and Vivian on the set of *London Town* was big news at the time. He knew better than to mention her name to Mom when they met. Anything to do with Vivian set her off and upset her so much that he thought it was best to keep that detail to himself."

"That's a big 'detail' to hide from your wife for fifty years—that you were married before, and to her mortal enemy," Ellie says.

"I still can't believe Mom has a 'mortal enemy,'" I add. "Before today, I would've said she didn't have an enemy in the world."

"I only picked up on her hatred of Vivian that day with Kate," Annie said. "Her name came up, and Mom was totally different. Later, when we were in the car, I asked her about it. She said in her whole life, Vivian is the only person she's ever truly hated. Then she told me why, and I totally understood why she felt the way she did about her."

"And today, she found out Dad was once married to her," Ellie said. "I feel sick."

Ellie sums up exactly how I feel.

Natalie squeezes my hand in support. This brings back awful memories of the brief time we split after we were first married. It's the same sense of helplessness and despair, only that was even worse because I thought I might've lost the love of my life forever.

"Check in with us after you see Mom, Annie," Aimee says.

"I will. Almost there."

"And I'll let you all know what Dad has to say when he arrives."

We end the call after promising to keep in close touch.

I lean my head on Natalie's shoulder. "I can't believe this is happening."

"It's surreal to me. I can't begin to know how awful it must be for you guys."

"I was just thinking that the sick feeling reminds me too much of the time we were briefly apart."

"I hope your parents put things back together the same way we did then. True love always wins. I have to believe that."

"I really hope you're right."

Stella

I CAME HOME RAVENOUSLY HUNGRY AFTER BARELY EATING ALL DAY, BUT now the thought of food makes me nauseated. A huge lump has taken up residence in my throat that makes it impossible for me to do anything other than focus on breathing and trying to swallow the bile that has my chest burning.

Or maybe it's the heartache that burns.

Max, *my* Max, was *married* to *Vivian Stevens*.

For the rest of my life, I don't think I'll ever be able to reconcile that sentence with the man, the life, the love I've known for fifty-two years. If you'd asked me this morning whether Max had ever lied to me about anything important, I would've bet my life the answer was no.

I'd be dead as a doornail, as my father used to say.

It's unfathomable.

It's revolting.

It's... *devastating.*

The awful feeling reminds me of the time, about twenty years ago, when a young actress accused Max of attacking her on a film set. I'll never forget the shock and fear of realizing an accusation alone can ruin a sterling reputation and a successful career. The press was relentless in their coverage of the story, and the woman was later discredited when it was proven that Max wasn't even on the set the day she claimed the attack occurred. She was run out of the business, but it took a long time for us to get past such an upsetting incident.

As bad as that was, however, this is worse in so many ways, because Max, my Max, is the source of my agony.

My phone chimes with a text I'm tempted to ignore, but I glance at it because it gives me something to do besides fume and grieve.

From my friend Kate Remington, ironically one of the top divorce attorneys in LA. *I just got a Facebook memory of your 40th anniversary celebration ten years ago, which means 50 is right around the corner. Happy anniversary to the golden couple (see what I did there with the gold?!). Love you both and hope you're celebrating with the family!*

I break down into deep, heart-wrenching sobs. I've been so looking forward to our fiftieth anniversary celebration and the massive party the kids have planned for Saturday, which is *two days* from now. With hundreds of our closest family and friends invited, including Kate, who must think it's a surprise, there's no way to call it off now. That's what I'd do if I could.

I've never been this hurt, angry or bewildered, even after the mess with Vivian and Jonah. That's nothing compared to finding out Max lied to me for all this time—and yes, a lie of omission is still a lie, even if done for altruistic reasons.

This weekend was supposed to have been an incredible celebration of an iconic, legendary marriage and family. Instead, I'm alone in our special sitting room, sipping a glass of whiskey that's making me feel sicker than I already do and contending with the unbelievable thing my husband of fifty years dropped on me out of the blue.

Vivian Fucking Stevens.

Of *all* people.

That he could've once loved *her* enough to *marry her* makes me want to vomit.

The realization that my Max once had sex with her takes me over the edge and has me running for the toilet to expel the meager contents of my stomach. The whiskey burns badly on the way out. I'm contending with dry heaves when I hear the chime of the security system, alerting me that someone has entered the house.

If Max has come back, hoping I'll change my mind about wanting him out of the house, he'll be very disappointed. I wipe my face and brush my teeth to get the foul taste out of my mouth. I'm emerging from the bathroom when I hear Annie calling for me.

"In here."

I return to my favorite chair and put my feet up on the stool. After a long day of rehearsals, I'm aching and exhausted, but more than anything, I'm heartsick and outraged, which is a tough combination to contend with all at once.

Annie comes in, looking as anxious as I've seen her since her son Garrett had meningitis two years ago. That was the scariest thing that's ever happened to our family.

"Mom," she says, tearfully. I hate to see my lovely girl upset over something to do with me or her father. She's tall like her dad, with blonde hair she got from me and blue eyes the same almond shape as Max's. Her delicate features are tight with anxiety that breaks my heart. Our fearless attorney is rarely ever rattled like she is now.

I move my feet over so she can sit on the footstool. "I guess you've heard, then."

She reaches for my hands. "What can I do?"

My huff of laughter sounds harsh. "Unless you can tell me this is a very bad dream, I'm not sure what anyone can do."

"I don't know what to say."

"Neither do I. What does one say when one learns that one's husband has lied to her for more than fifty years? Does Hallmark make a card for that?"

"Daddy loves you," she says softly. "He loves you so much."

"What would you do if Hugh told you—out of the blue—that he'd been married before to the one woman in this world you can't stand?"

"I, um… I don't know. But I think I'd try to remember… the, ah… the good things. There's been so much good."

"Yes, there has," I say with a sigh. "But it's now colored by the lie, Annie. How can it not be?"

"He didn't tell you because he knew it would upset you."

"That's no excuse! He *knew* how I felt about that woman. How could he have kept this from me for all this time? What if I'd heard about it when I was out to lunch or at the salon or anywhere else for the last fifty years? I've been juggling a live stick of dynamite that threatened to blow up my whole life for *fifty* years, and he never did a thing to protect me from that. *Not one thing.*"

"I can't imagine how you must feel."

"It's unbelievable. Just beyond comprehension."

"I'm sorry."

"Thank you for coming, sweetheart, but I'm all right." I've never lied to the precious face of one of my children the way I am now. "You should be with your family."

"I want to be here with you."

"That's so very kind of you—and your siblings, who I'm sure are awaiting your report with breathless anticipation. But I need some time to myself to process this. I'm sure you understand."

"I do."

I tuck a strand of her silky hair behind her ear and stroke her cheek. "I'll be okay. I promise. Please tell the others not to worry."

"How can we not worry? You and Dad are everything to us. Surely you must know..."

"We do. And the same goes for all of you. That'll never change."

"The party... Should we cancel it?"

"No. Don't do that. We don't need that kind of attention. We'll get through it. Somehow."

"We wanted you to enjoy it," she says, tearfully again.

"I'm sorry. That's going to be difficult in light of... Well, you know."

"Should we cancel the trip?"

"Absolutely not."

"But, Mom..."

"You're going to have to follow my lead on this, okay? Tell the others, too. I don't want you to cancel anything, but I would like to be alone. Okay?"

She wipes tears from her cheeks. "Sure. Whatever you need."

I lean forward to hug her. "Thank you again for coming. I really do appreciate you checking on me."

"I'm so sorry about this, Mom."

"I am, too. I'm very sorry indeed."

I'm sure she wants to ask me if I'm going to forgive him at some point, but I don't have the answer to that. Not now, anyway. I'm thankful the Hollywood Bowl rehearsals are finished until after the first of the year so I can fully wallow in my grief and anger. Maybe if I take some time to myself—on our actual anniversary, of all days—I can be ready to face whatever the kids have planned for us on Saturday.

As public figures, we have to be cognizant of things like subliminal messages. If we cancel our fiftieth-anniversary party for any reason, we'll be the lead story in Hollywood and beyond. I'd rather go through with the party than be the source of gossip. Even after all this time, that bitch Vivian would probably enjoy hearing there's trouble in my life.

I won't give her the satisfaction.

CHAPTER 5

Emmett

I've called in every favor anyone has ever owed me to find out more about Vivian Stevens's autobiography, but I've learned everything about the book is on lockdown. No advance copies have been issued, even to reviewers, which I'm told is exceedingly rare. This information only confirms that Max is right to be worried about what bombshells might be waiting to explode his life —and Stella's.

They're not my parents, but I love them like they are, and the thought of anything threatening them is unbearable to me. The term *salt of the earth* gets thrown around too much, if you ask me, but it suits them. They'd do anything for anyone, especially the people they love, and my family is fortunate to be among those ranks.

I can't stand calling any of the partners I work for with bad news, but I promised to keep Flynn informed, so I put through the call to him as I drive home from the office.

"Hey, Em. What'd you find out?"

"Nothing good." I fill him in on Vivian's memoir being the best-kept secret in publishing.

"*Fuck.*"

"My sentiments exactly. Did your dad tell your mom about what's going on?"

"He did."

"How'd that go?"

"Not well at all. She asked him to leave. He's on the way to my house now."

"No..." I can't imagine either of them without the other by their side. They're an institution. "I can't believe this."

"Right there with you."

"What about the party?"

"Annie was just with my mom, and she says to go ahead with it because canceling it would cause an uproar she doesn't need right now."

"I thought it was a surprise."

"Nah, we learned the hard way that Mom doesn't like being surprised like that."

"I hate that this is happening at a time when we should be celebrating them."

"I hate it, too. And I can't fucking believe it, to be honest."

I tighten my grip on the wheel as my stomach churns from hunger and distress on behalf of my friends. "How'd he keep this a secret for more than fifty years?"

"That's the question of the day. Shit like this doesn't stay buried in this town. How did it never get leaked before now? Makes me fear there's more to the story than what he told us."

"What else could there be?"

"I don't know, and the not-knowing is making me crazy. Oh hey, that's my dad now. I'll check in later. Thanks for everything you did today."

"I wish it could've been more."

"It was what we needed, as always. I'll talk to you tomorrow."

"Sounds good."

I end the call with him feeling unsettled, as if there's trouble between my own parents rather than my friend's. But Max and Stella have been in my life since high school. Their house was the preferred destination for Flynn's friends. They were always there for us and still are to this day. I simply can't fathom the thought of them on the outs with each other. It'd be like breaking up peanut butter and jelly, for crying out loud.

As I get closer to the home Leah and I recently purchased near Kristian and Aileen's house in Calabasas, I try to clear my mind of the day's distressing news so I can focus on my wife and son. Today was my fourth day back to work in the office after three months of paternity leave, during which I worked sporadically from home while my capable team handled most of the heavy lifting.

It was the first real break I've taken since I finished law school and went to work for Quantum, rising through the ranks to become the company's chief counsel less than four years later. The partners I work for are my closest friends, family in every sense of the word.

When one of them is threatened, so am I.

After I park in the garage, I sit for a second to gather myself, to change gears from office Emmett to husband-and-father Emmett. I never thought I'd find anything I loved more than my work, but then along came Leah and her special brand of insanity, which gave me no choice but to fall madly in love with her. And now... Now we have a son, and life has never been sweeter than it's been since Holt's arrival.

I grab my work bag and drop it inside the door, where it's apt to remain until the morning as I haven't spent one second on work any night this week. I'm so far behind on everything that I'll never catch up. Ask me if I care. That attitude would've been unthinkable before Leah and Holt. Now it's my way of life.

Luckily, I work for my best friends, who value family over everything, and none of them would want me to sacrifice time with mine to review contracts after hours. I'm always available to put out fires, but short of that, I'm off the clock when I get home. I bring the work home more out of habit than an actual plan to accomplish anything.

I walk through the spacious home that Leah still can't believe is hers after almost six months there, wondering where I'll find them.

They've been in a different spot every night, from Holt's nursery to our room to the office she keeps at home to maintain her job as Marlowe Sloane's assistant to the back patio that overlooks the pool.

Tonight I find them passed out on the sofa in my office, which is funny to me. Leah hardly ever steps foot in my domain, because she believes I need a space that belongs only to me, which is one of many ways that she's the perfect wife for me. As I pull at my tie and release the top button of my shirt, I wonder what brought them in here.

I'm sad they're asleep, because I've missed them like crazy all day, but I leave them to rest while they can. Holt is a lousy sleeper, which means we're sleep-deprived as well. Leah wants nothing to do with nannies or help of any kind, so we're powering through on our own, hoping he'll sleep through the night before he leaves for college.

Before he arrived, I had no idea it was possible to be so tired and continue to function somewhat normally. I refuse to leave it all to Leah to deal with, so we're in the trenches together, even when she insists I sleep because I have to work. I'd rather be with her—and our son—than asleep anyway. What's that old saying? I can sleep when I'm dead. For now, I'm just dead on my feet.

After I change into a T-shirt and track pants, I consider a workout in our home gym, but I'm just too fucking exhausted for anything more than dinner, a snuggle with my love and then as much sleep as I can get before Holt is awake again. It's just after seven o'clock, and I'm thinking about bed, which cracks me up. In the pre-baby years, I could stay up all night partying or fucking and then go to work in the morning. Somewhere along the way, I've turned into a seventy-year-old man, a thought that makes me chuckle as I pour myself a drink.

"What's so funny?" Leah asks as she comes into the living room and wraps herself around me from behind.

"I'm laughing at how all I want in the world is to go to bed right now."

Yawning, she says, "Right there with you, babe. This kid is killing us."

"We'll pay him back when we're crotchety senior citizens."

"Oh yeah, we'll drive him crazy then."

I turn to her, happy and relieved to see her after the long day apart. There was a time when the sight of her put me on edge because of how much I didn't want to want her. Yeah, make it make sense. She wore me down, and now I'm the happiest bastard who ever lived. After three months of spending twenty-four hours a day together, I miss her like crazy now that I'm back to work while she works for Marlowe from home for the time being.

"Missed you today," she says softly as she lays her head on my chest.

"I was just thinking how much I missed you, too. I got awfully addicted to being with you and the little mister all day, every day. Work is a drag now."

"Don't say that. You love your job."

"Not as much as I love my family."

"Aw, look at Emmett Burke, all domesticated and shit. Who'd a thunk it?"

"Not me until this pesky little fruit fly started buzzing around my head and wouldn't leave me alone until I fell in love with her."

She looks up at me and smiles widely, the way she always does when I recall how we began with her coming to me, the company's chief counsel—just about every day—with some stupid legal question she could've answered with a two-second web search. As I tried to resist her, she wore me down, and no one in the history of the world has ever been happier to have been worn down by a woman.

"You want a drink, babe?" I ask her.

"A short one. It might help him sleep through the night."

I pour her a glass of the orange-flavored vodka she likes. "Is that what we've come to? Getting him drunk?"

"Whatever works, right?"

We curl up together on the sofa, legs intertwined in a position that's become as familiar to me as anything in my life. There's nothing better than being wrapped up in my Leah.

"How was your day, dear?"

"Not so great."

"Why? What happened?"

"Flynn called me in a panic." I fill her in on the situation with Vivian Stevens and what occurred between Max and Stella today. We have a deal—I keep her in the loop about the things I can tell her, and she never repeats anything she knows about my work.

"She actually *kicked him out* of the house?" Leah sounds as floored by this as I've felt since I heard it.

"She did. He was on his way to Flynn's when I talked to him just now."

"Oh my God. Their anniversary... The party is Saturday!"

"Believe me, they're painfully aware of that."

"It hurts my heart to hear there's trouble between them. I can't imagine one of them without the other."

Like most of us in the Quantum family, Leah had a chaotic upbringing after her mother died when she was a teenager, leaving her with a father who was unprepared to manage her or anything else, for that matter. The Godfreys have filled that void for us and many others.

"I said the same thing to Flynn. It's unbelievable that something like this could happen to them."

"How could he keep that from her for all this time?"

"I think he did it initially because he felt he'd never have a chance with her if she knew he'd been married to Vivian. And then one year became two, which became fifty, and here we are."

"Damn." She looks up at me. "You're not holding on to anything like that, are you?"

"No," I say with a chuckle. "You know the good, the bad and the ugly. How about you? Any skeletons buried in your closet?"

"None that you don't already know about. My life was kinda boring until you came along."

"Likewise, my love."

"Your life was *not* boring before me."

"Yes, it was. The things I thought were exciting then have nothing on this life with you."

"Right... Getting puked on and peed on and pooped on and kept up all night... These are exciting times, I tell you."

I tip her chin up and kiss her. "These are the very best of times."

Flynn

THE MAN WHO WALKS INTO MY HOUSE BEARS NO RESEMBLANCE whatsoever to the Max Godfrey I've known and loved my entire life. This version of him is broken, and that breaks me, too. I go to him and hold him as he sobs.

I've never seen my dad cry over anything other than a happy occasion, such as one of our weddings or the birth of a new grandchild.

That he's clearly heartbroken and terrified sends my own anxiety through the roof. I simply can't conceive of a world in which my parents aren't happily married and as in love with each other as they've always been.

I lead him into the living room and sit with him on the sofa.

Natalie comes in, visibly crushed to see my dad in this condition. She pours our favorite drinks, puts them on the coffee table, kisses my dad's cheek and then leaves the room.

I pick up the glass of my dad's favorite gin and tonic and hand it to him. "Have a drink, Dad." I've yet to meet any challenge that a little bit of booze couldn't help, and besides, I don't know what else to do for him.

When I notice his hand is shaking as he raises the glass for a sip, my heart breaks all over again. I've never viewed him as fragile or elderly or noticed any of the traits most seventy-eight-year-old men exhibit on the regular. Normally, he's strong, dynamic and as far from elderly as it gets. But this day has knocked the legs out from under him. I'm trying to figure out what to say or do to help him and coming up blank.

He'd know what to say to me. He always does. I have to find some words that'll comfort him the way he does for me any time I'm in distress.

After a healthy sip of gin and tonic, he sits back against the sofa and closes his eyes. "I don't know what to do, son."

"Give her a minute to process this news, and then I'm sure she'll want to talk about it."

"I wish I could be so certain. I've never seen her like she was just now. Not once in fifty-plus years..."

"She's in shock, Dad. You have to give her some space to wrap her head around it."

"I fucked this up so bad. So, so bad."

"I keep going back to what you said earlier, that if you'd told her about Vivian when you first met her, you'd never have had a chance with her."

"That's true. The wound was still raw when we met on Merv's show when she was getting her singing career off the ground after the scene with Vivian had derailed her acting path. I knew better than to even mention her name around Stella."

"When she has time to think about it, she'll remember that. She'll remember how heated she was on that subject, and how there was no way you could've casually mentioned being married to Vivian *and* continued your relationship with her."

"No, there wasn't a way to do both. I chose her. I'd choose her a million times over."

"She knows that. Which one were you married to for five minutes and which one have you been married to for fifty years? Which one do you have four children and twelve grandchildren with?"

"Will any of that matter now that she knows I kept such a big thing from her the whole time we've been together?"

That's the great unknown. Will the lie... or the sin of omission... undo everything between them?

"Mom isn't known for being unreasonable."

"Except on the subject of Vivian. Any time her name is mentioned anywhere, she's revolted. That's all it takes. A mere *mention* of her."

"Does Vivian know that Mom hates her?"

"Oh hell yes. Any time we've crossed paths with her, Mom refuses to even look at her. Back then, the scene between the two of them was the talk of the town for a few weeks. By the time I met Mom, the full details of what'd gone down between her, Jonah and Vivian were well known. I didn't dare mention her name to Stella. Five minutes after I met her, I knew that secret would have to stay buried forever."

"What I don't get is how it's never come to light before now. Vivian is so proud of her six husbands and her checkered romantic past. They'll lead with that in her obituary, for Christ's sake. Why wouldn't she want the world to know she was also married to Max Godfrey? That there're actually *seven* ex-husbands?"

A look passes across his face that can be classified only as guilty.

"Dad... What else is there?"

He shakes his head. "I can't."

I blow out a deep breath. "If there's more to this story than you've let on, you have to come clean to Mom. You can't let her be blindsided."

"She'll hate me."

"No, she won't."

"She will. I'm sure of it."

"Is it something that could be in the book?"

"Possibly. Vivian has no reason to want to protect me, after all."

"Dad." I wait until he glances my way. "Tell me. Whatever it is, we can figure it out, but if I don't know, I can't help you."

"I'm ashamed to talk to you about this."

"You're my best friend in the whole world, and I'd like to think I'm yours."

Tears fill his already-raw eyes. "Of course you are, but you're also my son..."

"I'm a grown man. I can handle anything you want to talk to me about. I promise."

He shakes his head, and his apparent agony strikes new fear in my heart as I worry about how this terrible situation could actually get worse. "I was so young and stupid then. I did things I'm not proud of..."

"We all do things we're not proud of before we know better."

"Some things are worse than others."

"Tell me."

He doesn't want to. That's as obvious as the prominent nose on his face. After a long pause, he softly says, "Do you know what a sexual dominant is?"

CHAPTER 6

Max

$\mathcal{I}$ can't believe I'm having this discussion with my son, of all people, and the disbelief that registers on his face breaks my heart. I've never felt more ashamed than I do in this moment.

He stares at me, unblinking before he gives a slight nod. "I know what that is."

I hand him my glass. "Could I have a refill please?"

He takes the glass to the bar he and Natalie keep out of the reach of little hands. When he returns, he brings the gin bottle and puts it on the coffee table, probably realizing we're going to need additional reinforcements. He looks different to me, as if he's been through something traumatic.

What would it be like, I wonder, to hear such things from your father, the man you've looked up to all your life? I'm disgusted with myself, the same way I was way back when my first wife told me I was a sick fuck who had no business associating with polite society.

I take another drink, hoping the gin will take the edge off my nerves while Flynn waits to hear what other bombshells I might drop that'll change how he views me forever.

"Back in the day, when I was young, I... Well, I enjoyed that life-style. I know that may sound outrageous to you, but it was fun and exciting and—"

"Dad. Stop."

"I'm sorry. I hate this. You must be disgusted."

"I said to stop not because I'm disgusted, but because I understand."

I gasp as I look at him, feeling as if I'm seeing him for the first time or some crazy thing. "What do you mean you understand?"

"I'm a Dom."

"You... You're..."

"A Dom. I have been since my twenties. It ruined my marriage to Valerie, so when I say I understand, I truly do."

"I... Well... Wow. I didn't expect you to say that."

"Likewise. Must be in the blood or something."

For the first time since I arrived, I have cause to smile, which gives me hope that I might survive this day. Whether or not my marriage will survive remains to be seen.

"Tell me what happened and then we'll figure out how to handle it."

This is the very last thing I want to talk about with anyone, let alone my son. I love all my children passionately, but he's been special to me from the start—and not just because he's my only son. We've shared a bond that transcends the parent-child relationship, especially since he became an actor. How he handles a blockbuster, award-winning career, balancing professional and personal with extreme grace, is a source of tremendous pride to me. Being Flynn Godfrey's father is one of my favorite things in life.

"It would crush my soul if I ever disappointed you," I tell him.

"You couldn't."

"I could, and that's one of my greatest fears."

"Believe me when I tell you, there is nothing you could say or do that would change my opinion of you." He tips his head and looks at me with love, affection, respect and admiration. I see all those things expressed on his world-famous face. "You have no idea, do you?"

"Of what?"

"Of what you've meant to me, to the girls, to all of us…" His voice breaks ever so slightly, and his eyes fill with tears. "We love you so much. There's literally nothing you could do or say to change that. Please believe me when I tell you that."

"Even if my sexual predilections come to light? Some of the grandkids are old enough to read what's said online. The thought of that makes me sick."

"They love you as much as we do."

"I'm not sure I'd survive any of this becoming public."

"Yes, you would. There's nothing we can't get through as a family. We've proven that time and again."

"This is different, son. Tell me you see that."

"What I see is a vindictive woman out to destroy someone she hasn't talked to in more than fifty years. Who's going to look bad here? Not you."

"I don't even know for sure that she's coming for me, but I can't imagine she wouldn't if her goal is to sell books."

"Emmett and I agree that we need to prepare for the worst, and the way we do that is by having all the information we need to be ready for anything."

I refill my glass, needing all the liquid courage I can get to tell my son a story I never expected to share with anyone, let alone him.

"I was twenty-four, coming off the biggest year of my life after *Sandman* was a huge hit. Everyone wanted to work with me, to be close to me, to capture some of the pixie dust that comes from having a big hit. You know what that's like."

"Yes, I do."

"And the women… They threw themselves at me. It was like an all-you-can-eat buffet, and I was the main dish." God, I haven't thought about any of this in years. Why would I when I was happily married to the greatest woman on earth? A deep sigh rattles through me as I force myself to press on, to put words to my greatest shame so my son, of all people, can help me to keep that shame from ruining everything I hold dear.

"I did things I'm not proud of."

"We all have. I hope you know that's not uncommon. Celebrity is nothing more than insanity on steroids."

"It was uncommon for me. I kept thinking about what my mother would have to say if she knew what I was up to."

"I'm sure she knew. Not much got by her."

"No, it didn't, but in her wildest imagination, she wouldn't have put me at orgies... It was sheer debauchery, and I loved every bit of it."

"Most guys would," Flynn says with a wry grin. "Oh, they'd act appalled until they were offered the chance to participate, and then suddenly, their staunch ethics desert them and they're all in. I've seen that happen so many times, it's become comical."

"You're right, and I've seen it a lot, too, but the whole time I was cutting loose, I was also a bit ashamed of myself."

"Was everything consensual?"

"*Always.*"

"Then there's no reason for shame."

"I come from a different time, son. People didn't run around having group sex and partying like the apocalypse was coming and we all had to get as much as we could before time ran out, until the seventies in Hollywood."

"People have always done that stuff. It was just new to you."

"I suppose that's true."

"It's one hundred percent true. When I was new to the lifestyle, someone told me to never act like I was inventing this game. It's been played from the beginning of time, he said, and there's nothing more off-putting to longtime practitioners than some cocky new guy thinking he was the first to wield a flogger."

I grunt out a laugh at the way he phrases that. "That's good advice."

"I took it to heart."

"I wish someone had said that to me as I was indoctrinated into the lifestyle in the most decadent of ways. I might've avoided this whole situation we find ourselves in now."

"What do you mean?"

"I'm getting ahead of myself. So after *Sandman*, things were crazy in all areas of my life, personal and professional. I had a girlfriend for a year before *Sandman* hit. I'm not proud of how I walked away from that relationship like it meant nothing to me so I could run around and feed my ego and show my suddenly famous face everywhere I could. She was disgusted by me, and rightfully so."

"Remember what you said at the outset. You were young. We all do stupid things when we're young. I swear the twenties are all about stupid things."

"I was stupider than most. I let it all go to my head. I was so full of myself, there was no oxygen in the room for anyone else. My management team quit me three months after *Sandman*. I couldn't believe they'd walk away from a rising star. I was outraged. But they saw handwriting on the wall that I couldn't read yet because I was blinded by my own self-importance. I became insufferable. I lost some of the close friends I'd come up with in the business."

"You talked to me about not letting that happen when I first hit the big time. You said don't forget where you came from and who was on the journey with you."

"I can't believe you remember that."

"I remember all your spot-on advice. You made me who I am today, more so than anyone else in my life."

His words bring new tears to my eyes. "I'm so fucking proud of you."

"Same goes, Pops. I've always been proud to be Max Godfrey's son, and I always will be."

"I hope so."

"Some things you can count on to never change. That's one of them."

His assurances give me the courage to continue my story. "The more I learned, the more I became obsessed by the lifestyle. I couldn't get enough of the rush, the power... all of it. I was hooked on the high of it, the most natural drug in the world, the one that made me feel like I could conquer kingdoms rather than leaving me feeling like shit the way actual drugs did. But more than that, I felt like I'd come home to a place I'd always been meant to be. I know that sounds ridiculous..."

He puts his hand on top of mine. "It doesn't. I get it. I've been there, and I know that feeling all too well."

"It helps that you get it, as surprised as I am that you get it."

Flynn laughs. "The surprise works both ways here, but it also explains a few things, such as why it felt so natural to me from the start. It's in my DNA."

"I suppose it is. Anyway, because of my aforementioned big opinion of myself, I let the power go to my head and ended up scaring off a few early partners with my intensity."

"That happens."

"It never should've. I look back at that now with a sense of disbelief that I was ever that foolish or cavalier or stupid. That's one of my greatest shames in life, that I scared women who'd entrusted their pleasure to me."

"That's also far more common than you'd think. It happened to me, in fact. With Val."

I gasp. "Seriously?"

He nods and diverts his gaze, as if he understands the shame, too. "I was new to it when I was with her, still testing my own limits. I freaked her out, and she got even by cheating on me and making sure I found out about it. It ruined everything between us, not that we were that solid to begin with, but it never should've gone down like that."

"Wow."

"Everyone makes mistakes. The hope is that we learn from them and don't repeat them."

"Took me a while to learn the lessons. Too long." I take another sip of gin. The tonic is long gone. "I met Vivian at a party at Bobby Scott's and was instantly dazzled by her, the way every man alive was at the time. I lack the vocabulary to express how big of a star she was then. She was the most famous woman in the world for a time, eclipsing Queen Elizabeth and the stars of *Charlie's Angels* and anyone else you could name from that era. She was one of the first true superstars of the modern era, and I wanted her fiercely.

"The most shocking thing to happen to me, in an already shocking year, was that she wanted me, too. Bobby introduced us and offered to represent me. In fact, the minute she latched on to me, I got more new offers than I could handle. They didn't know we were together romantically, but if Vivian asked for a favor, it was granted. That's how powerful she'd become—and she was all of twenty-two years old.

"In private, we were on fire for each other. There's simply no other way to describe the attraction, the heat, the madness of that relationship. If we weren't working, we were, you know..."

"I know."

"It was sheer gluttony. We got married on a whim, with a justice of the peace called to her home and forced to sign an NDA before they were even a thing. She gave him twenty-five grand for his discretion, and surprisingly, he kept the secret when he probably could've sold it for millions. Even before the twenty-four-hour news cycle, the Hollywood press machine was ravenous—and Vivian getting married would've been a huge scoop."

"Did she know about the BDSM before the marriage?"

"God no. I kept that part of me on lockdown out of fear of driving her away. I was enthralled by her—and a little bit afraid of her, to be honest. Even as young as she was, she wore her power like chain mail, even if she was surprisingly innocent beneath the façade."

"So you tried to live without the lifestyle?"

"I did, and for a while, I was successful. And then, after a few months, I started to crave more, and that was the beginning of our undoing."

"How so?"

"We dressed up in disguises, and I took her to a club to show her what I wanted. That didn't go well at all. Where I was hoping she'd be intrigued, she was appalled. She said, '*This* is what you really want?' I'll never forget the disgust in her expression as she said that. It was devastating, and when I look back at it, that question was the end of us."

"So she never even tried it?"

"Oh, she tried, but it wasn't happening. Vivian Stevens was no one's submissive, and she couldn't get past the fact that I'd kept my true desires from her or the feeling that she'd never be enough for me without the rest of it. I tried to convince her that wasn't true, but nothing was ever the same after we visited the club. We tried getting our groove back, but it was gone, and soon she was, too. After we divorced, she had our marriage annulled as if it'd never happened. I'm still not sure how she did that without my involvement, but she was Vivian Stevens. Anything was possible for her." I glance at Flynn. "Do you see why I'm so terrified? If she tells the world we were married, she might also disclose what caused our breakup."

"Not necessarily."

"Why wouldn't she go there? Can you even imagine the headlines? MAX GODFREY RUINED MARRIAGE TO VIVIAN STEVENS WITH HIS SEXUAL DOMINANCE. AND PS—HIS WIFE HAS NO IDEA HE'S A DOM."

"So Mom doesn't know about the BDSM?"

I shake my head. "I like to think I learned my lesson with Vivian. I put that part of me on lockdown after that and never went near the lifestyle again."

"You just walked away from something that made you feel like you'd come home?"

"I'd seen the downside and was afraid to ruin another relationship. Didn't you feel that way after what happened with Val?"

"For a while, I did, but the BDSM was a symptom of a larger problem with Val. I didn't love her, and when she freaked out about the dominance, I cut the cord with her. She thought it was because of the sex, which is why she did what she did, but it was so much more than that."

"I hesitate to ask about how you handled it with Natalie."

"Badly. I kept it from her, assuming that because of her past as a sexual assault survivor, she wouldn't be able to handle it."

"Totally understandable. I would've done the same thing. How'd she find out?"

"Valerie told her."

"*What?*"

"Yep. She had the unmitigated nerve to confront my new wife in a ladies' room at an awards show and fill her in about my proclivities. At the time, Nat had no idea what to make of it. Then she discovered Hayden's room when we were staying at his house. When she asked me about it, I lied and said I didn't know about it."

"Cripes. Hayden, too?"

"All of us."

"Oh. Wow. Well..."

"Valerie called her and told her where to find proof in my house. It was my bad that I hadn't gotten rid of the room in the basement before Nat moved in, but needless to say, I wanted to kill my ex-wife for doing that, especially since Natalie left me for a time because I lied to her again when she confronted me about what she knew. Not my finest hour, to say the least."

"And on top of everything else you two were dealing with at the time."

"Exactly. That's how Valerie ended up on a reality TV show on a fishing boat in Alaska."

I laugh hard for the first time all day. "Brilliant."

"Hayden and I thought so, too. We made sure it was the only offer she got."

"And now she's hawking kitchen tools on QVC."

"Which is more than she deserves."

"Truly. I never would've suspected her of being so evil."

"I would, but you know what's funny? In a way, what she did sort of saved me with Nat. Her actions forced us to talk about it, to figure it out, and let me just say... That was *well* worth the time and effort."

"Was it now?"

"Oh yeah. She's my perfect partner in every way."

"You're a lucky man."

"And I know it. Believe me. Not that we have much time these days for anything more than the regular fun and games, which is more than fine."

"I can imagine it's hard to find time for yourselves with four little ones underfoot. I remember what that was like."

"I can't believe I'm actually going to say this, but has it ever occurred to you that Mom might be into it?"

"God no. She's not submissive to anyone. You know that."

"Would you have guessed that Natalie would be? That Addie, Aileen, Leah, Marlowe and Sebastian are? Although Mo and Seb switch."

I'm sure my face is blank with astonishment at hearing that list. "*All* of them?"

"Yep. Of course, you know I'm trusting you with other people's private business."

"I understand and will never breathe a word of it, but my God, son, how do such famous people keep a secret like that in this day and age?"

"Very, very carefully."

"I couldn't bear to be where you're at in this time in our culture."

"I try to ignore the noise and focus on my family and the work. What else can I do? If someone wants to blast me for being a Dom, then so be it. It's not going to change anything that truly matters to me."

"You're very evolved on the matter."

"I've been keeping this side of myself private for close to twenty years. My entire adult life, for the most part. It doesn't faze me the way it would have earlier in my career when I was less established. These days, I'm fresh out of fucks as to what people I'll never know think of me. The people who matter... Most of them know all my secrets, and the ones who don't... Well, they don't need to know."

He's referring to his mother and me, as well as his sisters.

"So if by *all of us*, you also include Jasper in the lifestyle, does that mean..."

Flynn laughs. "Don't ask questions you don't want the answers to."

I definitely can't think of my Ellie in this context.

After sharing my sordid story with my son, I'm completely spent. I feel as if I've run a marathon over the course of this day.

"What can I do for you tonight, Dad?"

"You've already done so much by inviting me here and listening. I'm sure it must be so shocking for you to learn this stuff about me at this point in your life."

"Is it shocking for you to learn what you did about me?"

"Surprising but not shocking."

"Same goes for me. Do you think you could sleep?"

"I suppose I could try."

"Nat made up the guest room for you."

"That was nice of her."

"She loves you as much as I do. You've been the father she never really had. I hope you know that."

That brings tears to my raw eyes. "Will she still love me when she hears all this?"

"Without a doubt. The way you and Mom stepped up for her and made her part of our family when her life blew up... She'll never not love you both with all her heart. No matter how terrible this gets, the people who love you and Mom always will because you've been there for us through everything. You can take comfort in that."

"I hope you're right about that."

"When have you known me not to be right about something?"

That makes me laugh, the way he knew it would. I've been telling him his whole life that he's too smart for his own good—and mine.

"Let's get you settled for the night. As you used to tell us, it'll be better in the morning."

"That was bullshit. You know that, right?"

We share a smile that goes a long way toward soothing my battered soul. My son knows the worst of me and still loves me. Perhaps the others will, too. Perhaps even Stella will. The possibility that she won't is more than I can bear to consider after this hellish day. I follow Flynn to the guest room, which has an adjoining bathroom.

"Thank you for everything today."

He hugs me. "I know it's hard not to think the worst at a time like this, but I refuse to believe there's anything my amazing parents can't get through together. Our room is across the hall if you need me for anything during the night."

"I'll be all right."

"Come get me if you need me. I mean it."

"I love you, son."

"Love you, too. Get some rest."

"I'll try."

CHAPTER 7

Flynn

My emotions are all over the place as I look in on my sleeping angels before I tiptoe into our room in case Nat is asleep. I'm relieved to see her sitting up in bed, feeding Ben and, by the expectant look on her face, obviously waiting for me. Fluff is curled up to her feet. As much as Fluff adores Cece, she still sleeps with her first love.

"How is he?"

"A mess, but we had a good talk, and he drank half a bottle of gin. I think he'll be able to sleep." As I unbutton my shirt, I'm completely drained after this eventful day. "I'm going to take a quick shower."

"We'll be here."

I run a gentle finger over Ben's soft cheek and kiss my beautiful wife. "At times like this, I don't know what I'd do without you. No matter what's going on, knowing you're here makes everything bearable."

Her warm green eyes go soft with emotion. "Same goes, love."

"Be right back."

I rush through a shower and shave, eager to hold her and talk it out with her, as always. I almost can't remember what my life was like before that momentous day in a New York City park when Fluff busted loose, burst into a scene Hayden and I were filming and ended up biting me. When I ran after them, Natalie feared I might sue her, which is too funny in retrospect. With one look at her, I'd seen everything I'd ever wanted. Somehow, I knew instantly that I'd regret letting her get away.

As I revisit the most important day of my life, I run the razor over my face and think about the days and weeks that followed our meeting. Our story never gets old to me, and soon, the rest of the world will see the film we made about her story—and ours.

Following months of debate, we changed the title from *Captivated* to *Valiant,* a word that accurately sums up the woman I love and her incredible tale of survival. The word is defined as boldly courageous, brave, which are the perfect words to describe my wife, and the studio liked that title much better than the original one. In all my years in this business, I've never anticipated a film's release more than this one. I'll never tell a more important story.

Even though Natalie was fully on board and consulted on every stage of the process, in the back of my mind, I worry it might've been a mistake to resurrect her painful past, even if it includes so much inspiration for other survivors. She swears she's fine with it, but still, I worry.

After today, among many other concerns, I'm also concerned about how a Godfrey family scandal might take the shine off the film. Some might call me selfish for having such a thought after everything that happened today, but after years of work on this project, I don't want anything to stand in the way of Natalie's big moment.

She's an executive producer on the film and has had an outsized role in shaping the narrative from the beginning. I want her to get all the accolades she deserves. With Natalie's youngest sister, Olivia, playing her, we're also about to watch a new star be born, and we couldn't be more excited about that either.

At a time like this, I hate to think about business, but in my world, the personal is tied to the professional. Of course, I'm far more concerned about my parents and the state of their marriage, but *Valiant* looms large in the background as we count down to the long-awaited release in March.

I towel off and walk into the bedroom in all my glory, noting that Ben is now in his bassinet and Natalie has turned on her side to wait for me.

I slide between the cool sheets and reach for her, wrapping myself around her and the comfort that comes with her. "God, I've needed this for hours." I breathe her in, and just that quickly, much of the tension I've been carrying since the call from my dad this morning slips away. I have no doubt it'll be back before long, but for now, I relax ever so slightly.

"I can't believe this is happening. If you'd asked me this morning if anything could ever come between them, I would've said nothing. Ever."

"I know." I run my fingers through her silky dark hair. "It's unfathomable."

"I can see both sides, though. Can you?"

"Definitely. I'm not sure my mom will ever get over him keeping this from her for their entire marriage." After a deep sigh, I add, "He told me something else that's going to come as a big and possibly unwelcome surprise to her." I keep nothing from her, ever, because I trust her with my life and all my secrets.

"What do you mean?"

"Back in the day, before he was married to Vivian and during, he was part of our lifestyle."

Natalie props herself up on an elbow, her expression conveying amazement. "And your mom doesn't know that?"

"Nope. It was a big part of what ruined his relationship with Vivian, so he decided to step back from it after he met Mom."

She drops back to the pillow. "Wow."

"What're you thinking?"

"That might be a tougher pill for your mom to swallow than him being married to Vivian."

"Why do you say that?"

"Her first thought, as a woman, will be that he did things with his ex-wife, who she can't stand, that he's never done with her. That he's kept that part of himself from her their entire married life. She'll wonder whether he was wanting more all that time. I would."

"I hadn't really thought of it that way, but you're right. She will wonder, and she'll probably be even more upset than she already is when she finds out there's more."

"That would probably rock me more than finding out there was an ex-wife I didn't know about."

"I don't know what to do to fix this," I say with a deep sigh.

"It's not up to you to fix it. Only they can do that."

"How will they do that if they're not living under the same roof or even communicating?"

"Your mom won't want to cancel the party or the rest of the plans. Doing that would send the media into a feeding frenzy that no one needs right now. They'll be forced to spend time together whether she wants to or not, and hopefully, they'll find a chance to talk."

"What'll we do if they split?"

"They won't. They can't. I refuse to believe that's even possible."

"According to Dad, it's more than possible."

"Everything is raw today. Your mom needs to sit with this for a minute and wrap her head around it. She's the most reasonable person I've ever known. I firmly believe she'll come to understand why he kept this from her. That may not happen right away, but it will. I'm sure of it."

"I wish I could be. I've never seen them on the outs. Not for one minute, let alone her kicking him out of the house."

"You're very fortunate to have lived for forty years without any trouble between your parents."

"I know that. Believe me, I do. I remember watching their friends, the Remingtons, tear each other apart for close to a decade and realizing how lucky I was to never have had to deal with something like that. Their kids were dragged through the mud with them. It was so ugly."

"Didn't they make a movie about that?"

"A TV show that lasted two seasons before the network decided the storyline was too toxic to be entertaining."

"Oh, right. I remember now. I think I watched some of it once and couldn't get through it for that same reason."

"My parents were good friends with Kate and Corbin before it went bad. They struggled to stay neutral and never chose sides. But they had strong opinions and were disgusted by what they put their children through."

"I can imagine that'd be hard to watch."

"It was. Dad used to say that as divorce attorneys, they should've known better."

"You'd think."

"Anyway," I say on another long sigh, "enough of all that. The last thing I want to talk about right now is divorce attorneys."

Nat chuckles at the face I make when I say that.

"What went on around here today? I hated being gone so long."

"I knew you would. Let's see... Cece got a one hundred on her spelling test."

"She's the most brilliant kindergartner in history."

"I couldn't agree more. Scarlett made a new friend named Aaron. Rowan played with the coolest truck *ever* at school, and Ben napped for ninety whole minutes, a new world's record."

"All that in one day." It never ceases to amaze me how much occurs in one twenty-four-hour period in the lives of young children. I find myself working less all the time, so I don't miss anything. I busted my ass for years before I had a family and am fortunate that I can now pick and choose projects that keep me close to home. It's been years since I filmed on location or worked for any company other than my own.

"What do we know about this Aaron character Scarlett is hanging out with?"

Natalie laughs. "He's four years old and has red hair."

"A ginger, huh? Can they be trusted?"

"He's a very sweet boy."

"Hmmm, I'll be the judge of that."

"Am I going to have to move out of here with the girls when they're teenagers?"

I pull her in closer to me. "You're not going anywhere."

"Then you'll have to tolerate boys in our daughters' lives."

"They don't need boys. They've got their daddy."

"Flynn..."

"Don't torture me at bedtime, sweetheart. I'll have nightmares."

She rocks with silent laughter as I try not to think about my angel babies fending off horny boys. The very thought of it gives me hives. Fortunately, we're quite a few years from when I'll have to actually deal with that horror.

In the meantime, I have to deal with the current horror of trouble between my parents and the very real possibility that it could get worse before—or if—it gets better.

Stella

I WAKE UP SMILING, THINKING ABOUT OUR PLANS FOR THE WEEKEND AND the upcoming Christmas holiday as well as Flynn's fortieth birthday. All four of our children will now be in their forties. How is that possible? After weeks of relentless rehearsals, I'm also ready for the holidays in Utah, followed by ten days in the Mexican sunshine with our extended family.

And then, with a sudden lurch that takes my breath away, I remember what happened yesterday. I'm crushed all over again to realize I've woken up alone on our fiftieth anniversary, in the home I've shared with Max for decades, while he sleeps somewhere else, probably at Flynn's, if I had to guess.

Max Godfrey.

The love of my life, the center of my universe, my everything...

And all this time, he was hiding a massive secret from me.

In my family—and in my life—I'm known as the fixer. I take care of whatever problem arises, efficiently and effectively, so we can get back to the business of living and loving and enjoying one another. I can't bear drama or manufactured bullshit, and my kids learned a long time ago to keep that crap far away from me. But when there's trouble of any kind? I'm their first call.

I like being the fixer. Rarely do I find myself in a situation where I don't know what to do.

As I confront this morning after yesterday's apocalypse, I have no idea what to do first.

My phone buzzes with texts, probably my children checking to make sure I survived the night. They're unaccustomed to trouble between their parents and have to be seriously undone by it. I feel for them. I really do, and I wish more than anything I could wave a wand and make it all better for them the way I normally would.

I wish someone would do that for *me*, but no one can. Only I can do it, and to be honest, I don't want to. I'm angry, hurt and betrayed. Why should I have to worry about fixing something I didn't cause?

The kids are probably also freaking out about the party. They'll want to know for certain that it's still on. If I could do anything I wanted today, I'd hop on a plane and go to Paris by myself and lose myself in galleries, museums, coffee shops and boutiques until the pain lessens.

If the pain ever lessens.

I won't do that to my kids and grandchildren, who are as excited as their parents to celebrate us and our long, successful marriage.

Oh God... I suddenly remember that the *People* magazine cover is due to drop today, lauding one of Hollywood's most enduring marriages. Max and I sat for the photo shoot a month ago, did the interview two months ago and haven't given it a thought since.

I try to remember what we talked about in the interview... Things like what it takes to stay married for fifty years while living and working in the Hollywood fishbowl. Respect, honesty, genuine love and humor. Lots of humor.

I'm going to be sick.

My Max was *married* to that *monster* Vivian Stevens.

Tears roll down my face that I bat away with aggravated swipes. Why am *I* crying when I haven't done anything other than love that man with all my heart for most of my life? Fueled by rage the likes of which I've rarely experienced, I get out of bed and get dressed, refusing to take to my bed like some sort of invalid when I'm anything but.

My muscles are sore from the relentless rehearsals over the last few weeks, but I power through the pain and get myself presentable for the visitors who are sure to come. They won't see me rolled up in a ball licking my wounds. That's for damned sure.

I'm headed downstairs when the doorbell rings. I think about ignoring it, but why should I? No one but our family knows about the current situation, so I have no fear of a reporter showing up at my door. Not yet, anyway.

I glance through the peephole to see a massive bouquet of white roses. Just that quickly, I'm angry again. Does he honestly think that's going to fix what's wrong here? I throw open the door, prepared to tell the delivery person to take them back, but it's a young woman looking at me with big, starstruck eyes, and I don't have the heart to reject her or her delivery. Besides, we don't need the publicity that would come from Stella Flynn rejecting a flower delivery from Max Godfrey. But I want to send them back and tell her to tell him to stuff it.

Ridiculous juvenile shit, but there you have it.

"D-delivery for you, Ms. Flynn."

I take the massive vase from her and nearly drop it when the weight settles on me.

"Do you need help?"

"I think I've got it. Thank you. I don't have any cash for a tip."

"Oh, it's all set, ma'am. You have a nice day, and if I can just say… I'm a big fan of your work. And your son's work. And your husband's." She blushes. "All of you."

"That's very kind of you to say. We appreciate it. I'm just going to go find a place to put these down."

"Yes, ma'am. Of course. I'll get the door for you."

"Thank you."

I carry them into the dining room and put them at the center of the huge table. We recently reconfigured the first floor to allow for the much bigger table as our family continues to grow. The card is nestled between two of the huge blooms that make up a bouquet of five dozen roses. I tear open the envelope to find a handwritten note from my husband that was obviously composed before yesterday.

My darling Stella... Fifty years ago today, you made me the happiest guy in the world when you married me and made my life complete. I'll never understand what I did to get so lucky as to spend my life with you, the most extraordinary woman I've ever known. You're the best wife, mother and grandmother any of us could ever wish for, and we love you with all our hearts. I love you with all of mine, my darling, now and forever. Max

I sink into one of the chairs, sobbing as I reread the note. He means every word of it. I have no doubt about that. I never have. But now I know something I didn't know before yesterday, and that one thing changes everything. I wish it didn't, but it does.

Tears continue to slide down my face, but I wipe them away and get up, determined to hold it together and get through this day that I thought would be filled with our own private celebration full of happy memories ahead of tonight's dinner with the family and tomorrow's party. I go through the motions of making coffee, which is normally Max's job as he gets up before me most days when we aren't working. Using my sleeve, I wipe away the tears that refuse to quit. Every one of them pisses me off, because under normal circumstances, I try to never waste my precious time weeping over things I can't control.

But this... This is a kick in the teeth the likes of which I've never experienced. Well, that's not entirely true... When Vivian swooped in and made off with my fiancé... That was a pretty big kick in the teeth, too. It's funny how I've rarely placed any of the blame on him, preferring to focus on her. She knew we were engaged, but that didn't stop her from taking what she wanted, and to hell with who got hurt.

The outrage of being stabbed in the back by another woman hurt worse than Jonah's weakness ever could have. It was almost immediately apparent that I hadn't truly loved him if I cared so little about losing him. Losing him to *her*, however... That's burned my ass for all the years since. To understand the why of that, one would have to understand what Vivian was like back then.

She was, without any doubt, the most beautiful woman to hit Hollywood in decades. Everyone who was anyone was dazzled by her. They wanted her in their beds and in their films—in that order—and were willing to do whatever it took to have her. Vivian, though, she was elusive and hard to get. One reporter at the time described her as smoke, impossible to capture or contain.

I'd rolled my eyes at that and all the other ridiculous ways the fawning press corps described her as something otherworldly, as if she'd descended from heaven itself to grace us all with her magic and beauty.

Long before I met her in person, I couldn't stand her. Not because she was beautiful or popular or all the rage with casting directors. No, it was because of the way she handled herself in a professional setting, as if she was the center of the universe and no one else involved in the project mattered as much as she did. Her ego always preceded her into any room and sucked up all the oxygen, leaving nothing left for others.

Filmmaking is a collaborative process, but you couldn't tell her that.

She was a selfish bitch, and everyone secretly hated her, but no one else would dare say it out loud until I did. I said what everyone else was thinking, and I said it in the most public way possible. Even though Vivian vindictively set out to ruin my career—and succeeded for a time—I've never regretted calling her out.

And into that vortex stepped Max Godfrey, rising star and sexiest man in the business at the time. I'll never forget the first time I saw him in person. He took my breath away, and I've never quite gotten it back in all the years since...

FIFTY-TWO YEARS AGO TODAY...

I'm in the Green Room at *The Merv Griffin Show*, the first major booking I've had since my explosive argument with Hollywood's golden girl, Vivian Stevens. Only because Dabney Richards is my manager have I gotten the chance to sing for Merv, since my acting career all but ended after I called Vivian a lying, cheating whore. I became the talk of the town for all the wrong reasons.

I found out how powerful Vivian is after I called her out for making off with my fiancé.

She's the worst kind of woman, in my opinion, one who acts like she's your best friend until she buries the knife between your shoulder blades and goes on with her gilded life like nothing untoward ever happened.

I, on the other hand, lost my fiancé, have been shunned by casting directors and even had a couple of pending contracts canceled.

While she's seemingly been cast in every project currently in development, I've been left on the sidelines fuming, punished for telling the truth.

Dabney suggested I go back to singing, which was how I supported myself during the early lean years after I first arrived in Hollywood off a bus from Dubuque, Iowa. I'd sacrificed everything for the dream that'd begun to come true until I dared tangle with Vivian Stevens.

My parents have never forgiven me for leaving home. Several of my siblings went on with their lives as if I was never one of them, while I stayed close to one of my sisters. Calls home became shorter as time went on, and in the third year, they didn't even ask if I was coming home for the holidays because they already knew what I'd say.

I don't blame them. How can I? They have no way to know what it's like in this town, how intense your focus must be to get anywhere, and then, even when you start to make inroads, it can all go to shit in the wake of one screaming fight with a nasty bitch who happens to be the new "it" girl.

I was never the "it" girl. I was the utility girl, cast as the sister or best friend to the ingenue. The epitome of supporting actress, even if my role in *London Town* was one of the biggest ones yet and was more substantial than Vivian's part in the film.

Vivian was a *star*.

I was just an actress trying to get by in a brutal business.

Until I wasn't even that anymore.

In Merv's Green Room, I help myself to a bowl of the fruit that's been put out for the talent appearing on the day's show, along with croissants, yogurt and bottles of champagne. I've lost more than fifteen pounds I didn't have to lose since the great blowup, as I refer to my career implosion. Eating, which used to be enjoyable, has become a chore. A lot of things are a chore that never used to be.

Thankfully, I was careful with the money I made before the great blowup and have been able to pay my share of the rent despite the downturn in my fortunes, but I'm always afraid that one more catastrophe will be the end of my Hollywood experiment, as my mother calls it. I'm cautious about everything—what I say, who I say it to, what I do and what I don't do.

The bad press has finally died down after endless headlines about the actress who dared to call the beloved Vivian Stevens a whore. No one cares that it's the truth. Why let that get in the way of a good story?

I need to be focused on what I'm here to do—launch my career in a new direction and focus on the music. Dabney was thrilled to tell me he'd gotten me on *The Merv Griffin Show*, the hottest ticket in the business, but I agreed to do it only after he promised I wouldn't be asked about *her* or what happened with *her*.

"You can't exactly afford to make demands, doll," Dabney said.

As if I need to be told that. "Either they agree to it, or I'm not doing it. I won't resurrect that nonsense when it's finally died down."

He came back with assurances, and here I am, hoping for a badly needed reset.

The door to the Green Room opens, and the peppy young staffer who brought me in earlier comes in with someone I instantly recognize: Max Godfrey, who's been the talk of the town lately after his starring turn in *Sandman*.

"Have you two met?" the young man asks.

"We haven't." Max comes toward me, extending his hand. "Max Godfrey."

"Stella Flynn."

"It's a pleasure to finally meet you."

I'm stunned that he knows who I am. "You as well."

Good Lord, the man is tall and handsome, with wavy dark hair, kind brown eyes and a showstopping, warm, genuine smile that lights up his face. Add a muscular physique to all that natural gorgeousness, and you've got the makings of a full-fledged movie star.

"I'll leave you to get acquainted," the admin says. "I'll be back for you shortly."

"Thanks, Brad," Max says.

It's no surprise to me that he's on a first-name basis with Merv's employee. He's on the show regularly, whereas this is my first time—and not for the reason I once hoped it would be. As Dabney said so eloquently when we realized I'd have to start over, *Thank God you can sing like an angel.*

Max helps himself to a croissant and some of the fruit. "Champagne?"

With so much riding on this appearance, I should decline. "Sure, thanks." Maybe a little bubbly will help my nerves.

He brings me the glass and takes a seat on the sofa next to me. "I thought you were great in *London Town.*"

I'm shocked because no one seemed to notice me in the film. No, they were all about *her.* "Oh. Thank you."

"You were the highlight."

"Sure I was."

"I thought so."

He's so beautiful, it almost hurts to look at him. Even though he's been everywhere lately, I know very little about him because he keeps his personal life locked down, unlike so many people in our business these days, who seem to enjoy being the subject of salacious rumors that keep their names in the news.

That's not him, and I respected him for the way he operates long before I met him in person.

"Thank you. It's kind of you to say so."

With kindness in short supply in my life lately, I'm deeply grateful for his.

"I heard you're singing today. I didn't know you were also a singer."

I'm shocked that he knows anything at all about me, except, of course, the bad stuff that everyone knows. "That's where I started out, and it's always been my first love." That's not true. I desperately wanted to be an actress. The music was a means to an end at first. Now it's my only option, which makes me bitter.

"I can't wait to hear you."

Now I'm even more nervous than I was before. I take a sip of the champagne, praying for some badly needed liquid courage as we watch Merv's opening on a monitor.

Brad returns for me ten minutes later.

Max flashes that warm smile my way. "See you out there. Break a leg."

"Thank you."

He'll never know what his kindness means to me. That he treated me like a colleague and not a walking, talking scandal is a special gift during this difficult time.

I rehearsed yesterday with Merv's musicians, who are ready for me to sing "I Don't Know How to Love Him" from *Jesus Christ Superstar*.

Dabney hopes I'll attract the attention of Broadway producers with this performance and encouraged me to sing something from one of the big shows. The last thing I want is a move to New York City, but I'll do it if it comes to that. Whatever it takes to stay in the business and to make enough to support myself.

I've worn a slinky silver gown and had my hair and makeup done professionally, which cost a pretty penny, but everything about this opportunity has to go perfectly if I'm to have a chance at career rehabilitation.

Merv is warm and welcoming as he introduces me and my "hidden talent" to a studio audience that greets me with applause that's a big relief. I was afraid they might boo me because they love *her* so much.

The song allows me to show my considerable vocal range, which was another goal, and is met with enthusiastic applause after the final note.

Merv walks toward me, clapping and smiling, and gives me a hug. "Stella Flynn, ladies and gentlemen."

He invites me to the sofa for a chat, which wasn't promised, and I take the arm he offers me to walk to the seating area.

When we're settled, he says, "Well, who knew that Stella Flynn could *sing*?"

I laugh as the audience applauds again. "It's my big secret."

"Not anymore, my dear."

I've offered a few funny stories he can ask me about, and he chooses the one about the bus ride from Dubuque in which one of my fellow travelers was car sick almost the entire way. "I'm a sympathetic puker. If you puke, I puke, so needless to say, this was a bit of a problem for me."

Merv laughs along with the audience.

I'm glad he chose that story, because it's funny and relatable, and it's not about show business. "Here I was, this young girl from Iowa, striking out for Hollywood, and the first twenty hours are all about puke."

"An inauspicious start," Merv says, smiling.

"To say the least."

"Can you stick around for a bit?"

"Absolutely."

"Great. We'll be right back with Stella Flynn and Max Godfrey up next."

That's the first time our names are mentioned in the same sentence.

When we cut to commercial break, Merv says, "You'll be in hot demand after that performance."

"I hope so."

He leans in and lowers his voice, so he won't be overheard. "For what it's worth, I think she's a total bitch."

"It's worth a lot."

"You'll be okay, Stella, and you're welcome back here any time."

"That means so much to me. Thank you, Merv."

"My pleasure, sweetheart."

When we return from the break, Merv introduces Max to thundering applause and wolf whistles from a few of the women.

He's changed into a gray turtleneck and black slacks. He looks positively dreamy, and I'm not the only woman in the room who thinks so.

"You met Stella backstage?" Merv asks.

He glances my way. "I did, and wow, that song... Beautiful."

"Thank you." I hope I'm not blushing.

"I can't believe you've been hiding a talent like that from all of us," Max adds. "Have you always been a singer?"

He's using his time on the show to help me. Why would he do that?

"I, um, well... Yes, I used to sing in church and in shows at school."

"What a voice you have. Incredible range."

I'm speechless. And incredibly grateful. I'm also slightly ashamed to be in a situation in which someone like him feels the need to help me. But whatever. I'll take what I can get.

Merv and Max are witty and fun and obviously good friends as they talk about a memorable night they spent together in Vegas.

When the show wraps, Max walks me back to the Green Room, where we left our things.

Once we're inside the room with the door closed, I turn to him. "Thank you for that out there."

He looks genuinely confused. "For what?"

"You didn't have to use your time with Merv to help me, but I appreciate it."

"That's not what I was doing. At least not intentionally. I was genuinely blown away by your talent."

"That's nice to hear. Thank you."

"You're welcome. What're you up to after this? Want to grab a drink?"

"Oh, um..." Is he asking me out? *Max Godfrey* is asking me out?

He tips his head, flashing that potent smile. "You're not going to leave me hanging here, are you?"

"No, of course not. I'd love to get a drink."

"Excellent. Let's go."

TEARS SLIDE DOWN MY FACE AS I REMEMBER THAT FIRST MEETING WITH Max. One drink led to two, which led to forever. We were together from that day on, the first three days without coming up for air. My appearance on *The Merv Griffin Show* had the desired effect as my singing career took off, and I've never looked back.

Every year on our anniversary, the kids play the video of us on Merv's show. How many children have video of the day their parents met, they like to say.

Merv attended our wedding two years to the day later on December 19 and sang a duet with me at the reception. He became a close, treasured friend to us, and we mourned his passing when we lost him. I haven't thought of that day since our anniversary last year. We didn't care that it was six days before Christmas and both our mothers objected to the timing. The date meant something to us. It always has.

Until today.

Fifty years of marriage, fifty-two years together, and this is the first time we've woken up on this day without each other. I always thought only the death of one of us could cause that to happen.

In some ways, hearing he was *married* to Vivian before he met me is a death of sorts, the death of my innocence where Max is concerned. I thought I knew him better than anyone on earth.

Finding out otherwise has been brutal. *She* knew something about him for all this time that I didn't. That burns like acid inside me.

I go into the kitchen, boil water and wait for my tea to steep while I ponder the unbelievable situation I find myself in. Tomorrow, our closest family and friends will gather to celebrate us, and we're on the outs.

How is that even possible?

Max and I have never been on the outs, not for more than an hour here or there in all these years. Our infrequent arguments tend to blow over quickly because, under normal circumstances, neither of us can bear to be upset with the other.

What does it say about me that even after everything that's happened, I want to call and beg him to come home to me?

I take my tea to sit at the cozy table in the kitchen where we have breakfast together every morning. He scans the *Los Angeles Times* and the industry trades while I scroll through Facebook on my iPad. We chat about everything and nothing. I show him pictures the girls have posted of the kids, and he muses about the state of the world.

His empty chair across the table feels so incredibly wrong, especially on this particular day, which we fully planned months ago. We've been looking forward to a couple's massage, a champagne lunch and then dinner with the family at Frankie's later.

I drop my head into my hands. People will talk if we don't show up for any of those things.

My phone chimes with a text. I glance at it, expecting it to be one of the girls. They must be out of their minds over this. Of course they are. In all their charmed lives, they've never known their parents to be anything other than blissfully happy and in love. Always in love.

The text isn't from the girls.

It's from Max.

I read it like the woman who'll be in love with him until I draw my last breath, regardless of what he failed to tell me.

My darling, fifty-two years ago today, my life changed forever when I walked into Merv Griffin's Green Room and met my destiny. Fifty years ago today, I was on top of the world because I got to marry my dream girl.

Every single day since then has been better than the one before because I got to spend 18,250 days with you. Today I'd planned to thank you for fifty-two years of everything good and sweet and perfect in my life, for our four exceptional children, our twelve incredible grandchildren, the legion of friends and experiences and adventures.

I still want to thank you for all of that. None of it happens without you. I quite simply can't imagine what my life would've been without you by my side. Whatever that picture looks like, I'm not interested. The only life I want is the one I've had with you, my beautiful wife, my soul mate, my best friend, my forever love. When I tell you there's no one but you, that there has NEVER been anyone but you in my heart or soul, I hope you believe me, even though you have no reason to after what you learned yesterday. That person is less than nothing to me. A blip. A mistake. A moment in time I never think about. For all intents and purposes, in my mind, she doesn't exist, she never existed. Meeting you was like staring directly into the sun. Everything else was blotted out by the brilliant, bright light of you.

I knew then and I know now that I don't deserve you, but for some reason, you love me, and that's the greatest single gift in my life. None of the other beautiful things happen without you. You are everything to me. You always have been, and you always will be. It breaks my heart that I have hurt you, especially with so much to celebrate this weekend.

I'll never forgive myself for this, even if you do.

I love you, Stel. Fifty-two years and counting.

Max

I read it three times, blinking through the tears that try to blind me.

He can see that I've read it.

I picture him, probably at Flynn's, holding his breath, hoping I'll reply.

After another reread of his heartfelt note, I have only one thing to say.

CHAPTER 8

Max

Waking up in Flynn's guest room is surreal. The events of yesterday replay in my mind like a slow-moving train wreck I wish I could forget. I already know I'll never forget the sick feeling in my stomach from knowing I hurt the person I love the most in this world. I love my kids and grandchildren passionately, but Stella... She's the sun around which my whole world rotates.

The horrified look on her face when my words registered with her, when she learned I was once married to the only person in this world she hates, will stay with me always.

Having to tell her that will go down as the worst moment of my life, and yes, I know it makes me incredibly privileged to not have had something worse happen to me. I've been incredibly blessed in this life, thanks in large part to her.

I can hear Flynn shushing his kids, telling them there's a surprise guest and they have to be quiet until the guest wakes up to play with them.

Smiling, I brush aside the tears that wet my cheeks and force myself to get up to see the kids and figure out what the hell I'm going to do about my wife, our anniversary, the party, Christmas, the trip to Mexico…

Not to mention the rest of my life.

I shower, shave and get myself together so I won't scare the babies, who'll expect their usual jubilant Pappy and not the sad sack I am on the inside. When I'm as ready as I'll ever be to face this day without my Stella, I walk into the living room where Flynn is on the floor, surrounded by kids, while Natalie snuggles with baby Ben on the sofa.

Flynn sits up, concern etched into the expression on his handsome face. "Did you sleep?"

"A little."

The kids require my full attention, and I give it to them the way I always do.

Flynn brings me a cup of coffee that I drink carefully, between hugs and kisses from the girls and wrestling with Rowan.

"Don't hurt Pappy, Rowan," Natalie says.

He's so different from his gentle sisters, who'd rather give me a manicure than wrestle.

"Where's Grammy?" Cece asks.

"She had rehearsal." I feel guilty for lying to her. But I can't very well tell her that Pappy fucked up bad and Grammy kicked me out of the house on the eve of our fiftieth anniversary.

"Dad," Flynn says, "come into the office."

I give Cece a kiss on her silky dark head. "I'll be back."

I follow Flynn into his home office and shut the door. "I've got the others ready for a conference call to plot our strategy."

"I guess that means they all know?"

My son gives a grim nod. "We need their help."

This entire situation is mortifying, and that Flynn feels it's serious enough to call in our cavalry makes it that much worse. I'm well aware that his partners and friends look up to Stella and me and consider our marriage one to emulate. Many of them came from difficult upbringings and have often told us how much our family means to them. I hate feeling like I've disappointed them in addition to my own kids. "Are the girls on the call?"

"We're here, Dad," Aimee says.

I'm so ashamed by the sadness and fear I hear in her voice.

"We're damned sorry to hear about all this, Max," Kristian Bowen says.

"Hard to believe it's anything more than a blip," Hayden Roth adds.

"I appreciate the support, and I know Stella would, too."

"What can we do?" my son-in-law, Jasper Kingsley, asks in the crisp British accent we all adore so much.

"I've been thinking about that," Flynn says, "and I've decided I'd like to try to see Vivian and get a sense of what we need to be prepared for—"

"Absolutely not," I say before he finishes the sentence. "We're not going anywhere near that woman. Do you have any idea how much she'd enjoy having you show up on her doorstep, hat in hand, asking her to tell you how badly she's going to annihilate your father? No way. And don't you dare get any ideas about defying me on this."

I don't care that he's a superstar in his own right. At the moment, he's my son, and I'm still the dad around here. Involving her is a hard no for me.

"Simmer down, Dad," Flynn says. "It was just an idea."

"I have a thought," Marlowe Sloane says.

She's our honorary fourth daughter, so I welcome her input. "What're you thinking, sweetheart?"

"What if you make a joke of it? When the book goes public with whatever secrets she's daring to tell, act like Stella has known all along and how you regularly have a good laugh about you once being married to Vivian."

"I really like that idea, Mo," Flynn says. "What do you say, Dad?"

"I love it, but I'm not sure if your mother would go along with it."

"She was a heck of an actress back in the day," Hayden says. "I bet she could pull it off. It's not like the rest of the world knows how much she continues to revile Vivian after all these years."

"That's true." I pick it over from all angles, and the more I think about it, the more I like it.

"Dad, you have to take a huge mea culpa on this." As the lawyer of the family, Annie is looking at it logically as well as emotionally. "You have to pour your heart out to Mom and tell her how the only reason you kept this from her was because you feared you'd never have a shot with her if she knew."

"I agree," Ellie says. "You have to take all the blame and tell her anything else she doesn't know before that book hits the shelves."

"You're right, and I will. If I can get her to talk to me."

"Text her," Annie says. "Put it all out there, and don't leave anything unsaid."

"I'll do that. Thank you for the good advice."

"What're we doing about the party?" Ellie asks in a small voice that's so unlike her, it pains me to hear it.

"Mom said to go ahead with it," Annie says. "Canceling would draw attention no one needs."

"I want to bring Liza in on this," Hayden says of the Quantum Productions publicist. "She can help us plan a strategy, and if we're going ahead with the party, I'd like to suggest we sell exclusive photos to *People* or some other top-shelf outfit. Let's get those amazing family photos published before that book hits."

"That's an excellent point," Emmett says. "It'd put you and your happy marriage out there ahead of the book."

Stella and I disdain celebrities who seek out publicity for everything they do, especially private family events, but in this case, it could only help. I hope my wife will agree when I nod to give the go-ahead to bring in the publicist.

"That's a yes to Liza," Flynn says to the others. "Where are we with the injunction, Emmett?"

"Getting nowhere fast. It's very tricky to stop a book from being published if the info in question is true."

"Even if it libels someone else?" Aimee asks.

"It's not libel if it's true," Emmett says.

"He's right," Annie adds. "Dad was married to her, so if she reports that, she's not lying."

"What I want to know," Hayden says, "is how did that never come out, especially after you got together with Stella? I did some reading about what went down between Stella and Vivian back in the day, and it was big news. To have one up-and-coming actress call another a whore in public was a huge deal in the seventies. How were you not outed right then and there?"

"As a condition of our divorce, I made Vivian sign a nondisclosure agreement that basically said she could never talk about our marriage. I didn't want to be tied to her after the way it ended. I'd completely forgotten about that until this very moment, which says a lot about my state of mind."

"Wait," Emmett says. "Do you still have a copy of that?"

"Oh jeez. I wouldn't know where to look. It was fifty-three years ago."

"Max... If you can find that NDA, we can stop the publication of the book if it mentions you or your marriage."

My mind races with thoughts about where it could be, but I'm fairly certain I left all the documentation of my brief marriage to Vivian with my attorney at the time. But that attorney's son, my friend Corbin Remington, might be able to help me. "I'll see what I can do."

"Hurry, Max," Emmett says. "We need to act fast to stop the book's publication on January twentieth."

"God," Flynn says, "that's right around the corner."

"If it's still findable, I'll get it." It's comforting to think there may be something I can do to stop the publication of the book, even as I realize that won't fix what's wrong in my marriage. Only I can do that. "Thank you all for rallying around us. It means the world."

"I know I speak for everyone when I say we love you and Stella very much," Kris says, "and we'll do whatever it takes to protect you and our family."

Once upon a time, I caught Kristian Bowen stealing food from a craft services table on a set in Compton. That he's now one of Hollywood's top producers is due in part to my interest in a kid who showed potential. "Thank you, Kris," I say in a hushed tone. My emotions are raw after the last surreal twenty-four hours.

"Whatever we can do," Hayden adds. "You need only ask."

"Love you all," I say.

"We love you, too," Marlowe says for all of them.

"We'll be in touch," Flynn says before he ends the call. "Where would that NDA be, Dad?"

"It might be in Corbin's archives with the divorce decree. I'll call him right now."

When I pull my phone out of my pocket, I see a text that lets me know the flowers I ordered weeks ago for Stella have been delivered.

I hope she didn't put them in the trash, not that I'd blame her if she did.

I find Corbin Remington's number in my contacts and make the call. His assistant tells me he's with a client and will get back to me shortly. I convey that information to Flynn.

"Should we go over there?"

My son is like the proverbial cat on a hot tin roof this morning, and I hate to be the cause of that. "I'll wait for him to call and go from there. In the meantime, I'd appreciate a few minutes alone so I can compose that text to your mom that the girls suggested."

"Sure, Dad." He gets up, comes around the desk and squeezes my shoulder. "Take all the time you need."

I look up at him, amazed as always about the handsome, kind, talented, loving man he grew up to be. "Thank you for bringing in the others. I feel better after talking to them."

"I'm glad. The whole family is here for whatever you and Mom need. I hope you know that."

"I do, and it's very much appreciated."

Flynn looks at me with his heart in his warm brown eyes. "My father likes to say that you reap what you sow in this life. You've sown nothing but love and kindness and support to all of us. It's the least we can do to return the favor."

"Your father is a wise man," I say with a small smile.

"He's the wisest man I know, and if he kept this from his wife for all this time, he must've had a very good reason."

"She wouldn't have even talked to me if she'd known."

"When you remind her of that, it'll help. Right?"

"I guess we'll find out."

"Take all the time you need. My home is your home."

"Love you, son."

"Love you more."

After Flynn leaves the room, shutting the door, I close my eyes and try to calm my racing thoughts so I can say what needs to be said to my precious wife. I stare at the blank text message screen, trying to find the words to repair the damage I've done to the most important thing in my life. Knowing what's at stake, I leave nothing on the field.

My face is damp with tears as I press Send on the message.

Almost immediately, I can see that she's read it.

For long minutes, I stare at the phone, holding my breath, praying she'll reply, that she'll talk to me, that maybe someday she'll forgive me for ruining what should've been one of the best days of our lives together.

The wait is interminable.

At one point, I see bubbles appear that indicate she's replying, but then they disappear, which crushes me.

Then the bubbles reappear right before a two-word message arrives, the best two words I've ever seen in my life.

Come home.

I burst into tears the likes of which I haven't shed since our four babies were born. My shoulders shake with sobs of relief as I drop my head into my hands. It takes a full ten minutes to get myself together, to wipe my face and catch my breath. I go into the bathroom attached to Flynn's office and splash cold water on my face. When I look in the mirror, I gasp at the ravaged look on my face.

I go back to the office to retrieve my phone. *I'm coming,* I say in response to her.

I'm afraid I'll scare the kids if I go out there looking like this.

I text Flynn. *I sent the text to Mom. She asked me to come home. I look rough... Will you tell the kids I'll see them tonight at dinner? Tell them I had something I had to go do and I'm sorry I left without saying goodbye? Thank you—and Natalie—for having me. I love you all.*

Of course. Go take care of things with Mom and keep us posted. I'm glad you're going home.

Me, too, but still anxious about it all.

One step at a time. You've got this.

I guess we'll see, won't we?

Stella

AFTER I GET MAX'S MESSAGE THAT HE'S ON THE WAY, I RUN UPSTAIRS TO make myself presentable, which, at seventy-five, is harder than it used to be, especially after a nearly sleepless night. I employ all the tricks I've learned over decades in makeup chairs to hide the dark circles under my eyes and to play up all my still-considerable assets. I spray my signature scent of Joy onto my neck and wrists. I've always thought it was a fitting fragrance for a life mostly filled with joy.

As my peers were running to the plastic surgeons to ward off the ravages of time, I took a subtler approach with some Botox here and there, but nothing too dramatic. While I'd never be mistaken for fifty, I probably could pass for early sixties, which works for me. I get dressed in the outfit I bought for today... sleek black pants and a top that flatters the rest of me. I've managed to stay mostly slim and trim through yoga and regular workouts with my trainer, but I'm under no illusions there either.

Time is catching up to me, as it does to all of us.

As I get myself ready for what could be the most important conversation of my life, I much prefer to think about things that don't matter than to worry about what else I might hear that can never be unheard or forgotten.

I'm going to want details. About her. And him. And them

together. I probably shouldn't go there, but the not-knowing will drive me mad. He'll say it doesn't matter, that it was a lifetime ago, before he knew me, before there was an us.

I still want to know.

I'm a bit ashamed of the rancor I still feel toward her. I've never held on to a grudge in my life like the one I have toward her. In the seventies, women were still coming into their power and were often treated as second-class citizens in life and in show business, even as we were conquering the town with massive hit shows like *Charlie's Angels*.

My close friends in the business were like me, the kind of women who stuck together, who had one another's backs and didn't add to the problems we all faced on sets run by misogynistic men in a business dominated by them. We'd all run up against producers, directors and casting agents who wanted a sexual quid pro quo in exchange for a part. When that happened, far more often than it should have, we'd turn to one another to vent our outrage while keeping our mouths shut about it publicly, lest we be branded troublesome to work with.

So to have Vivian storm onto the set where I was working, take one look at the man she knew I was engaged to and decide she wanted him for herself, disregarding me and the girl code most of us tried to live by, was galling to say the very least. I'd heard she was more like a guy than a gal in how she approached her career, but until I experienced it for myself, I didn't believe any self-respecting woman would want to be viewed as such.

Vivian was a different breed. Men and women alike were bowled over by her beauty, her brashness, her brazen sexuality and her take-no-prisoners approach to life and work. Had she not stabbed me in the back and then reveled in my downfall after I called her out, I might've admired the way she handled herself.

As it was, I despised her with every cell in my body, and I still do all these years later.

She's the worst kind of woman, one who takes what she wants with no care or concern for anyone else's feelings. The pattern might've started with me, but it certainly didn't end with me. It happened repeatedly as she stepped on one person after another to reach the pinnacle of the A list. And now she has the audacity to release a memoir that'll probably detail the arduous journey she undertook to become a star.

Please.

Twenty minutes later, I'm downstairs, steeping my second cup of tea and still stewing over things I haven't thought about in years, when I hear the garage door open.

I take a deep breath and hold it for a long moment before I release it slowly, as if that can prepare me for what's about to happen. Nothing can prepare me to have this conversation with my husband.

He comes into the kitchen, and with one glance, I can tell he hasn't slept much. He looks terrible, and my heart goes out to him the way it has from the very beginning.

For the longest time, we stand there staring at each other, neither of us seeming to breathe or blink. We've never once been in a situation like this, and neither of us knows how to handle real trouble between us. Part of me would like to throw my arms around him, tell him it doesn't matter and get on with our plans for the day we've looked forward to for months.

But I can't do that.

I just can't, as much as I want to.

He breaks the long silence. "Stel…" The agony I hear in that single syllable is unbearable.

"Have you eaten?"

"I couldn't possibly."

"Sit." I gesture to the table and go to the stove to make him some eggs.

He comes up behind me, wraps his arms around me and rests his head on my shoulder. "I'm so, so sorry, honey. That I could've hurt you this way wrecks me."

I place my hand over his and am immediately comforted.

"Especially on this of all days. Happy anniversary, my darling."

"Happy anniversary to you, too. Thank you for the flowers." That I wanted to send them back seems like a long time ago now that he's wrapped around me. "Let me make you something to eat."

"I can't eat or breathe or function until I know we're going to be okay."

"We're going to be okay, but it might take some time."

"I've got nothing but time to give to you."

"Will you also give me answers to my many, many questions?"

"I'll tell you anything you want to know and do anything it takes to make things right with you. Being away from you, for even one night..."

"I know."

He turns me so I'm facing him and tilts my chin up to receive his kiss. "I love you more than my own life. I have since Merv's Green Room. Please tell me you know that."

"I do."

After inhaling a deep breath, he releases it slowly. "Can you forgive me for keeping this from you?"

"I'm trying. I've been thinking a lot about what went on back then and how raw it still was when we met."

"That's the only time in all the years I've known you that I ever would've described you as fragile."

"I was fragile back then. I felt like I was going to shatter at any second. That appearance on Merv's show was so, so important to reviving the career that'd been decimated by..."

"By her. It's okay. You can say it. I'm well aware of why you had to reinvent yourself."

"I just can't, for the life of me..." My eyes fill despite my intense desire to get through this without tears.

"What, my darling?"

"I can't picture you with her. I don't *want* to picture you with her." I shudder at the thought of it.

"It was over almost as soon as it began with her."

"But you were *married* to her. How did no one ever know that?"

"Bobby insisted on secrecy because of where we were in our careers when we spontaneously got married. Besides, neither of us wanted to deal with the shitstorm it would've been if that news got out. I insisted on privacy as part of the divorce, and she agreed because we didn't want it known we were or had been married. Back then, being married—or divorced—wasn't good for the career, as you certainly know."

"Yes, I do." Marriage made us less appealing to the public, or some such nonsense.

"In fact, I remembered this morning that I made her sign an NDA as part of the divorce proceedings, and Emmett said if we can find that document, we might be able to get an injunction to stop the publication of the book. If I'm mentioned in the book, that is. We still don't know that. The details are on total lockdown, apparently."

"She'd want everyone she's ever tangled with to be sweating those details." I glance up at him. "So, Emmett knows. Who else does?"

"Their whole team was on a call with me and the kids earlier, talking strategy."

I cringe at the thought of my extra kids, as I think of them, knowing about this, but they're also the savviest people I've ever met. "What'd they have to say?"

"Marlowe had an interesting idea." He takes my hand and my cup of tea and settles us in our usual seats at the table.

For the first time since all hell broke loose yesterday, I feel calm inside, seeing us where we belong.

"What did our Marlowe suggest?"

"Making a big joke of it. How we laugh about me once being married to her, how we always have."

"That's a deliciously evil idea, and I love it."

He offers a true, genuine smile. "Had a feeling you would."

"It'll drive her mad to think of us making fun of her for fifty-odd years."

When he reaches for my hand, I curl mine around his. "After everything we've had, there's no one and nothing that can come between us, and that's the message we'll put forward."

"But we're still going to try to stop it if it mentions you?"

"You're damned right we are. I'm not letting her drag me or us through the mud without a fight." He looks down at the table and then back at me, his eyes haunted once again. "I'm more afraid of the reason we split becoming public than I am of the marriage itself."

Just that quickly, I go cold all over as the sense of dread fills me anew. "What're you talking about?"

CHAPTER 9

Stella

His gaze is fixed on our joined hands.

I wonder if my hand feels cold to him or if it's only cold on the inside.

"When I was a young man, I was full of myself, especially as my career took off and fame set in."

"I've never known you to be full of yourself."

"I'd learned a few hard lessons by the time we met."

"What lessons?"

"It's mortifying to even think about it now, let alone talk about."

"I still want to know. I want all the details, even the ones you'd rather not share. I think you owe me that much."

"I owe you everything, Stel. Every single good thing in my life is because of you."

I stare at him, letting him know I'm not letting this go. Whatever he's ashamed of, whatever might go public in that freaking book of hers... I want to know.

After a long pause in which he can't seem to look at me, he takes another deep breath and releases it in an anguished-sounding sigh.

"Back in the day, when I was young and dumb, I dabbled in what some would call... kinky sex."

Nothing he could've said would've surprised me more than that. "What does that mean?" I barely get the words out around the astonishment.

"I liked it a little rough. I was a, um, a Dominant. I was into light bondage, toys, denying pleasure to my partner until she was begging for it. That kind of thing."

His words land like knives to my heart. I have more questions than answers after hearing this, and I don't know where to begin.

I pull my hand back from him. "Did I ever really know you?" That's the only question I can form and the only one that really matters when it comes right down to it.

"*Yes.* God yes. You know me better than anyone ever has."

"Not as well as Vivian knew you, apparently."

He shakes his head. "She knew a fraction of what you do."

"I take it you practiced this so-called kinky sex with her."

His cheeks flush with color, which happens so rarely it's astounding to me. "Yes."

"I'm afraid I might be sick."

Max jumps up, grabs a bowl off the counter and brings it to me just as his phone rings. He glances at the screen. "That's Corbin about the NDA."

"Jeez, even he knows?"

"I need his help to access the records, if they even still exist."

"Take the call."

I notice his hand is shaky as he reaches for the phone and puts it on speaker so I can hear, too, which I appreciate. "Corbin. Thanks for returning my call."

"Of course. My assistant just handed me the new issue of *People* with you and Stella on the cover. What a gorgeous photo of you two, not that you guys ever take a bad picture. Happy anniversary, my friends."

"Thank you."

I drop my head into my hands when I hear the magazine is out.

Another thing we were so excited about has been tainted by this nightmare.

"You two are the benchmark in every way."

"That's nice to hear."

"What can I do for you, pal?"

"It's a very delicate matter."

"Most of them are."

"And highly confidential."

"I'm a lawyer, Max. Anything we discuss is confidential."

"I have something I need you to handle personally for me. No delegating to anyone, even one of your sons."

"I'll do whatever I can for you, my friend. You should know that by now."

"This is nuclear, Corbin."

"And it shall be handled as such."

"Before I met Stella..."

Saying these words out loud, even to a friend, is killing him. That's plainly obvious, and it doesn't bring me any pleasure to see him in such distress. That's how much I love him.

"I was married to Vivian Stevens for eight months."

Corbin lets out a low whistle. "Holy bombshell, Batman. How'd you keep that under wraps all this time?"

"Through an NDA your dad had her sign as part of our divorce settlement. Now there's a memoir coming, and I'm told that NDA could halt publication of the book if my name is mentioned."

"Sure as hell could."

"Your dad kept all the files. I need a copy of the NDA if it still exists."

"We don't destroy any records. We've got a whole floor of our building devoted to archives."

Max releases a deep breath full of relief as he returns to his seat. "How hard would it be to put your hand on that document?"

"It might take a little longer if I do it myself, but I know where to look. I'll get right on it and call you back as soon as I have something to report."

"I appreciate this very much, and I'm sorry to interrupt your day this way."

"Think nothing of it. What're old friends for if not for something like this? I'll be back in touch shortly."

After the line goes dead, Max glances at me. "Well, that's one piece of good news."

"If he can find it."

"I'm sure he will. His father was meticulous and saw to every detail, just like Corbin."

"And Kate."

"Yes, and Kate."

Corbin's ex-wife runs the other Remington law firm, in partnership with their three daughters and two of her nieces, while their six sons work with Corbin. The two firms often face off against each other in some of the most contentious Hollywood divorces.

"Anyway," I say, "back to what we were talking about before he called."

Max stands so abruptly, he knocks over the chair, which crashes to the floor, rattling my nerves even further. He bends to pick it up. "I need some air. Let's go outside."

Max

I CANNOT BELIEVE I HAVE TO TALK ABOUT THIS SHIT WITH STELLA, OF all people. I feel like I'm disrespecting her with every word I say as I head outside to our gorgeous pool deck, where the palms sway softly in the breeze of a lovely Southern California day.

She follows me, bringing the bowl.

I'm making her sick, which is not at all how I'd hoped to spend this momentous day.

As I run my fingers through my hair, I remember our plans for the day. "What're we doing about the spa appointment?"

"I canceled it this morning. I paid for it and gave them a hefty tip."

Which is code for *I paid them not to tell anyone we canceled on our anniversary.*

"I also canceled the lunch reservation but kept the plan at Frankie's for later. The grandkids wouldn't understand if we cancel that."

"No, they wouldn't."

"And the party is still on for tomorrow. Too late to cancel that at this point, without having the whole town talking about us."

"I'm very sorry about all this, especially the timing of it when we should be celebrating."

"I know you're sorry, and I want to accept your apology and move past this, but I'm having a heck of a time wrapping my head around you keeping it from me for all this time."

He drops into a seat next to mine and looks over at me. "Was there any time in the last fifty-two years that would've been a good time to tell you this?"

I can't help but smile at the expression on his face when he says that—and he makes a good point. "Probably not."

"Would I have had a snowball's chance in hell with you if I mentioned, say, the first week or so we were together, 'By the way, Stel, I was once married to the woman you despise who helped to ruin your career'? The first career anyway."

"No, you wouldn't. The snowball would've melted under the heat of my fury."

"Exactly. In all our years together, you've never disliked anyone the way you do her, and there was never a time to slide that into the conversation with you." He turns in his seat so he's facing me. "I want you to know that I *hated* keeping it from you. It felt wrong to me from the start, but I've been so damned happy with you. From the get-go... Happy like I'd never been. The thought of doing anything to mess with that was unimaginable. And then, as the years rolled on, I never thought about it anymore. What did it matter in the grand scheme of things?"

"Tell me about the kinky stuff."

"Do I have to?"

I give him the look wives have been giving husbands since the beginning of time. He told me once that look makes his balls shrivel. I hope that's the case now, too.

He sighs, seeming to resign himself to coming clean about something he'd much rather never talk about, especially with me. "It was a phase, a short-lived one at that. Some guys I hung out with back in the day were into it, they introduced me to it, and I enjoyed it. Until I didn't."

"What did you enjoy about it?" she asks with shyness that's unusual between us.

But I suppose it's to be expected, since it's not every day I talk to my wife of fifty years about my past interest in kinky sex.

"I liked the taboo of it, although it's hardly taboo these days. It's much more mainstream than it was then. I enjoyed the explicit communication with a partner about what would happen in a scene. Everything is agreed to ahead of time, so there're no surprises. I found that to be intriguing. I liked delaying gratification for myself and my partner, and the toys were always fun."

"So you liked it a lot."

"I did. For a time."

"What changed?"

"Vivian wasn't into it. She said I was a sick fuck, she wasn't submissive to anyone, and at the time, I thought I needed it, so it made us incompatible in the long run."

"Like what happened with Flynn and Valerie."

I'm stunned. "How do you know that?"

"I'm a mother. I pay attention."

"So you know…"

"About him and the others? Yes, I've known for a long time."

"*How?*"

"Vibes I've picked up on, snatches of conversations I wasn't supposed to hear. I worried terribly about how Natalie would handle it in light of her past, but they're so happy together. They obviously figured it out."

"The first I heard of it with him was yesterday."

"When you told him you used to be kinky before you met me and settled into vanilla monogamy?"

"That's not what happened."

"Isn't it?"

"I'd given up the kink at least a year before we met. The thrill was gone."

"And you've never wanted it again?"

"No, I haven't." I reach for her hand. "What I've wanted is everything I've had with you. In all these years, I haven't had one minute of discontentment with the woman I chose to spend my life with. I haven't ever looked at someone else's life and thought, 'Hey, he's got it better than me,' because no one does. I've always known how lucky I am to be with you." I kiss the back of her hand. "This, you and me, and our family... It's everything to me."

"It's everything to me, too."

I want to ask her if we're okay now, if we can move past the last twenty-four hours or if there's more she wants to talk about. But I'm afraid to mess with the fragile feeling of accord we've achieved over the last hour.

As the silence stretches on, I find it increasingly distressing. Not that we aren't capable of companionable silence, but nothing about this is normal. Finally, I can't take it anymore. "So what now? Where do we go from here?"

"I don't know."

That's as upsetting as anything else that's happened during this surreal event. Stella *always* knows what to do. In fact, it's something I've come to count on during our life together. Any time I don't know the answers, I turn to her, because she has them. That she doesn't know is deeply unsettling.

My stomach chooses that moment to growl loudly, which serves to break the tension somewhat as she smiles at me.

"You should eat something so your blood sugar doesn't act up."

She's right, as usual, but I'm still so churned up that I'm not sure I could eat.

When she gets up to go inside, I follow her. I don't know what else to do, and as usual, I want to be wherever she is.

In the kitchen, she makes me a sandwich from the leftover tenderloin Ada made for us the other night. "Where's Ada today?"

"On vacation, remember? We're not going to be here, so we told her to take the time off."

"That's right. Are we still going? To Utah and Mexico?"

She puts a plate on the table in front of me. In addition to the sandwich, she's added my favorite dill pickles and a few chips. "Of course we are. I wouldn't miss that time with the family for anything." She sits in her seat, bringing her own plate. "Eat. We don't need a trip to the ER on top of everything else."

The first bite goes down okay, so I take another. "Thank you for the sandwich."

"You're welcome."

It's all so polite and weird and so removed from our usual casual vibe as to be painful in the differences. But what did I think would happen when she found out I'd kept a first wife secret from her for our entire lives, especially considering who that first wife was?

In truth, I never expected to ever have to tell her about Vivian. And yes, I would've gone to my final reward and taken that secret with me if it meant not hurting the person I love best with information that didn't matter. I still say it doesn't matter.

My phone rings, startling us both.

I withdraw it from my pocket. "It's Flynn."

"Take it. He'll want to know if we're on for dinner."

I put the phone on speaker. "Hey, son."

"Hey yourself. What's going on over there?"

"Having a bite of lunch with your mother."

"Oh. Okay. Are you guys doing all right?"

I glance at Stella, hoping she'll reply for us.

"We are," she says.

Those two little words mean the world to me, and apparently to our son, too, as he exhales an audible sigh of relief.

"Glad to hear it," Flynn says. "The girls and I are hoping we're still on for tonight."

Again, I look to Stella to confirm.

"We're looking forward to seeing you all."

"Do you need anything?"

"No, thank you," she says. "We'll see you in a couple of hours."

"We'll be there. We love you both."

"We love you, too," I tell him.

"See you soon."

I end the call and glance at her. "What a kid." We say that all the time about him and the girls.

"What a kid, indeed."

I'm surprised I'm able to eat the entire sandwich as well as the chips and pickles and that I feel a thousand times better afterward, only because she's still here, still sitting across from me, still talking to me.

We're not out of the woods by a long shot, but we're still *in* the woods, and we're there together, which is all that matters.

CHAPTER 10

Flynn

$\mathcal{I}$'m weak with relief after talking to my parents, even if I'm under no illusion that everything is suddenly fixed between them. But at least they're together and hopefully working it out.

Natalie comes into our room after putting the kids down for naps or "quiet time," since it's going to be a late night celebrating their grandparents. She crawls onto the bed next to me and cuddles up to me.

"Where's Benny Boy?"

"Napping in his crib for the first time."

"A momentous occasion."

"For sure. How're you doing?"

"I just talked to them. They sounded remarkably normal. All systems go for tonight."

"I'm glad to hear it."

"I can't believe how much this has rattled me."

"Of course it has."

"If there was anything in this world I could always count on, it was them being solid as a rock."

"They still are underneath it all. The foundation will hold, and the storm will pass."

"You really think so?"

"I'm sure of it."

I turn to her and draw her in close to me, taking comfort from her nearness, her scent and the silk of her dark hair against my cheek.

"You're sure you're not hiding any deep, dark secrets from me?" she asks.

I laugh. "You know them all, sweetheart, and they nearly wrecked us once upon a time."

"That seems like a long time ago now."

"It was a long time ago. I've never forgotten what it felt like to fear I'd lost you forever. It's a feeling I hope to never have again."

"Same. It was dreadful."

"Thankfully, it didn't last long for us, and it seems like it won't last long for them either."

"I...um..."

"What's up?" I ask.

"I don't want to be a downer or anything, but I think you should expect there to still be a few bumps ahead for them. This was a big thing for him to have kept from her for all this time, even if he did it for what he thought were the right reasons."

"Yeah, I suppose that's true. It's just so hard for me to fathom real trouble between them, you know?"

"I do," Nat says. "I look up to their marriage as the ideal, too. I certainly didn't have that kind of example growing up, and like many of our friends, I've latched on to them as the how-to manual."

"They love the parental role they play for you and our friends."

"And we love them as much as you and your sisters do."

"I know that—and they do, too."

"We'll rally around them until they work this out, no matter what we have to do."

"I'm so glad I have you to talk to about this. I'd be losing my mind without you here to tell me everything is going to be okay."

"I'll always be here to tell you that."

I nuzzle her neck and kiss her soft skin. "The kids are all napping."

"We don't know that for certain."

"We could lock the door."

"You know how I feel about locking them out of our room."

"And you know how I feel about making love to my wife as often as I possibly can."

"Let's wait until later, when we know for sure they're asleep."

I respond to that with a moan that makes her laugh.

"You'll survive."

"Not sure I will." I continue to kiss her and caress her. If that's all I'm allowed to do—for now—I want to make it count.

"Flynn..."

"Yes, my love?"

"What're you doing?"

"Touching my wife."

"That's not all you're doing."

"Whatever do you mean?"

"You're getting me interested when I told you we can't."

"How's that my fault?"

She snorts with laughter. "Whose fault is it? The guy next door?"

I freeze. "I knew you had a thing for him. Are you having a fling with him? Tell me the truth right now."

Her laughter lights up her gorgeous face. "He's ninety, and you're being ridiculous."

"I bet he can still get it up, especially for a babe like you."

"Oh yeah, I'm a real babe with breast milk going sour on my shirt and my hair looking like it was dried in a blender and—"

I kiss her because I can't bear to hear her say a single negative thing about herself. "Stop that. You're the hottest babe in town, and I'd better never hear you say otherwise or else."

She gives me the challenging look I love so much. "Or else what?"

"I might have to give you a good spanking."

"Oh no, not that."

Knowing how much she loves to be spanked does nothing to dim my ardor. Anyone who tells you that having four kids in six years doesn't do a number on your sex life hasn't had four kids in six years.

"I love you so much, Nat. So, so much."

"I know you do, and I love you just as much."

"That's not possible."

"Yes, it is." As she closes her eyes, she exhales a sigh of contentment.

"You're the best wife and mommy and foundation president and friend. You're everything."

When she opens her eyes, her gaze meets mine with the same impact it had that first frigid day in a New York City park. "This life with you is my dream come true. Every messy second of it is perfection."

"It sure is, except for the part about your children being cock-blockers."

She laughs. "Your cock is doing just fine in this world."

"Don't talk about him if you don't intend to follow through."

"I'll follow through. Later."

Since my lovely wife always keeps her promises, I decide to take the rare opportunity to nap before tonight's festivities.

Hayden

AFTER PUTTING IN A FEW HOURS AT THE OFFICE THIS MORNING, I STAND in the window at the back of our home in Calabasas and watch as workers finish setting up inside the massive tent on the lawn for the Godfreys' fiftieth anniversary party tomorrow. From what Flynn tells me, we're going ahead with the party, which is a huge relief.

Like most of our friends, who were raised in families nothing like the Godfreys, I need Max and Stella together and happy. Max Godfrey has shown me, as well as Kristian, Emmett, Jasper and

Sebastian, how to do marriage and fatherhood successfully. He's always there for us when we need him, as if he raised us himself.

In many ways, he did.

I met Flynn in middle school and spent more time at his house in the ensuing years than I did at either of my parents' homes. Max and Stella were warm, welcoming and there for me in ways my own parents never were. I was lucky that my father's housekeeper, Sebastian's mother, Graciela, took an interest in me and made sure I didn't go without birthday parties or someone cheering on the sidelines at my soccer games.

But the Godfreys showed me how family life is done right, and only because of them am I able to be the husband and father I am today. I'm pretty good at both, if I do say so myself. My five ladies have me wrapped completely around all their perfect fingers and regularly make me their bitch.

I'm the happiest bitch you've ever met.

Addie startles me when she wraps her arms around me from behind.

"Where'd you come from? Two minutes ago, you were outside with a bullhorn."

"I heard you were home. What're you thinking about in here all by yourself?"

"Max and Stella."

"They're all I can think about today, too. It's unreal. The whole thing."

"The crazy thing is, I can see why he kept it from her and why she'd be furious to find out this way."

"Me, too. I heard Stella talk about Vivian once, years ago. She can't stand her, and then to find out her husband of fifty years was once married to her... Yeah, she has every right to be outraged, but... I see his reasoning, too."

"I can't believe how upsetting it is for me to know there's the slightest bit of trouble between them."

"They were your stability before we were."

She gets it. Of course she does. She gets me. Always has, and once

I decided to allow her all the way into my life and my heart, everything has been a million times better than it was before her.

I raise my arm, and she snuggles up to me as I bring her in close. I kiss the top of her head. "How's it going out there, General Roth?"

"Everything is on schedule."

Though she's my full-time wife and the mother of our four girls, she's still Flynn's full-time assistant and wants everything to be perfect for him and his family tomorrow.

"Of course it is. General Addison York Roth is in charge."

"I love that nickname."

"It suits you."

"Do you think they'll be able to enjoy the party with this happening in the background?"

"Max and Stella are both accomplished actors. If they're unhappy or out of sorts, no one will know that."

"That's true. This is when their talent really comes in handy."

"If I know them at all, and I think I know them pretty well, it won't all be an act. They're crazy about each other, and I can't imagine anything could truly change that. Even something like this."

"I really hope not. I don't want to think of them as anything other than blissfully happy and showing us all how to go the distance."

"We don't need anyone to show us how."

She smiles up at me. "No, we don't."

"Where have you stashed our ladies today?"

"Peyton and Lily are with Aileen. Marlowe has Bella and Tessa."

"How long are they going to be there?"

"Aileen and Marlowe told me to take as much time as I need to finish getting ready for tomorrow."

I drop the arm that was around her shoulders to her waist and lift her right off her feet.

She lets out a huff of protest. "What the hell are you doing?"

I head for the stairs and don't put her down until we're in our room with the door closed and locked against the crowd of workers that's overtaken our house.

"Hayden."

"Yes, Addison?"

"I have fourteen million things to do. Whatever you're thinking, I don't have time for it."

I kiss her neck and nibble on her delicate earlobe. "Our children aren't home."

"Yes, I'm aware. I usually know where they are."

I find the hem of her T-shirt and lift it over her head. "Surely you can handle fourteen million and *one* things today. You're my general." I make quick work of her bra and my T-shirt and gasp when her breasts rub against my chest. The feel of her soft skin against mine never gets old. Nothing about being with the magnificent Addison York Roth ever gets old.

"Can I tell you something?" I ask her as I lower her to our bed and slide formfitting leggings over luscious curves.

"Anything you want."

I run my tongue over the tight tip of her nipple.

She raises her hips and presses her heat against my hard cock.

"Even after you gave me no choice but to fall in love with you, I wasn't entirely sure I had forever in me."

Her fingers delve into my hair, which sends a shiver of sensation through me. "I was sure enough for both of us."

Since her phone is buzzing incessantly, I move things along, sliding into her tight heat with a feeling of completion that never fails to take my breath away.

I love when she wraps her arms and legs around me and holds on tight for a quick, intense ride that has us both straining and gasping and crying out at the end of it.

I come down on top of her and breathe in the fresh, clean scent of my love, my life, my everything.

Her phone rings and buzzes with more texts.

"The whole world is going mad as I get it on with you."

"The whole world can wait while I take one more minute with my gorgeous, sexy, brilliant wife."

She starts to squirm when she realizes I'm still hard. "You'd better not be angling for round two, mister."

"I'm sorry if I messed with your schedule."

"You're not at all sorry."

She knows me better than I know myself. "I'm really not. We haven't had five minutes to ourselves in weeks."

"It's been *days*, Hayden. Not weeks."

"Too many days. Feels like weeks. Remember when we used to make a 'quickie' last for hours?"

"I vaguely recall that. Guess what?"

"What?"

"Dad and Jan offered to take the girls for the night so we can see to the final details for tomorrow."

My mom married Addie's dad three years ago, which is one of the more amazing developments to come from our marriage.

"So what you're saying is we'll have a whole night kid-free?"

"That's what I'm saying."

"Have I mentioned how much I love that our parents married each other and take our kids whenever we need them to?"

"You've said that a few times."

"What would we do without them?"

She runs her hand in soft, soothing circles on my back. "Ten minutes after they leave with the girls, you'll be pouting and asking me when they're coming home."

"The ultimate parental dichotomy. I can't wait for time alone with my wife, and I can't wait to have my princesses back home with me where they belong."

"And you thought you didn't have forever in you."

"If I do, it's in no small part because of Max and Stella's example."

"They'll get through this. I'm sure of it. They're too amazing together not to."

"I really hope you're right."

"When have you ever known me not to be?"

Since I can't argue with that, I laugh, kiss her and let her up to go back to work while I get busy planning a romantic evening for us— another thing I'd never done until I had her to inspire me.

CHAPTER 11

Stella

In the shower, I'm careful not to get my hair wet. It's still perfect from yesterday's dress rehearsal, which now seems like a hundred years ago in light of what's happened since I arrived home last night. While I was in the shower I decided how we're going to proceed from here.

With Max in the shower in his bathroom, I stand before the mirror in my dressing room and contemplate my reflection.

Not bad for seventy-five, all things considered.

Thanks to good genes and rigorous avoidance of sun, I've been luckier than most, including Vivian Stevens. She hasn't aged well at all, and I haven't heard a word about her in years. Not that I take pleasure from that.

Much.

The thought makes me laugh. I'm such a nasty bitch when it comes to her, but oh well. I'm ninety-nine percent harmless.

The one percent of me that still holds a grudge against her doesn't get much attention in the grand scheme of things. Who has time to dwell on shit that happened more than fifty years ago when there're so many more productive things to focus on, such as love and family and work that still satisfies me?

I might've never given her another thought if I hadn't learned that Max, *my* Max, was once *married* to her.

Twenty-four hours later, that fact still boggles my mind.

I smooth moisturizer onto my face, followed by concealer and foundation that hides a world of sin. There's nothing quite like the right foundation and powder. I'd rather think about trivial things like that than picture my husband in bed with that woman, even if that happened before he met me.

It's so revolting to me.

Eyeliner is followed by shadow, mascara and lipstick.

A splash of Joy completes the package as I move on to the outfit I bought with tonight in mind. Slinky black slacks are topped with a snazzy gold top in honor of the occasion. I place the gold bangle Max bought me for an anniversary years ago on my wrist and put on earrings from another occasion, each item bringing with it memories of a happy marriage with a generous, loving husband. We promised each other there'd be no big gifts for this anniversary. We both have everything we need, and the time with our family is the only gift we wanted.

I grew up with a tightfisted, stingy father who never did a single nice thing for my hardworking mother. I vowed I'd never marry a man like him, and instead, I married his polar opposite, a man who cares more about my happiness than anything else in this world. I've never taken him or what we have for granted, especially as so many of my friends went through ugly, public divorces from men who treated them like shit.

The jewelry is yet another reminder of how incredibly blessed I've been to have him as my partner in life. I need to tell him that and forgive him for the secret he kept from me, but I have a condition.

I slip on black heels, pack the black Tory Burch clutch purse Aimee's kids gave me for my birthday and sit to wait for him to come out of the shower.

When Max walks in with a towel around his waist, I take note of the body that's still toned by regular exercise. Thick gray hair is combed back off an arresting face. That face was the first thing I loved about him. I'd never met a handsomer, kinder man, and that's still true today.

"What?" he asks when he catches me looking at him.

"I'm thinking about your handsome face and how much I've loved it from the first time I ever saw you in Merv's Green Room."

The comment stops him short. "Is that right?"

"Uh-huh."

"You look gorgeous, as always."

"Thank you." I stand and go to him, laying my hands flat on his chest, which is covered in gray hair that used to be dark. "I want to tell you something."

"Okay..."

"I forgive you for not telling me the thing you didn't tell me."

He's stunned to hear that. "Really?"

Looking up at him, I nod. "You were right that if you'd told me at the beginning I wouldn't have given you a chance."

"I can't bear to think about spending the last fifty-two years with anyone but you."

"Same."

"Thank you for forgiving me."

"I do have one condition."

"What's that?"

"Whatever you did with her, you're going to do with me."

He wasn't expecting that.

Good. I wanted to take him by surprise.

"Um, we're old, Stella. That's a young person's game."

"We're not too old for sex, as you well know. Everything still works, and I want to understand that side of you, the side that's... dominant."

I feel my cheeks get warm, which he'll see, makeup or not.

"I'm not that guy anymore. I haven't been that guy in so long, I'm not even sure I'd remember how."

"You need to remember. We're going to do this in Mexico."

His eyes bug. "When we're surrounded by our family and the others?"

"We'll be in the guesthouse, far enough away from everyone else to do what we want."

Flynn always puts us there when the family is at his place in Mexico, so the kids won't drive us nuts with their early wakeups.

"Where do you propose I get the uh... *supplies*... needed for such a thing? I can't very well order them online."

He's right about that. Since Flynn became a superstar, our public profiles are higher than ever, and our careers are also hotter than they've ever been. Which means the interest in us can be far more intense than we'd prefer.

"Ask your son how he manages that."

Again, his face goes flat with shock. "You want me to ask Flynn how he..."

"Gets what he needs to play this game with his wife. Yes, I do."

"I... I don't think I can do that. I'd be mortified!"

I pat his face like he's a little boy. "You'll figure it out. I have faith in you. Now hurry up and get ready before we're late to our own party."

Max

SON OF A BITCH. SHE EXPECTS ME TO FUNCTION AFTER SHE LAID THAT challenge on me? I'm electrified just thinking about it. The thought of actually doing it, however... I can't let myself go there. Not now, when our family is expecting us for dinner.

The headline of the last ten minutes should be that she's decided to forgive me, but as I dress in a dark suit with a white dress shirt and the gold tie Stella bought me to wear tonight, I'm thinking about dominance, not forgiveness.

I'm incredibly thankful for the forgiveness. This time last night, I thought we might be over, and that was among the worst feelings I've ever had.

Her forgiveness means *everything* to me.

But as we drive to Frankie's Steak House, the site of our first date and every major celebration since, all I can think about is the condition of her forgiveness. While she seems remarkably relaxed and excited for the evening with the family, I'm wound tighter than a drum. How in the actual hell am I going to pull this off without causing another scandal?

We're almost to Frankie's when I get a text from Corbin. *Still looking but making progress. Will update you tomorrow.*

I respond to him at a red light. *Thanks for the effort.*

Anything for you, my friend.

I was hoping he'd put his hand right on the file we needed, but I suppose that was wishful thinking in light of how long ago the divorce happened. In today's digital world, we'd have the document in minutes, which is a good and bad thing, depending on how you look at it.

I'd rather think about divorce records and the digital age than figure out how I'm going to get the things I need to dominate my wife.

Holy hell. That's a sentence I never thought would cross my mind.

It'd be funny if she wasn't dead serious about this. She can live with knowing I was once married to her enemy, but not that I had a kind of sex with Vivian that we've never had. As if that matters.

It does to her, so that's what counts.

And what if all this is for nothing? What if I'm not even mentioned in Vivan's book, and I've set off a bomb in my life for no good reason? That's probably not likely. Knowing Vivian like I once did, it would give her great pleasure to name me as the ex-husband no one ever knew about, especially in light of how famous my son has become. Not to mention, she'd probably delight in sticking it to Stella.

It's delusional to presume we're not named in her memoir.

If she's looking for the book to be a blockbuster, dragging the Godfreys through the mud would help make that happen. People are so hungry for celebrity gossip, as if we're not just regular people putting our pants on one leg at a time like everyone else despite whatever success we may have enjoyed in the business that made us famous.

"Max."

I'm startled out of my thoughts to realize I've settled into one hell of a brood as I hand over the Escalade with a tip for one of Frankie's valets, who greets us like the regulars we are.

"Let it go for now. The kids are anxious enough as it is."

She's right, as usual.

I hold out a hand to her and feel tremendous relief when she curls her hand around mine to walk into the restaurant that holds such a special place in our hearts.

After being met inside by another member of Frankie's staff, we're directed to the back room, where so many of our most important events have transpired.

We turn heads as we make our way through the restaurant, but we keep our focus on the destination, so we won't be stopped.

"Happy anniversary," a woman calls out to us, which sets off a chorus of other good wishes from patrons.

We give them a wave and a smile but keep moving, aware of people taking photos and video that'll appear online within minutes. Such is the world we live in. I miss the days when it took a week or two for pictures to go public. Now, it's a matter of seconds, and no one bothers to make sure the photos are good ones before they go live, which means you never know what nightmare image might appear on TMZ.

We'd become mostly immune from celebrity stalking until our son became a star. It got even wilder for all of us after he and his producing partners swept the Oscars two years in a row, launching us into an all-new stratosphere that we're still getting used to.

Speak of the devil. Our handsome son greets us at the door, wearing a dark suit and burgundy tie, looking relieved to see us holding hands as we come toward him. He hugs and kisses us both, holding on a little longer than usual in light of current events.

"Happy anniversary, you two."

"Thank you, son," Stella says.

"Everything okay?" he asks, his brow furrowed as his gaze darts between us.

"We're working it out," Stella says to his great relief.

"That's the best news I've had all day."

"Me, too," I say with a smile for my wife.

"Welcome to bedlam." Flynn steps back to admit us into the room, where our youngest grandchildren are chasing one another around the second table we now require. Scarlett, Cece and Rowan are playing with Ellie and Jasper's kids, Harry and Matilda, as well as Marlowe and Sebastian's three-year-old twins, Domenic and Delaney.

As our honorary fourth daughter, we're delighted to have Marlowe and her family with us tonight. The rest of the crew will be at tomorrow's party.

Our older grandchildren, Ian, India, Ivy, Connor, Garrett and Mason, are doing their best to keep the little ones out of trouble.

In the corner, a TV has been set up with the video of us on the *Merv Griffin Show* playing on repeat. The kids thought of everything.

"Holy moly," I say to Flynn as I take in the chaos.

"All this from one marriage," he says. "What a legacy."

"It's a *loud* legacy," Stella says as she accepts hugs from Aimee, Annie and Ellie, as well as their husbands Trent, Hugh and Jasper, and then Natalie, Marlowe and Sebastian.

The grandkids rush us with hugs and kisses.

We wouldn't have it any other way.

It takes the better part of twenty minutes to corral kids and get everyone seated for appetizers and drinks. With the little ones in mind, everything was ordered in advance so it would be ready for a speedy delivery. We wanted the kids with us tonight, no matter what it took.

Once we're seated, a member of Frankie's staff rolls the man himself into the room in the transport chair he now relies upon. He'll be ninety at his next birthday, which is hard to believe.

Stella and I get up to greet one of our oldest friends with hugs and thanks for having us tonight.

"My pleasure, as always, to host my favorite family."

We settle him at the table next to me. His caretaker knows I'll tend to him and make sure his food is cut and that he has what he needs. We still play cards with a group of guys at least twice a month right in this room, and it's time with old friends that I cherish.

Waiters come in with glasses of champagne on trays, which wasn't part of our order.

Frankie raises his glass to us. "Happy anniversary, my dear friends. And cheers to the next fifty years."

"Thank you, Frankie, for all the years of celebrations right here at our home away from home," Stella says. "We love you."

"Love you right back," Frankie says.

"While we've got champagne," Flynn says as he stands, making his sisters groan predictably.

"Why does he get to make the toast when he's the baby?" Aimee asks.

"It's because I'm the most eloquent," he says, making a face at her as his sisters boo him.

The kids giggle at their parents' antics. I catch little Rowan's belly laugh, delighted as always by that guffaw of his.

Bennett, the newest addition to our family, is asleep on his mother's shoulder.

"I introduced Natalie to the madness that is the Godfrey family right in this very room. Funny how that was nothing compared to the madness of today."

"We're not the ones who added four new kids in five minutes," Annie says, receiving a high five from Aimee.

"No, you added the first round of kids and all their chaos," Stella says.

"She's got you there, Aunt Annie—and Mom," our eldest grandchild, Ian, says with a smirk.

I can't believe he's seventeen now and due to graduate from high school in June. He's planning to attend film school at USC in the fall. I love that he's going into the family business, even as I hope it treats him kindly. The older he gets, the more he resembles his uncle Flynn, which he tells us is an asset with the ladies.

"As I was saying," Flynn says with a glare for his sisters, "in the years since Natalie's first evening with us, our family has grown and expanded to include her, Jasper and Sebastian, as well as Cece, Scarlett, Rowan, Benny, Henry, Matilda, Domenic and Delaney, and all of us, everyone in this room, are here tonight because of the extraordinary couple who exchanged vows fifty years ago today.

"The life you've led, the family you've created, the legacy of your love and commitment will live within us forever. Happy Golden Anniversary to Max and Stella, with all our love."

"Damn him," Ellie said as she wipes away tears.

"Right?" Annie blows her nose and dabs at her eyes. "He ought to go into show business."

That sets the girls off laughing at their brother, one of their favorite pastimes.

It warms my heart to know that despite their nonstop mockery and play-bickering, they'd do anything for one another. Keeping it real with his sisters has been critical to Flynn successfully navigating superstardom. They haven't let any of it go to his head.

Once the tomfoolery dies down, I stand with my glass in hand. "I'd like to propose a toast to my bride, the love of my life, the remarkable, beautiful, talented Stella Flynn."

The family applauds raucously for the woman who holds us all together.

"As you all know, it's been an interesting couple of days for us, but even when things are unsettled or uncertain, there's no one I'd rather be working it out with than you, Stel. You're my everything. You're everything to all of us. I love you. Now and forever. To Stella!"

She stands to kiss me, leading to more applause and tears from our four children, who have to be beyond relieved to see our loving affection after the scare we put them—and ourselves—through.

"Thank you for your beautiful words and fifty years of sweet love, Max. You give me all the credit, but none of this happens without the best husband, father and grandfather any of us ever could've wished for. We've been blessed with a life of joy, love and purpose and with children, grandchildren and friends who've made our lives complete. We love you all so very much."

I embrace my wife, thankful for her love, for fifty-two years together and for everything still to come, even if the apprehension remains over whether I can keep up my end of our deal.

CHAPTER 12

Kristian

I'm incredibly relieved to hear that the Godfrey family dinner at Frankie's went off as scheduled last night, with the guests of honor in attendance and happy to be there together. It might seem odd to be so upset by the thought of trouble between my friend's parents, but they're the only parents I've ever had, too.

Max Godfrey saved my life after he caught me stealing food from his Compton movie set. Rather than turn me in to the authorities, like most famous people would've, he took me into his trailer, got me the first real meal I'd had in weeks and asked me what I planned to do with my life.

From that day forward, he took an interest in a street kid, mentored me and helped me find my way into the business that's made me wealthy beyond my wildest dreams—and not just financially. I have plenty of that, but more important—to me, anyway—is the family I've created for myself, first with Flynn, Hayden, Jasper, Marlowe, Emmett and the entire Quantum Productions team, and now with Aileen, Logan and Maddie, who I adopted shortly after

Aileen and I were married, and our soon-to-be five-year-old daughter, Joy, who lives up to her name every day of her life.

She's the sunshine of all our lives, and as I make her pancakes early this Saturday morning, I don't even mind that it's been years since I slept in because I'd rather be with her than be asleep. I'm ridiculously over the moon for her, but then again, everyone is.

"Do I get to wear my new party dress today, Daddy?" Her blonde hair is a mass of tangled curls, and her cheeks are rosy from sleep. In my unbiased opinion, she's the most beautiful little girl in the entire world.

"Yep. Today's the day for Grammy Stella and Pappy Max's big party."

"Will there be cake?"

"I'm sure there'll be lots of cake."

"I love cake."

"I know you do, pumpkin." I serve her pancakes just the way she likes them, with melted butter, syrup and a dusting of confectioners' sugar. Girlfriend likes her sugar any way she can get it. Aileen does her best to limit it, but I'm not as good at saying no to her as her mommy is. I joke that Aileen is the only thing keeping her from being completely spoiled.

"Yummy. Thank you, Daddy."

"My pleasure, sweetheart."

"Are you having some, too?"

"You bet." I bring my plate and coffee to sit next to her at the kitchen island.

"Pancakes are my favorite."

"Mine, too, but only when I get to have them with you."

"You're silly, Daddy. They taste the same no matter who you eat them with."

"Nope. They're much sweeter with you."

She rolls her eyes, which is something she learned from her sister. At twelve, Maddie has become a delightful preteen who cracks us up with her quick wit. She's in sixth grade, while Logan is in ninth. He's become one hell of a soccer player and watching him play is one of my favorite things. They're both out at sleepovers, which I hate, but Aileen tells me it's a normal thing that kids do. I know nothing about such things because I was never a normal kid. Everything feels wrong to me when they're not sleeping under our roof. I encourage them to invite their friends to our house as often as possible.

Rufus the dog rubs up against my leg to remind me he's there.

"Ruffy, want some pancakes?" Joy slips him a bite before I can object, not that I would. The two of them are best friends.

"No pancakes for Rufus," Aileen says when she comes into the room just in time to catch me asleep at the parenting wheel.

That happens a lot.

"Unless you want to clean up his puke, Miss Joy."

"Morning, Mommy." That angelic smile makes Aileen melt. She's only human, after all.

"Morning, my littlest love." She kisses Joy and makes her giggle with whatever she whispers into her ear.

"How's everything?" Aileen asks me as she kisses my cheek and fixes my hair.

I wrap an arm around her and give her a proper kiss. "All good. Flynn said they had a great night at Frankie's."

"Well, that's a relief."

"You said it."

We've all been anxious, waiting to hear if the Godfreys would be able to resolve things in time for their anniversary celebration, not to mention the rest of their lives.

"The thought of them not together and happy was super upsetting to me," Aileen says as she pours a cup of coffee and tops off my mug.

"Same, babe. It's amazing how it feels like they belong to all of us, you know?"

"I do, for sure. They're always there for us when we need them. As they get on in years, they'll have an army of kids tending to them. I hope they're prepared for that."

"I'm sure they'll love it, but we're a long way from them needing tended to."

"Definitely," she says. "Well, now I can look forward to today without the feeling of dread I've had since I heard the news."

"Apparently, there's an NDA from Max's divorce from Vivian that the lawyers are looking for. If they can find it, we might be able to stop the publication of the book."

"That'd be something." She sips her coffee and then hands Joy a wet paper towel to wash the stickiness off her hands.

I use it to wash her face, too. I help her down to go play, and she takes off with Rufus in hot pursuit. The two of them are inseparable.

"I still can't believe Max was once married to Vivian Stevens."

"It's so weird to think of him married to anyone other than Stella." She sits next to me. "I know! They're an institution."

"I really hope they can find a way to keep his marriage to Vivian under wraps. That'd be a massive story in this town."

Aileen cringes. "I'm sure it would be. The media would turn it into a BFD."

I take her hand and link my fingers with hers. "Any news yet?"

She shakes her head.

The waiting for the results of her now-annual breast cancer checkups is torturous. You'd think I'd be used to it after all these years, but you'd be wrong. Technically, she's "cured" since she's been in remission for more than five years, but the annual checkups will happen for the rest of her life. Each one of them takes ten years off my life.

"I'm sure we'll hear something soon."

"I sure as hell hope so." I slide my hand up her leg, moving quickly until she stops me. "Not in front of the child."

"She's not paying any attention to us."

She squeezes my hand. "Put it on ice, buddy. We've got stuff to do."

I make a pout face. "I hate when we have anything to do other than each other."

Her laughter is the best sound in the world to me.

"You're ridiculous."

"I love my wife."

She leans in to kiss me. "She loves you right back. Now go get dressed."

Stella

THE KIDS SEND A CHAUFFEURED BENTLEY FOR THE RIDE TO HAYDEN AND Addie's home in Calabasas. We've been instructed to act surprised because the guests were told to keep the secret. My hair stylist was the first to "give it away" when she asked if I wanted to set something up for today just in case.

Belinda has been doing my hair for forty years, so of course she's invited to the party, along with my makeup queen, Michelle. They're close friends after all these years, and they spent the morning at the house making me pretty. My kids know I don't love surprise parties, but they like to do nice things for me, so I try to be a good sport about it. They meet me halfway by telling me the basic details of what they have planned so I can properly prepare.

As an aging celebrity, I'm careful not to appear in public looking less than my best to keep the tabloids from publishing unflattering photos of me. Could I retire and be done with it all? Sure, but as long as I still enjoy my work, I'm not making any plans to slow down. These days, however, Max and I accept only the offers that interest us rather than feeling like we need to grab everything that comes along like we did when we were younger.

I'm looking forward to the televised concert at the Hollywood Bowl, set for late January, and I'll be glad when the rigorous final rehearsals for the show are done. I'm taking a few months off afterward to rest and figure out my next move. I have offers pending for everything from movies to television shows to Broadway, which doesn't interest me at all. I have no desire to be away from my family for months on end, especially with a whole new group of grandbabies to dote on while the older ones mature into young adults.

Life goes by too quickly to miss anything.

Max reaches for my hand. "What're you thinking about over there?"

"About how fast the time has gone and what I might do after the concert."

"Dani told me you're in hot demand," he says of the manager we share with Flynn. "You have your pick of projects."

"I told her I'm taking a break after the Hollywood Bowl. I want to spend some time with the grandkids and futz around the house."

"You're not thinking about the R-word, are you?"

"Good Lord, no. I'd be bored out of my mind if I never worked again. You know that."

"Phew, you scared me for a second there."

"Don't worry. I'm not punching out quite yet."

"You can, you know. If you wanted to. Nothing says you have to keep up the current pace."

"Trust me, I know that. I'm not ready to be done for good. Maybe in a few years, I will be, but I'm not there yet."

"Me either. I still enjoy the game."

We played ourselves in *Valiant* and were thrilled to be part of the film that tells Natalie's amazing story. Production was delayed first by the pandemic and then by the strikes. It'll finally be released in March with an amazing new actress playing our courageous daughter-in-law—Natalie's youngest sister, Olivia.

In the years since she accepted her first modeling job, Olivia has become one of the hottest young stars on the scene, and we've been thrilled to have front-row seats as she took the town by storm with an award-winning turn in a TV series, followed by a movie role that significantly raised her profile. *Valiant* is her first starring role, and we're so excited to watch her shine.

Their middle sister, Candace, is Olivia's manager. Both girls are like daughters to us and even have the security code to our home and orders to come and go as if they were raised there. Their mother visits from time to time, and Natalie has forged a new relationship with her, even if they'll never be close after both her parents abandoned her when she needed them most.

I'm able to be cordial to the woman for Natalie's sake, but I have no respect for her, and I never will. That she could walk away from her child after she'd been raped and beaten by her husband's friend... No, I can't forgive that as a mother or as a woman. I give Natalie credit for finding it in her to forgive her mother. She's a better person than I would've been, not that I'd ever express those thoughts to her. After everything she went through, Natalie deserves a peaceful, happy life. If reconnecting with her mother helps achieve that goal, then I totally understand.

We'll get to see the film for the first time when we're in Utah for Christmas, and none of us can wait to see the finished product.

"Are you ready for this?" Max asks as we arrive at the gates to Hayden and Addie's seaside home.

"As ready as I'll ever be."

He smiles at me. "Let's enjoy every minute of it."

"That's the plan."

We're met by a young man in a tuxedo, who offers a hand to help me out.

After Max emerges from the back seat, our four children appear with their partners at the front door.

A lump forms in my throat as they come toward me, wearing formal dresses and tuxedos.

"What a gorgeous group," I say as I accept hugs and kisses from each of them.

"You're looking rather stunning yourselves," Aimee says as she smooths her hands over Max's lapels. "That gown is exquisite, Mom."

"This old thing?"

They laugh, and I do a little spin to show them how my gold gown shimmers when it moves. I loved it the second our favorite stylist, Tenley Black, suggested it for the "surprise" party. The people closest to me know it's not a surprise, but we'll act the part for our other guests. I'm looking forward to seeing Tenley and her handsome husband, Devon, at the party.

We're led through Hayden and Addie's palatial home to the backyard, where a massive tent occupies much of the yard. At the bottom of the stairs, we're greeted by our grandchildren. Ian has baby Ben in his arms, all of them in formal attire, even the baby. I have tears in my eyes as I take a moment to cherish each of them with a hug and kiss. Just when we thought we had everything, our grandchildren arrived to show us there was so much more.

The kids take us by the hands to walk us into the tent, where the rest of our guests yell "Surprise," and throw gold confetti as we make our way inside, stopping to hug our friends and extended family. Gold is the theme as tiny tea lights sparkle above, and lush floral centerpieces sitting on gold tablecloths give off the fragrant scents of lilies and roses. I want to look at everything, but we're surrounded by so many people who've been part of our fifty-year journey, and each of them wants a moment with the guests of honor.

It takes more than an hour to greet everyone, and by then, we've consumed several glasses of champagne.

We're led to the front of the big tent, where our close friend Superior Court Judge Rosalee Davis leads us through the renewal of our vows, something we've never done before. After the last couple of days, it seems somewhat fitting that we should reconfirm our commitment to each other.

We decided to go with traditional vows rather than trying to come up with something on our own. As it is, I'm astounded by how emotional even the most traditional of vows makes me as I stare into the eyes of the only man I've ever loved and promise to love him and only him for the rest of my life.

Even with everything I know now, it's still the easiest vow I've ever made—both times.

It's not lost on me that having the Vivian bomb dropped on me on the eve of this momentous anniversary was probably a good thing. At any other time, I might've made the grievous mistake of punishing him for much longer than a day for something he did a lifetime ago that doesn't matter much in the grand scheme of things. Yes, I'm still shocked by it, but not so shocked or angry that I'd throw away all the good I've had with him. The anniversary festivities have forced me to focus on the good, and there's so much of that.

Before we're seated for dinner, we step outside into a gorgeous sunset over the Pacific for a family photo that'll be my most treasured keepsake from this day and will be the only image released to the media to mark the occasion.

Surrounded by the ones I love best, I'm at peace after a tumultuous couple of days. Yes, the news about Vivian was stunning and disappointing, but I'll get over it. Eventually. For now, I'm delighted to be spending this evening with all my favorite people.

CHAPTER 13

Max

*A*fter a delicious dinner of filet mignon and lobster, as well as heartfelt toasts from family and friends, I'm leaning against the bar with a glass of whiskey in hand when Corbin Remington approaches, shaking my hand as he offers his congratulations. "What an amazing celebration. I stand in awe of you and Stella for going the distance, especially in this town."

"Thank you, my friend. I'm so glad you and the family could be here today."

"We wouldn't have missed it." He reaches into the inside pocket of his suit coat, removes a piece of paper and puts it into the same pocket inside my coat. "The item you requested."

"You found it! Thank goodness."

"I found it, and it's airtight with no expiration date. If you're mentioned in her book, you can stop it."

"I can't thank you enough for this, Corb. And for your discretion in handling it personally."

"Our archivist was surprised when the senior partner turned up in her domain, but she was very helpful in pointing me in the right direction."

"I bet she doesn't see you in her world very often."

"I hadn't been in that part of the office in years. It was humbling to have to do some real work for a change."

Laughing, I place a hand over the spot where the document resides inside my coat. "It's such a relief to have a way to fight back. The last thing I want is to be dragged into her web of drama."

"I get it. Trust me."

"Have you run into Kate?"

"I saw her across the room, but I haven't talked to her."

If you ask me, Corbin is still in love with his ex-wife, and she's still in love with him, despite their acrimonious divorce. Neither of them has ever remarried or had another serious relationship—that I know of, anyway.

Corbin's eldest son, Julian, approaches us.

Out of respect for my friend, I'm cordial to his son, but I'll never forget the way he hurt my Aimee once upon a time. He's the epitome of tall, dark and handsome, more so than usual in a tuxedo. In the years since I last saw him, he's become as celebrated an attorney as his father.

"Congratulations, Mr. Godfrey."

"I think you're old enough to call me Max, Julian."

"I don't know if I could bring myself to do that."

"Try."

"Congratulations, Max."

"There. Was that so hard?"

"Not so bad." Julian's smile has made him one of Hollywood's most eligible bachelors, but from what Corbin tells me, his sons intend to remain unmarried. Their father carries tremendous guilt over the example of marriage his nine children were raised with, giving each of them an aversion to the institution. It probably doesn't help that they spend their days dissolving marriages and working on complex family law cases.

"My bride beckons," I tell them when Stella waves me over to her.

"Congratulations again, old friend," Corbin says. "And many happy returns on the day."

I shake his hand and Julian's. "Thanks for being here to help us celebrate."

"We wouldn't have missed it," Julian says.

When I rejoin Stella, the musicians launch into our wedding song, "You're the First, the Last, My Everything," and we step onto the dance floor to the applause of our guests. We fall right into the jazzy dance routine we did at our wedding, without any practice. Some things you never forget.

"The kids went all out, huh?" I ask as the music slows and I draw her in close.

"Did you expect anything less?"

"I wasn't sure what to expect, but this is truly magnificent."

"Yes, it is. The best part is the babies."

We look over to where the little ones are gathered in a tight group of cousins and children who'll grow up to be best friends like their parents are. Little Rowan has shed most of his suit and unbuttoned his shirt.

"How much do we love that our son has a son who's just like he was?"

"We love that very much. No one deserves a wild child more than he does."

"I fear he's going to be every bit as handsome as our Flynn, too."

"No question about that." I pull back to look down at her. "Are you happy, my darling?"

"I am. Are you?"

"If you are, I am, and I have good news. Corbin found the NDA."

"Oh wow. That's great news indeed. What happens now?"

"I'll turn it over to Emmett and get the ball rolling on putting a stop to this memoir of hers."

"What do you think about Flynn paying her a visit?"

"He offered that, but I nixed it."

"What if I wanted that to happen, for Flynn to show up at her door in all his glory and for her to think he's come to speak to her about a part in one of his films, but in reality, he's come to stop her book?"

"My vindictive little she-cat."

She laughs. "I can't help that she brings out the worst in me."

"This is the only proof I've ever had that you're not perfect."

"Oh please. There's been lots more proof than that over the years."

I shake my head as I gaze at her warmly. "Nope. You're perfect for me in every way, including your vindictive streak where she's concerned."

"Our many children are looking on with relief."

"I'll bet they are. We gave them a scare."

"We gave ourselves a scare."

"I'd say we can celebrate a fairly good run if our first major scare happened at the end of year fifty."

She laughs. "For sure, and it's been much better than a fairly good run. It's been magical. Every minute of it, well, except for a few minutes this week."

"Magical is a good word."

"It's the only word."

I hold her close as the remaining members of our wedding party join us on the dance floor—my brother, her sister and some of our oldest and dearest friends. We've lost five of the others who stood up for us that day.

Our family and friends come to the dance floor as the band plays a medley of songs from the year we were married: "Love Will Keep Us Together," "Laughter in the Rain," "You Are So Beautiful," "Some Kind of Wonderful," "How Sweet It Is (To Be Loved by You)" and "This Will Be (An Everlasting Love)," among others.

We dance for an hour full of love, laughter and happily ever after.

Marlowe

"A<small>RE YOU FEELING BETTER</small>, <small>HON</small>?" S<small>EBASTIAN ASKS AS WE ENJOY THE</small> dance party of seventies hits.

"Much better." The trouble between Max and Stella rocked my world like nothing has in longer than I can remember and made me sick to my stomach. They're my family as much as they're Flynn's, and I love them dearly. Ever since my mother died shortly after I came to Hollywood to chase the dream, Max and Stella have stepped up for me in so many ways that've meant the world to me. I couldn't bear to think of something coming between them.

"We all need them strong and happy and taking care of us."

"Absolutely."

I notice Sebastian's parents, Graciela and José, dancing cheek to cheek on the other side of the dance floor. "Your folks look happy."

"They really do. If you'd have asked me years ago if they'd ever figure out their shit, I would've said no way. Look at them now."

"True love wins."

He hugs me tighter. "Sure does."

"Have you seen our children recently?"

"Ivy's got them. Don't worry."

He had the brilliant idea to pay Ivy to watch our little monsters, as we affectionately refer to the three-year-old twins who've turned our lives upside down in every possible way. We joke that they touched down like an EF5 tornado and have had us spinning ever since, but we love every minute with them—and every break we get from the intense demands of parenthood.

"I have a surprise for you," he whispers in my ear, sending a shiver down my spine.

"What kind of surprise?"

"The kind that has my parents taking the monsters home with them tonight."

"For reals?"

"Would I lie about that?"

"No, you wouldn't. Best surprise ever."

"How long will it take for us to miss them?"

"About fifteen minutes."

We laugh together, something we do every day as we march through life hand in hand. Since our twins, Domenic and Delaney, arrived three years ago, I've taken a break from acting to give them my full attention. As soon as they start school, I'll look around for something to keep me busy. For now, I'm loving life as a full-time wife and mother and occasional producer while Sebastian continues to manage Club Quantum.

"Flynn calls it the ultimate paradox. You can't wait for a break from them, but the minute you get one, you just want to get back to them as soon as possible."

"That's a perfect summary. We'll have a belly full of kids in Utah and Mexico."

"But they'll have all their friends to play with, which makes it so much easier."

"For sure."

There's nothing our babies love more than time with their pals. They ask for Joy, Cece, Scarlett, Rowan, Henry and Matilda first thing every morning. We see them as often as we can because the kids love one another as much as their parents do. The little ones are obsessed with the older ones, and vice versa. Aileen has said that she suspects Logan and Maddie are an easier preteen and teenager than they might've been because they're aware of the little ones looking up to them. I say that's bull because Logan and Maddie would've been awesome no matter what.

"It's a helluva gift we're giving them, growing up surrounded by so much family," Seb says.

"I know. I never had anything like that, and it's so beautiful to see their bonds already forming."

"Those bonds will last a lifetime."

I look up at my handsome husband, who was right there for years, waiting for me to find him and the kind of happiness I once thought would never happen for me. "I can't wait for Utah and Mexico and two whole weeks together."

He kisses me. "I can't wait for everything together."

Julian

I SHOULDN'T HAVE COME TO THIS PARTY, BUT BOTH MY PARENTS checked in to make sure I'd be here, and since it means so much to them, here I am. Max and Flynn Godfrey were polite to me, shook my hand and said all the right things, but they've never forgiven the way I broke Aimee's heart back in the day. Even if it was almost twenty years ago, a devoted father and brother don't forget.

Hell, I haven't forgotten either.

She's as beautiful as ever, dancing with her tall, handsome husband and equally attractive children. I'm amazed by how much her son looks like his uncle Flynn. Years ago, the family sued the publication that all but said her son was really Flynn's—and they won.

Disgusting episode all around, and I cheered for her and her family from the sidelines.

Aimee Godfrey is my one major regret in life, not that we didn't go the distance so much as how we ended. I handled it badly, for reasons that made sense to me at the time. But with the benefit of hindsight, I hate myself for the way I hurt her.

We met when I played high school baseball with Flynn. I'm five years younger than Aimee, which gave her pause at the beginning, but I was mature for my age after what my parents had put us through by then. Aimee and I were like a rocket ship right out of the gate, madly in love and in over our heads from the get-go.

I had no intention then—or now—of falling in love with anyone. After what we went through watching our parents tear each other— and our family—apart for the better part of a decade, marriage and forever isn't in the cards for me. When you spend your days dissolving marriages, the last thing you want for yourself is that kind of shackle around your leg. My brothers wholeheartedly agree with me. Our goal in life is never to find ourselves in the situation our parents were in when they split up, putting nine kids through the wringer fighting over us and everything else for ten long years.

No, thank you.

That's never going to be me—or Griffin, Carson, Ethan, Jackson or Roman. The six of us have a pact—none of us will ever get married. Our three sisters, Jordan, Kaidan and Gillian, more or less agree with us, but they haven't taken the same vow we have. I suspect they'll be more likely to give in, but we never will.

The very thought of being legally bound to a woman is so preposterous to me as to be repulsive. Marriage ruins everything. I've seen that my whole life, and even all the happy couples I see before me on the dance floor can't convince me otherwise.

Once upon a time, I ran around with Flynn Godfrey, Hayden Roth and Emmett Burke, and I know stuff about them—and their partners in crime at Quantum—that would set off a world-class scandal if it ever got out. No one will hear it from me, especially since I enjoy the same lifestyle they did before they became happily domesticated.

I negotiated Flynn's divorce from Valerie Ward, which turned ugly, as most of them do.

Even though I don't believe in the institution, it's nice to see Flynn happily married to Natalie now. I didn't believe him when he said he'd never get married again after the Valerie disaster. But Hayden? That was a true shocker. His family of origin is even more fucked up than mine—and that's saying something. He's happy as a pig in shit with his Addison and four beautiful little girls who follow him around, looking up to him like the superhero he is to them.

Good for him—and Emmett, who allegedly married a spitfire in Leah. Their little guy, Holt, is a cutie, and Emmett seems happier than I've ever seen him.

They all deserve happiness, no doubt about it. Hell, everyone does. But not everyone needs a wife or even a long-term partner to be truly happy. I love my life as a single man about town, dating anyone who catches my eye, moving through life unencumbered, able to do whatever the fuck I want whenever the fuck I want without answering to anyone. It works for me—and for my brothers.

The six of us work for my dad—or will as soon as Roman finishes law school at Stanford—at Remington & Sons, the firm our grandfather founded more than sixty years ago. Only Carson isn't an attorney. He's our chief investigator and is damn good in that role. Our sisters and two of our cousins work for our mom's boutique firm, Kate Remington & Associates, making us frequent rivals in divorce cases. Even as we face off as adversaries in court, we go out of our way to stay close as siblings. That was critical to our mental health during the long custody battle, and our group of nine has remained tight well into adulthood.

This is the first time all eleven of us have been in the same room at the same time since Roman graduated from UCLA almost three years ago. That's fine with us. Our parents are barely able to be civil to each other, leaving us to dread days when we're together. The funniest part of it, if you can call it funny, is that we all believe they're as in love with each other as they ever were.

We have no idea what came between them to blow up their marriage into a modern-day *War of the Roses*. Neither of them has ever divulged that detail, not that it matters now. But they've never remarried, nor has either had a serious partner in the years since they split.

I finish my fourth—or is it fifth?—glass of champagne and head for the restroom to take a leak. Like everything else about this party, even the rented bathrooms are classy. As I'm heading back to the tent a few minutes later, I nearly crash into Aimee as she comes toward me, not paying attention to where she's going.

"Hey." She would've stumbled had I not reached out to her. The second my hands touch her skin I realize my mistake.

Her audible gasp indicates I'm not alone in feeling the punch of connection we've always shared.

The second she's steady, I release her.

"How are you?" I ask her.

She crosses her arms, as if she needs the protection. "Fine. You?"

"Good."

"Glad to hear it."

"Nice party for your folks."

She can barely bring herself to look at me, even after all this time. "Uh-huh."

"Your kids are all grown up."

"Yes, they are."

"Congratulations on your beautiful family."

"Thank you."

"I... um... It's nice to see you, Aimee."

"Uh-huh." She moves to step around me, and I take the hint that this conversation she didn't want to have is over.

I head back into the tent.

"Julian."

I turn back to her, brow raised.

"It's nice to see you, too."

She walks away, leaving me with a feeling of deep regret that's so foreign to me as to belong to someone else entirely. As a rule, I don't believe in regrets.

"Were you talking to Aimee Godfrey?" Carson asks when I return to our table.

Like me, he has brown eyes and dark hair, but where mine is cut every four weeks by a professional, his is long, unruly and often looks as if he cuts it himself. He probably does. He teases me for being metro. I tease him about being a slob.

"Yeah." I signal the waiter for another drink. Ethan is our designated driver tonight, so I'm free to indulge.

"How was that?"

"Awkward."

Carson winces. He knows better than anyone how it went down with her. "She seems happy."

"She does. I'm glad for her."

"Don't let her get under your skin. You made your choices for good reason."

"I know."

"Julian..."

"I hear you. I'm okay."

I watch Aimee come back into the tent and go straight for the table where her devoted husband waits for her. She slides onto his lap, smiling as she wraps her arms around him. Across the massive tent, her gaze connects with mine. I feel her in every corner of my body, something I've never experienced with anyone but her.

Thank God for that, because I have no desire to feel wild and out of control like I did with her.

"You're better off without her," Carson reminds me. "You're better off by yourself than with someone who fucks up your head the way she did."

"You're right."

"You're goddamned right I am."

Everything is better this way, or so I tell myself, but when Aimee finally looks away, I feel like I've lost something special, something I never wanted in the first place.

CHAPTER 14

Flynn

*A*s the celebration begins to wind down, my dad asks for a minute with me. We find a quiet corner in the tent, and he hands me a folded piece of paper. "What's this?"

"The NDA Vivian Stevens signed as a condition of our divorce."

"Oh wow. Why're you giving it to me?"

"I talked it over with Mom, and we decided we like the idea of you asking for a meeting and presenting it to her. I know there's not much time until we leave for Utah, but if you can squeeze that in before we go, we'd appreciate it."

"I'll make it happen."

"Thank you, son, for all your support during this difficult situation."

"Whatever you guys need, whenever you need it."

He hugs me tightly, bringing a huge lump to my throat.

"Love you so much," he whispers gruffly. "You'll never know how much or how proud of you we are."

"I know, Dad. I've been blessed to always know that."

When he pulls back from me, he has tears in his eyes that gut me. "Are you okay?"

"I'm better than I was, that's for sure."

"And things with Mom..."

"We're working it out."

"Thank God for that. There's a whole tentful of people who need you two to keep showing us how it's done."

"I made a huge mistake keeping this from her for so long."

"No, you didn't. Like you said, if you'd told her back then, she wouldn't have given you a chance." I gesture to the room full of loved ones. "Look at what you would've missed out on. Not that I'm any kind of proponent of secrets in a marriage, but in this case, the truth would've done more harm than good back then."

"Yeah, for sure. The funniest part—if any of this is funny—is that I hadn't given Vivian a thought in years until I read about her memoir. She never crosses my mind."

"Why would she?"

"When you show up there, she's going to think you want to work with her."

I smile. "I thought of that."

"Make sure she knows we both sent you to take care of this for us."

"I'll do that. If she plans to run my parents through the wringer, I'll make sure to thoroughly ruin her fun."

My dad's smile lights up his eyes. "We'll look forward to a full report."

"You'll have it as soon as the deed is done."

"Thank you again for everything these last few days, including this glorious party with all our favorite people."

"The girls had more to do with that than I did."

"I'm sure you had a hand in it."

"A little bit, when they'd let me. Between them and Addie, I didn't get much say in any of it."

He laughs, knowing how bossy my sisters and Addie are with me. "It was a beautiful celebration."

"Of a beautiful couple and marriage." I glance over to where Natalie is dealing with four kids about to melt down since it's way past their bedtime.

"Hey," Dad says, "while I have you, let me ask you something else that's been on my mind since our frank discussion the other day."

"What's that?"

"The lifestyle..."

I cringe. "Are we really going to talk about that again? Once was more than enough for me."

He laughs at the face I make. "Me, too, but I've been wondering... If one is Flynn Godfrey, superstar, how does one go about procuring the... items... needed to practice said lifestyle?"

"A fake name and a PO box," he says bluntly.

"Ah, I see. Well, that's a relief. I had nightmares about a warehouse employee somewhere telling the world what he was shipping to you."

"Please. No chance of that."

"I should've known you had every base covered."

"Always. Got to protect the ones I love. Speaking of that, I'd better go rescue Nat from the kids. They're running on fumes."

"Time for bed."

"It was time an hour ago, but we weren't ready to leave yet." I tuck the document into my inside coat pocket and then pat my chest. "I'll reach out to her in the morning and get the ball rolling."

"Thank you again, son."

"Love you, Dad. Anything for you."

He kisses my cheek and walks away, leaving me feeling emotional about one of the greatest blessings of my charmed life—being born to him and my mom. So many of my closest friends grew up in turbulent homes with parents constantly at each other's throats, such as the Remingtons, who are all here tonight to support my parents when theirs have been the exact opposite of mine.

I'm sad for the people who didn't get to grow up with parents like Max and Stella. Natalie and her sisters had the opposite of them, as did Hayden, Kristian and Jasper. Although Jasper's mom is awesome, his dad was a freaking monster. Marlowe's father refused to support her desire to move to Hollywood and become a star. Her mom brought her, and the two of them lived out of their car for a year while Mo chased the dream. No sooner had the dream begun to come true than she lost her mom to cancer.

Sebastian's dad wasn't in his life for most of it, Kristian watched as his mom was murdered, and Hayden's parents have been married and divorced so many times, none of us can keep count. It's nice to see his mom, Jan, healthy after a long struggle with addiction and happy with Addie's dad, Simon, who was widowed young when Addie's mom died suddenly. We sure as hell didn't see Jan and Simon coming, but the relationship has been great for them and everyone who loves them.

When Natalie comes toward me, carrying a sleeping baby with three little ones trailing behind her, I realize I tuned out for a second into my own thoughts. "Everything okay with your dad?"

"Yep." I bend to pick up Rowan, who's asleep on his feet. "Let's get this crew home to bed, shall we?"

"Yes, please."

After we say good night to my parents, sisters and many friends, another half hour has gone by, and the kids are all but asleep as we buckle them into car seats in the Mercedes SUV.

We wave to Marlowe and Sebastian as they walk to Graciela's car with Domenic and Delaney passed out on their shoulders. They told us they're excited to have a night alone together since his parents are taking the twins.

"Looks like everyone ran out of gas around the same time as ours did," Natalie says. "The kids had the best time. Addie got an awesome picture of all of them together before they lost the suit coats and bow ties."

"I was hoping someone got a pic." The minute we clear Hayden's gate I take her hand.

She cradles my hand between both of hers, the way she always does. "That one will be historic."

I chuckle. "I can't wait to see it."

"I look at them all and wonder what they'll grow up to be and which of them will follow their parents into show business."

"None of them if I have my way about it."

"I'm sure they'll listen to you the same way you listened to your parents' warnings when you wanted to be an actor."

"They were totally opposed to it at first."

"Your mom said they were until the first time they saw you onstage in the eighth grade and realized how wildly talented you are."

"I had the lead in the middle school production of *Guys and Dolls*. That was the start of it. After that, all I wanted was more of it. I didn't want to play sports anymore or surf or do anything but perform."

"So you know there's no stopping a child with a dream, even if you might want an easier life for them."

We've gone to enormous lengths to keep our kids mostly out of the media, which is easier said than done. Photographers have managed to get the occasional photo of them, but for the most part, they're leading private lives, at least for now. We're under no illusions about what our entire crew of kids is in for as they get older. My parents asked for permission to release the family photo to the media, and we gave it, somewhat reluctantly.

"I want them to have a normal life."

"They're having a very normal life, full of all the things childhood should be about."

"All thanks to their amazing mother."

"Thanks to both of us. You're every bit as wonderful with them as I am."

"This is my favorite time in my life."

"Driving the family SUV rather than the Bugatti?" she asks, smiling at me.

"Hell yes. As great as the Bugatti is, there's nothing quite like having the whole family riding shotgun."

"Aw, that's nice to hear. Sometimes you must look back at the Bugatti days and wonder what became of your orderly, sensible life."

I look over at her, surprised to hear her say that. "I never, ever look back at those years with any kind of yearning. You know that, right?"

"I do, but still, we have to be a huge shock to your system. You went from never wanting to be married again to having a wife and four kids."

"Best years of my entire life, hands down."

"Mine, too."

"Don't ever, *ever* think I wish for my old life, because I don't. When I'm not with you guys, all I want is to get home to you as fast as I can."

"We all look forward to Daddy coming home, no one more so than Mommy."

"Because she can't wait to turn the wild ones over to me."

"That's not the only reason."

"Oh no?"

"I still get all fluttery in the belly when you walk in and look at me the way you do."

"How do I look at you?"

"Like I'm your whole world and you're so happy to see me."

"You are my whole world, and I'm always thrilled to see you. That hasn't changed one bit since that first day."

"We're so lucky."

"And we know it. Working on *Valiant* has brought it all back, the thrill of those early days, the madness that followed the Golden Globes, getting married in Vegas and shocking the world."

"Sometimes I still can't believe it all happened to me."

"The best day of my life was the day Fluff brought you to me, topped by every day since then. Being with you is like living my dream come true—a dream I didn't even know I had until I had you."

"That's very sweet of you to say, but I'm still annoyed with Fluff for biting you. How funny is it that you're the only person she's ever bitten? Three times!"

"It's hilarious."

She cackles with laughter.

"What's so funny, Mommy?" Cece asks.

I can't believe she's still awake.

"We're talking about the day that Fluff bit Daddy—the first time."

"But that's how you met Daddy," Cece says.

She never tires of hearing about how we met and fell in love.

"So it was a good thing that Fluff bit him."

"It was a very good thing," I tell my baby girl.

"Biting is naughty," Natalie says, "and Fluff was in big trouble for biting Daddy. All three times."

"She's the goodest girl," Fluff's attorney, Cece, says emphatically. "She's not naughty."

Natalie and I dread the day when Fluff crosses the rainbow bridge. Cece will be devastated—and so will we. But the old battle-ax is going strong, despite her advanced age, so we're not worried yet.

"That's right, honey." I glance in the mirror to catch her sweet smile. "We love Fluff for bringing Mommy to meet me."

"As long as we all agree, biting is bad," Natalie says.

"Biting good," Rowan says sleepily.

"Honestly," Natalie mutters as I silently laugh my ass off. "That boy is going to be the death of me, just like his Daddy."

"I bet Benny's gonna be just like him."

"Heaven help me."

Jasper

WITH OUR KIDS FAST ASLEEP INSIDE, ELLIE AND I HANG OUT FOR A BIT at Hayden's after most of the guests have departed. Hayden lights the firepit, and we gather around, most of us with baby monitors in hand so we can listen for our kids.

"The front door is locked, right?" Addie asks her husband.

"I checked it twice. Everyone is gone, and the gate is locked. All good, hon."

We've helped ourselves to drinks and the fresh-baked cookies the caterers brought out as a late-night snack.

"What a party," Hayden says.

"It was everything we'd hoped it would be—and then some," Ellie says.

My love is exhausted but exhilarated after a successful evening—and from the relief of seeing her parents together and happy. We're all grateful for that.

"I *loved* the video," Aileen says.

Joy is asleep in Kristian's arms. Logan went home with Annie's boys for a sleepover and Maddie with Aimee's girls.

"The video was all Annie's doing," Ellie says, "with some help from Hayden."

"I just edited what she did and added music."

"According to her, you brought it to life."

"I was just so freaking happy to see your parents laughing and having a great time," Leah says.

I suspect she's breastfeeding baby Holt under the blanket that's over him.

"No kidding," Aileen says. "I didn't know what to expect tonight."

"I think the timing of the anniversary helped us avert potential disaster," Ellie says. "They knew they had to get it together in time for this weekend."

"That may be true," Hayden says, "but they would've figured it out sooner rather than later, anniversary or not. If any two people belong together, it's them."

"And us," Addie says with a grin for Hayden.

"And us, babe. That's a given."

"Good save, my man," Kris says, laughing.

Hayden grins. "I like to think I can be trained."

Addie pats him on the head. "You're my very well-trained house pet."

That sets us off into hysterical laughter that disturbs the sleeping kids.

"Simmer down, y'all," Kris says as he soothes Joy.

He's so gone over his little girl. I love watching him in daddy mode. No one deserves a happy life more than my best friend does after a horrific childhood. The man who killed his mother more than thirty-five years ago was convicted and sentenced to life in prison with no chance of parole. While it was agonizing for him to testify about the murder he witnessed as a three-year-old, getting justice for her has helped Kristian put the past behind him where it belongs.

Nights like this, spent with my closest friends, the family of my heart, make all the hell and heartache I went through with my father blackmailing me worth it. My sister Gwen has done an amazing job running Kingsley Enterprises since our father retired, while I continue to live my dream here in LA with Ellie, Harry, Matilda, and our Quantum family. I'm still in line to be the tenth Duke of Wethersby when my father passes away, but I don't waste any time worrying about the future when the present is so sweet.

"Can you guys even imagine being married for *fifty years*?" Leah asks as she burps Holt.

Emmett gives her a playful scowl. "Not thinking you can stand me that long, honey?"

"I wouldn't be able to," Hayden says to more laughter.

"I never said that," Leah replies. "Fifty years, though. That's just incredible."

"My dad's parents were married for sixty-five," Ellie says.

"Longevity runs in your family," Leah says. "You're lucky."

"And we know it," Ellie says. "I have no idea what any of us would be without Max and Stella leading the way."

I raise my glass. "To Max and Stella, the best parents, grandparents, in-laws and friends anyone could have."

"Cheers."

CHAPTER 15

Max

Stella is exhausted and heads up to bed when we get home. I tell her I'll be up shortly and go into my office, fire up my laptop and get busy setting up accounts under the name I use when I check into a hotel. That's a trick celebrities use to keep the paparazzi from finding us when we don't want to be found. My Edwin Johnson persona has a fake California driver's license and everything, which makes this process much easier than it would've been otherwise.

Within thirty minutes, Edwin has an account at an online vendor and a new box at the Beverly Hills Post Office.

I'm quite pleased with myself until I dive into the actual shopping portion of the program. The vast array of options is mind-boggling. Clearly, the lifestyle has evolved and expanded—greatly—in the years since I last dabbled. At that time, it was exciting, exhilarating and a bit taboo. Now, it's mortifying.

I'm far too old for this shit.

The thought of actually using these things in bed with Stella makes me feel like I'm having a heart attack.

She says she wants this, but does she really? Does she fully understand what it means to be submissive?

We're going to have to have that conversation, in addition to several others.

When I was younger, the conversation alone would be enough to get my motor running on all cylinders. As I contemplate "going there" with my lovely wife, I break out in a cold sweat, and any desire I might've felt is swept away by a sick feeling.

The worst part is Stella thinking that I've ever been unsatisfied with our always-healthy sex life. That's simply not true. Long after most of our friends settled into seemingly platonic marriages, ours is still romantic and sexy and everything it's always been.

I mean, we're not doing it like we did back in the day when we were newly in love and couldn't get enough of each other. Four kids arriving in quick succession put a damper on our ardor for a time, but we never lost that loving feeling like so many people do as they age.

In fact, two Saturday nights ago, we came home from dinner with friends and had ourselves a private after party that went on until well after midnight. We laughed about that the next day, how we'd stayed up long after our usual bedtime. "We've still got it," I'd said.

She'd agreed. "Damn straight we do."

Before this condition of hers goes any further, it's imperative to me that she know, without any shadow of any doubt, that I've never wanted anything more than what she and I have had. We've had as close to perfect a married life as it's possible to have, full of love, laughter, intimacy and great sex. We've supported each other through all the highs and lows of a lifetime, from losing our parents to missing out on coveted parts to challenges with our kids. Having her in my corner has been as important to me as having her in my bed, and she has to know that.

I order a few basic items and have them sent to my new PO box using expedited next-day shipping, so they'll arrive in time for the trip.

Then I clear the search history on my laptop, not that anyone but me ever uses it, but one can't be too careful about these things. I power it down, shut off the lights on the main floor, check to make sure all the doors are locked and head upstairs, hoping Stella is still awake.

In our room, the bedside light is out.

I'm disappointed, but the conversation will keep until the morning. I get ready for bed, brush my teeth and reflect on the beautiful celebration the kids threw for us.

I slide into bed carefully, so I won't disturb her.

She turns over and curls up to me.

I make her welcome in my arms, as always. "Are you ready to sleep?"

"You know me and sleep these days. It's a nightly battle."

"I don't want to disturb you."

"It's fine. Did you take something for the champagne headache?"

"Shit. No. Let me do that so tomorrow's not a total loss."

I get up and go into the bathroom to take two ibuprofen and return to bed. "Come back."

She returns to her spot next to me, her head on my chest and my arm around her. "What's on your mind?"

"Since you laid out your condition for forgiveness, it's been bothering me ever since that you might think I've found anything lacking in what I've had with you. Because I haven't. I've never once thought, after making love with you, gee, I wish that was different or more or anything other than exactly what it's always been. I need you to know that."

"Of course I know. I was there, remember? I know how it is between us."

"After hearing about what came between Vivian and me, you didn't think that maybe I wanted something more?"

"I mean... It's a little unsettling that she saw a side of you that I never have, and it's made me curious, as anyone would be."

"That side of me was short-lived."

"Still... It interests me."

"Do you understand what it means to be submissive to your Dom in bed?"

"I, um, I think so."

"You'd turn over your pleasure to me and trust me to take care of you."

"How is that any different from what we already do?"

"It's different because I may ask you to do things we don't normally do, all of which would be discussed and agreed to in advance, and you'd have the power to stop everything with a single word."

"A safe word."

"Yes, exactly."

"I've read books that featured the lifestyle, so I have some idea of what to expect."

"What would your safe word be?"

She thinks about that for a second. "Green Room."

"I love that, but green usually means go in this game."

"As long as it's paired with room it works."

"Fair enough. When you read the books, did the BDSM turn you on?"

"It did. You usually benefited from that."

"I wish you'd told me what'd fired you up. We might've tried this long before now."

"I would've been embarrassed to tell you that."

"See? That's the beauty of the lifestyle. We put it all on the table and talk about everything, even things that might normally be embarrassing to discuss with a partner. Especially those things. The free exchange of communication and information helps me under-stand what really works for you and helps you to know what to expect in a scene."

"You sound excited to be talking about it."

"Do I?"

"Yes."

"I suppose it's easier to talk about and to be excited about it with the lights off."

She laughs. "Everything is easier in the dark." Her hand moves in circles on my chest. "I've been proud of the fact that there was nothing we couldn't talk about, even the difficult stuff."

"That's true, and there's no one I'd rather talk to about anything than you."

"Same, which is why it should be somewhat easy for us to make the transition to something new and different. We're already good at the most important part."

"You're right."

"You say that like it's a new development."

"Ha! I walked right into that one."

"Yes, you did."

I tip her chin up to receive my kiss. "My beautiful wife is almost always right."

"Almost always... Whatever you say, stud."

"That's the spirit. Whatever I say goes."

"Only in here. I'm in charge everywhere else."

"I wouldn't have it any other way, my darling."

Flynn

IN THE MORNING, I TEXT MY MANAGER, DANI, AND ASK HER TO GO through Vivian Stevens's management to set up an ASAP meeting. *Needs to happen before Christmas, and I'd like it to happen at her house, if possible. Tell her I have something important to discuss with her.*

On it, Dani replies minutes later.

Thanks.

The message should make Vivian want to see me right away. I don't mean to be arrogant, but after the successes we've seen at Quantum in recent years, everyone wants to work with us. That reminds me that Hayden mentioned Cammy Smith the other day—and I haven't thought of it again. I text to ask if he set something up with her.

Marlowe and I are having lunch with her tomorrow. Don't worry about it. I think it's just a get-acquainted thing so she's on our radar for future projects.

Got it.

How are things today?

Okay, I guess. Haven't talked to them this morning yet, but I'm working another angle to put a stop to the memoir.

Let me know how you make out. Last night was amazing, but none of us will relax until we're sure there's no threat to them.

Agreed. Same here. I'm on it.

Then it's in good hands.

Thanks again to you and Addie for letting us invade your home over the last week.

Our home is your home. You know that.

Likewise, my friend.

With chaos unfolding in the living room, I leave my office to help Natalie get the kids fed and dressed. Until I had four little kids, I wouldn't have thought either of those things was particularly difficult to accomplish. However, I've learned that those two tasks make for a crazy morning.

We get through it with jokes the kids are too young to understand and nonstop banter that makes the wildest part of the day also the most entertaining.

Natalie usually turns Rowan over to me while she focuses on the little ladies, who require much more assistance because they care about what they wear and how their hair is done.

Rowan couldn't care less as long as the getting-dressed portion of the program is done quickly so he can get back to leaving a path of destruction in his wake. With Cece and Scarlett, we said the terrible twos were wildly overrated. Rowan is proving otherwise. It's a good thing he's the cutest little guy ever, or we might have to send him back for a refund, which is another joke we often make.

I grab him before he can get away from me, hoist him onto my shoulder and buzz him through the house. That's all I have to do to make him happier than a pig in shit. As long as it's fast and rough, he's thoroughly entertained.

I'm getting way too old to keep up with a two-year-old with his kind of energy.

Natalie says the kids will keep me young. I'm feeling every one of my forty years these days, but life has never been sweeter. Nat is right when she says it'll go by in a blur. It already has. How is Cece already almost *six*?

Hayden jokes that we had Bennett only because I didn't want to be outdone in the kid department by him. We thought we were done after Rowan blasted into our lives, until Bennett made fools of us by slipping past the goalie.

Nat says she's given birth four times, so it's up to me to make sure there isn't a fifth time—or else. I have an appointment to discuss the dreaded big V after the trip.

I settle on the sofa with Rowan and put on *Paw Patrol*, which turns him into a zombie for a few minutes. That's the only break we get from his nonstop pace, other than when he runs out of gas and collapses right where he is to nap.

My son is a character, to say the least.

Since he's settled for a minute or two, I take a call from Dani. "Hey."

"You're set to meet Vivian at noon tomorrow at her home in Bel Air. I'll text you the address. Nelson, her longtime manager, said she's excited to meet you."

"Great."

"What's this about anyway?"

"Nothing I can talk about yet. I'll let you know if it goes beyond conversation."

"Do you need someone with you for the meeting?"

She can't possibly know that's the last thing I want. "Nope. I can handle this one on my own."

"Sounds good. Let me know if you need anything else."

"Will do. Thanks for the quick work."

"Sure thing. Hope you guys have a Merry Christmas."

"Same to you and your family."

"Talk to you in the New Year."

I text my dad to let him know the meeting is set for tomorrow.

He responds with a thumbs up.

Everyone I talk to this week signs off until after the holidays. Our business mostly grinds to a halt this time of year, which is a welcome break from the often-relentless pace. We emerge from the holidays and go straight into awards season. This year, we're not in the running for any of the big awards, which is actually a relief as we can sit out the merry-go-round of formal events that come one right after the other for weeks on end.

I was asked to present at the Golden Globes, but I declined since I'd rather be home with my family these days than spend a night rubbing elbows in Hollywood.

Natalie sits next to me on the sofa.

I take Ben from her and give him a nuzzle. He's so flipping cute and smiley. I've been amazed at how my heart has expanded to admit each of our precious babies as they arrived. Just when you think you've given away all the love you have to give, you find out there's more.

"I have a surprise for you," Nat says.

"What's that?"

"Candace and Olivia asked if they could babysit for us tonight because they miss the kids."

"They saw them two days ago."

"Parents of four young children do *not* look gift aunties in the mouth."

I chuckle at the forceful way she says that. "Right. As you were saying..."

"I made us a reservation at the Maybourne."

I raise a brow. "Did you now?"

"I did. Good surprise?"

"Best surprise ever."

"Are you up for it with everything that's going on?"

I take her hand and put it over the proof of how "up for it" I am to spend a night alone with her.

"That's all it takes?" she asks, laughing.

"That actually happened when you sat next to me."

"You're so easy."

"Only for you." I lean in to kiss her. "What brought this on?"

"We'll be surrounded by kids and people over the next couple of weeks. I wanted a minute to ourselves before the madness begins."

"I have the best wife in the history of wives."

"I'm glad you think so."

"I definitely think so. I have a meeting with Vivian Stevens at noon in Bel Air tomorrow."

"I can wait for you at the hotel."

"What about Mr. Bennett?"

"He'll have to come with us, but he's no trouble."

I kiss the downy softness at the top of his head. "No, he isn't. Remember how freaked out we were any time we had to leave home with Cece?"

"We were newbies then. We're old pros now."

"Where are my little ladies?"

"Playing in their room with the gate up so Rowan can't get to them."

"They're wising up and playing defense. What time are we planning to leave?"

"The girls will be here at four."

"Have I mentioned today how much I love your sisters?"

"They love you right back."

Candace and Olivia are regulars at our house, coming and going as if they live there, which is just how we like it. Natalie wants as much time with them as she can get after spending so many years without them in her life.

I've enjoyed nurturing Olivia's career and acting as her chief adviser/big brother/overall protector. She's carved out a nice niche for herself and is in hot demand. She'd tell you that's because of her connection to me, but that's not why. She's sublimely talented, and her screen presence is magical, the kind of "it" factor that's either there or isn't. I expect her to become a big star the minute *Valiant* is released in March, and I can't wait to watch it happen.

Our work on the film was delayed first by the pandemic and then by the strikes. When we were finally able to begin production, the actress we'd chosen to play Natalie was unavailable. Hayden suggested we talk to Olivia about the role. While I loved the idea, I wasn't without reservations. Mostly, I was concerned about reopening old wounds, but Olivia assured me—and Natalie—that she could handle it.

And boy, did she. Her performance was everything I hoped it would be and then some. She delivered a tour de force playing her sister through the worst and best parts of her life. While parts of the story were harrowing to revisit, I've never had more fun doing anything than I did re-creating the incredible early days with Natalie, from our first auspicious meeting in the New York City park to the Golden Globes to getting married in Vegas.

Hayden plans to show us the final cut when we're in Utah. I can't wait to see it all put together and to show it to Natalie, who's maintained a bit of distance from the project since she approved the final script. We asked her if she wanted to see it for the first time in private, but she said she'd rather see it with her closest people by her side, so that's what we're doing.

Bennett has dozed off in my arms, Rowan is snuggled up to my left side, while Natalie is on my right. I can hear the girls in their room playing make-believe with their toys, and Fluff is snoring like a buzz saw, per usual, on the other end of the sectional sofa.

I could have anything I want, anything in the whole goddamned world, and this, right here... This is all I want or need.

CHAPTER 16

Flynn

The aunties arrive with the usual madness of excitement they bring to every visit with the kids, who are simply wild about them—and vice versa. Candace has long auburn hair and hazel eyes, while Olivia has dark hair and brown eyes. She looks much more like Natalie than Candace does, but there's a definite resemblance between the three of them and in Cece, who favors them.

The kids are all over them, and both aunties are thrilled by the reception they get from the kids. Within seconds, Candace is on the floor wrestling with Rowan while the girls drag Olivia toward their room to play.

"Wait a minute," Natalie says. "I need a second with my sisters before you guys steal them."

"No, Mommy," Rowan says, "no seconds."

That kid... He cracks me up, but if I laugh at him saying no to his mother, I'll be in trouble with Mommy. "Rowan, let Auntie Candace see Mommy, and then you can have her all to yourself."

"Fine."

I make a face at him. "Fine."

He giggles. My day is made.

Natalie herds her sisters into the kitchen, and I follow them so we can catch up for a second before we leave. Nat gives them the rundown on the meal she prepared for all of them and reminds them of the "suggested" bedtime, which the aunties don't enforce with the same vigor as Mommy does. They're here so often that they know where everything is and what all the kids like and don't like.

"We'll make sure they're not up for a minute after nine," Candace says.

Natalie gasps. "Nine? I said *seven thirty*!"

"I heard nine." Candace glances at Olivia. "Right?"

"I heard ten."

"You guys! Stop!"

"Relax," Candace says. "They'll crash long before we're done playing."

"The back door is locked," I tell them. "I checked it twice." We have alarms on top of alarms with the pool in the backyard.

"We'll stay inside," Olivia says. "Don't worry."

"We never worry when they're with you guys," Natalie says. "Except about the level of spoiling."

Candace smirks. "That's what aunties are for."

"Payback will be a bitch when you guys have kids," Nat says.

"Oh yeah," I add. "We're so gonna get you back."

"Tell them your big news," Candace says to her sister.

"*Variety* wants to do a cover on me when *Valiant* is released," Olivia says with the shy wonder that continues to endear her to all of us as her career takes off. "They said that me playing Nat is the biggest story in town this year."

"That's amazing, Livvy." Natalie hugs her baby sister. "I'm so proud of you."

"I'm trying to tell myself I'm prepared for this, but…"

I hook an arm around her and give her a squeeze. "There's no way to prepare for what's about to happen to you, kid."

"Gee, that's comforting. Thanks."

Laughing, I say, "Trust me. Just strap in and enjoy the ride. There's nothing else you can do."

"Gulp. Okay."

"You need to be ready, too," I tell Candace.

"For what?"

"You're going to become as famous as your sister."

"No way."

"Mark my words, the two of you will become Hollywood power-houses. One of you in front of the camera and the other behind the scenes, which is every bit as important around here."

Candace opens a bag of Goldfish. "Whatever you say."

I love, love, *love* the way they treat me like I'm nothing special. That's exactly how I want it, and they know it. They can say anything they want to me, the way they would to their own brother if they had one. And when they refer to me as their brother-in-love... I adore them.

Rowan comes bombing into the kitchen. "Mommy! No more seconds!" He grabs Candace by the hand and all but drags her to the family room for more wrestling.

"Go with God," I tell her.

"Thoughts and prayers," Nat calls out to them as Olivia follows Candace.

We've already put our stuff in the car while the kids were napping. As much as we want to hug and kiss them all for the hundredth time today, we take Bennett and sneak out through the garage so there won't be any tears about Mommy and Daddy leaving for the night.

The girls will keep them so well entertained that they won't even know we're gone.

As we drive toward town from the Hollywood Hills, I'm excited for some time mostly alone with Nat. I love that she planned a getaway for us and surprised me with it. I recall a time when she would've hesitated to spend a dime on anything that wasn't essential. It took a while to adapt to her new circumstances, but she's never become frivolous or extravagant with money.

She's also held the line on me spoiling her with jewelry and other things she says she doesn't want or need. I like to think I can be trained, and she's made me more frugal while I've made her a little less so.

Before we punch out for the night, I call my dad to check in.

"Hey, son. How are you today?"

"That's what I was calling to ask you."

"We've had a nice day getting stuff done around here and talking. We're okay. Try not to worry."

"As long as you're not hiring attorneys, I won't worry."

"No one is talking about that."

"Good to know."

"What're you guys up to?"

"My lovely wife planned a little getaway for us tonight. The younger aunties are babysitting the older three hooligans. We've got Bennett with us."

"That sounds like fun. Enjoy yourselves and don't worry about us. We're working it out."

"That's the best news I've had all day. I'll check in after my meeting tomorrow."

"I can't wait to hear how it goes."

"You'll be my first call when I leave there."

"Thank you for handling this, son. We appreciate it."

"There's nothing I wouldn't do for you two."

"Likewise, my friend. Have a wonderful evening with Natalie. Tell the girls to call us if they need anything."

"I'll do that, but I'm sure they'll be fine. Talk to you tomorrow."

"Love you."

"Love you, too."

I end the call and glance at Nat for her take.

"I'd rather picture them puttering around the house than at odds with each other."

"Me, too. This whole situation really rocked me. Just when you think the most solid thing in your life could never be vulnerable…"

"*One* of the most solid things in your life. You have a lot of solid things."

"That's true, but they're the glue, you know?"

"I do. I get it. They are for me, too." She looks over at me. "What do you plan to say to Vivian?"

"I'm going to pour on the Godfrey charm, let her think I'm interested in working with her and then tell her the real reason I'm there."

She has nothing to say to that, which means she has something to say. My wife is rarely silent.

"What?"

"I don't like you letting her think you want to work with her. It feels mean."

"What about her potentially dragging my father through fifty-year-old mud?"

"You don't know for sure about that."

"If you were her, a fading movie star trying to remain relevant, would you include mention of your brief, unknown marriage to Max Godfrey in your bombshell memoir, or would you take the high road and leave it out?"

After a pause, she says, "I suppose I'd include it."

"And what would be your primary motivation in doing that?"

"Probably to sell books as well as get back at the woman who called me a whore once upon a time," she says hesitantly.

"Precisely, so I don't think it's mean to present somewhat false pretenses for our meeting."

"I still say it's beneath you to mislead an elderly woman, regardless of what she's done in the past."

"It's not beneath me to want to protect my parents." The words come out sharper than I intended. "I'm sorry. I don't mean to be testy with you."

"It's fine."

"No, it isn't, honey. You're just trying to help me."

"I don't want you to take the low road with her, even if you have good reason to. That's not who you are."

"In this case, it might be."

"It's not. You're too good for something like this. Just tell her why you've come and show her the NDA. Don't pretend to be interested in working with her. I don't like that angle."

One of the things I love best about her is that she's never intimidated by my success, my celebrity or any of the bullshit that comes with it. She tells it to me straight, and she has from the start.

"Okay."

"That's it? Just okay?"

"I can't appreciate your advice only when I agree with it."

Her smile lights up her gorgeous face.

"Don't be smug," I say with a chuckle.

"Me? Smug? Never."

"Right."

We laugh together. We do that a lot, which is another thing I love about her.

When we arrive at the hotel, we're met by a bellman who recognizes me but doesn't make a thing of it as he efficiently ushers us inside. I'm carrying Bennett while Natalie takes the backpack she uses as a diaper bag.

He hands a keycard to Natalie.

"We'll have your bags sent up, Mrs. Godfrey."

"Thank you so much, William."

"My pleasure, ma'am."

I've enjoyed watching Natalie come into her own in dealing with being married to me. She simply takes care of business and doesn't suffer fools, but she's always nice to everyone we encounter. People have nothing but great things to say about Flynn Godfrey's lovely wife, especially Flynn Godfrey.

"Smoothly done, my love," I tell her when we're in the elevator.

"I asked for expedited check-in because I know you hate the fuss."

"My wife gets things done."

"I'd like to think so after all these years." She uses the keycard to gain entrance to a lovely suite that looks out over the Hollywood Hills. "We can almost see the house from here."

"Close but so far away."

"That was the idea."

Bennett is snoozing, so I place him carefully on the sofa to continue his nap.

I keep an eye on him as I go to Natalie to put my arms around her. "Thank you for this. I had no idea I needed it until you told me we were going."

"We both needed a break, especially before the trip."

Vacation isn't as relaxing as it used to be, before our group of friends was overtaken by a huge posse of kids. Everyone pitches in, and we give each other breaks where we can, but it's nonstop madness. Despite the chaos, we love being together as much as we did when we were footloose, single and child-free. Our annual tradition of spending Christmas in St. George, Utah, where we were marooned due to a blizzard the first Christmas Natalie and I spent together, is one of our favorite things.

We'd been on our way to my place in Aspen when we encountered rough air due to the storm and were forced to land. This will be our sixth Christmas at the Castaway Inn, and our original group has expanded to include my parents, my sisters and their families, Simon and Jan, Sebastian's parents, and even Jasper's mom came one year. We've got the whole place reserved, along with a plane big enough to transport us.

"Vacation isn't what it used to be," I say.

"I was just thinking the same thing. In a few years, we'll be sad the kids aren't little anymore."

"That's true, but for right now, pack the headache pills."

She laughs. "They're already in the bag, along with the heartburn meds you require these days."

"Haha, very funny. Mexican food and I have had a falling-out."

"It's tragic."

"Sure is. I'm getting old."

"I still love you."

"Thank goodness for that. Speaking of me getting old, promise me no fuss about the big four-oh."

She looks away. "Um... Well..."

I groan. "Nat... Come on. You know I hate my Christmas birthday. It's all about the kids, as it should be."

"And a little about you."

"A very little."

"Maybe a *tiny bit* more than usual this year."

"Let's forget about the whole thing."

"After that epic thirtieth birthday party you threw me?"

"That's different."

"How?"

"It was for you and not me."

She laughs. "Are you listening to yourself?"

I nuzzle her neck and love the shiver that runs through her. "I don't want to talk about my birthday."

"What do you want to talk about?"

"My beautiful wife and hours and *hours* to spend alone together."

She looks over at Bennett, who's out cold. "Not completely alone."

"He's no trouble, and he's too young to remember what goes on here."

"What's going on here?" she asks, looking up at me with green eyes full of love as she rubs shamelessly against my erection. It took me a minute to get used to the green after she got rid of the brown contacts she'd once used to disguise her appearance. Now the whole world knows her story, and there's no need to hide. I'd never want it to happen the way it did, but she says it's a relief not to worry about it anymore.

"Are you in the mood for some fun?"

"I will be as soon as we have our stuff."

I can't believe I've forgotten that our luggage is on the way up.

The doorbell to the suite chimes through the big room.

"There it is." She kisses my cheek. "I'll get it since you're in no condition."

"Haha, who put me in that condition?"

She flashes a smile over her shoulder as she goes to the door.

I take a seat on the sofa as she chats with the bellman and hands him a tip.

"Thank you, Mrs. Godfrey. Have a nice evening."

"You do the same."

When the door clicks shut, I get up to help her with the bags.

"Give me fifteen minutes," she says.

"When I come in, will you be on your knees waiting for me?"

"Is that what you want, sir?"

I'm immediately hard as a rock at the way she looks at me as she says those incendiary words. "That's what I want."

She runs her finger from my throat, down to my chest and abdomen, hooking it in my belt. "It's been a while. You might have to refresh my memory on the rules of how we play this game."

"It's like riding a bike. It'll all come back to you."

"If you say so."

"What's your safe word?"

"Fluff."

I kiss her sweet lips. "See? You remember." I steal another kiss and then a third. "Fifteen minutes?"

"Uh-huh."

"Will Benny be okay where he is?"

"Yep. He's still too young to move on his own, and he's good for another ninety minutes or so."

"Mmmm, ninety whole minutes alone with my love."

"Let's make it count, shall we?"

She renders me speechless with the way she looks at me.

"Absolutely."

CHAPTER 17

Flynn

Fifteen minutes have never passed so slowly. I use the time to rifle through my suitcase to find the items I packed hoping we'd have a chance to play our favorite games. It's been almost a year since we indulged. Between the demands of her work on the foundation and our three older kids keeping her busy, Natalie had her most difficult pregnancy yet with Bennett. She was exhausted and nauseated for most of it and run ragged from dealing with the kids.

One of the few real fights we've ever had was over me wanting to get some help for her during that difficult time, but she still wasn't having it.

Rather, her sisters and my parents pitched in when they could, and our friends stepped up to help out, too. She spent every minute she got away from the kids catching up on sleep.

I also packed dreaded condoms because we're done having kids. Until I get the snip, I'm gloving up and hoping for the best. I was supposed to have the procedure after Rowan but never got around to it and then came Bennett.

We're both thrilled to have a second son, but she'll murder me if I get her pregnant again.

The thought of that makes me laugh as I strip down to boxers and deal with a couple of work-related texts and emails to kill the last few minutes.

Bennett is sound asleep, arms thrown over his head, his tiny lips moving, as if he's telling a story in his sleep. He's a cute little guy, with a delightful, easygoing way about him that makes him the perfect addition to our family.

At exactly fifteen minutes, I adjust Bennett's blanket and leave him to sleep in full view of the bedroom, where I find my wife exactly where I told her to be. She's wearing a silky red thing that barely covers her with her glorious dark hair contained in a bun.

"Has my love been doing some shopping?"

"Perhaps."

"I approve."

She looks up at me. "I'm glad to hear it."

I extend a hand to help her up and wrap my arms around her, loving the way she fits in my embrace. She's the other half of me, the best part of me. "I've missed you, sweetheart."

"You see me every day."

"I've missed *this*, time to ourselves to be alone together."

Our playroom in the basement is long gone, replaced by an actual playroom with toys for children rather than adults.

"I've missed it, too. Feels like it's been forever since we were really alone."

"And we're still not completely alone," I remind her.

"This is as good as it gets these days."

"Everything about these days, this life, is the best time ever."

"For me, too. I love it all, especially my partner in crime."

Smiling, I raise her chin to receive my kiss.

She wraps her arms around my neck and opens her mouth to my tongue, rubbing hers against mine and making me light-headed with desire.

Knowing we have all night to indulge is as much of a turn-on as having her warm and soft in my arms, kissing me like she hasn't seen me in a year. Even as life and kids and work make it more difficult to find time alone, the sizzling chemistry between us has never waned. We're as hot for each other as when we were first together, which is how we ended up with four kids.

"What does my baby want tonight?" I ask her when we come up for air.

"Whatever my sir has in mind."

"Anything?"

"I trust you to make it good for both of us."

Those words, the way she looks at me when she says them, the trust, the love... "You continue to amaze me, my love."

"How so?"

"It would take me all night to give you the full list of ways. But the way you trust me is so... It wrecks me."

"I trust you more than anyone in this entire world."

"That makes me the luckiest guy ever."

"We're both lucky."

"And about to get luckier." I back her up to the bed and run my hands over the silky slip of material before I remove it and toss it aside. "You're so beautiful, Nat. I could look at you and only you for the rest of my life and never get tired of the view."

"You'd get tired of it."

Cupping her breasts, I tease her nipples with my thumbs. "No, I wouldn't."

She gasps, and her body goes tense.

I freeze. "What?"

"We forgot condoms."

"No, we didn't."

Relaxing again, she says, "Oh, thank goodness."

"Don't worry about anything, sweetheart. I've got you." I ease her back on the bed and drop to my knees before her. "Hands over your head. Eyes closed."

That this strong, capable, courageous, resilient woman turns over her pleasure to me is still one of the greatest gifts I've ever been given.

As I love her with my tongue and fingers, the sounds she makes are like gas on a fire. I can't ever get enough of her, but when she's lost in pleasure that only I provide... That's a whole other level of satisfaction.

Normally, I like to drag it out, to make her "suffer" before I deliver the payoff, but I want her so badly that I bring her to a quick orgasm and then roll on a condom. I bend to taste her nipple, and she gasps. "Still with me, love?"

"Mmm, I'm here. Can I use my arms?"

"Whatever you want."

She opens her eyes, and her gaze collides with mine in a moment of absolute rightness. And then she smiles, and I'm as lost to her as I've been from the start.

"I was going for all the bells and whistles tonight," I whisper against her lips as I push into her, slowly and carefully. Even months after she gave birth, I still worry about hurting her.

"I don't need anything other than you and this." She wraps her arms and legs around me, trapping me in every way.

Once upon a time, I needed the bells and whistles. I needed the kink and the variety. Now, there's only her and us and this. It's all I'll ever want or need.

Stella

I'M TRYING TO GET BACK TO NORMAL, BUT I DON'T KNOW WHAT THAT IS anymore. The foundation under me has been rocked by the things I've learned about my husband. I wish I could stop picturing him in bed with young, beautiful, sexy Vivian. The woman had positively exuded sex, even when she did nothing more than enter a room.

While Max is in his office tending to last-minute business matters before we leave town for a couple of weeks, I fix a cup of tea and sit at the kitchen table, lost in thoughts of a past I thought I'd long ago left behind. If only I could stop thinking about *her* and my husband...

Married.

Every man I knew at that time was wild for her. They stopped what they were doing when she appeared, practically drooling over her like horny dogs who couldn't control their baser impulses.

I saw it happen many times. A man in the middle of a conversation would lose his train of thought and every brain cell in his head when Vivian walked in. She was the literal meaning of the term showstopper.

At first, I too was awestruck by her. Back then, most women weren't powerful like they are now. We didn't command rooms full of men and make them stupid in the head with our presence. Not like Vivian did. Other actresses envied the seemingly effortless command she exuded like no other woman ever had, except maybe Marilyn Monroe.

Whereas Marilyn put off an almost untouchable aura of mystery, Vivian was "real." She was in on the joke—especially the off-color ones. She could be one of the guys as easily as she was one of the girls, even if most of the girls secretly despised her because they'd never be her. They said awful things about her even as they laughed at her ribald commentary and pretended to be her friend.

Before I met her, I felt a little sorry for her because I'd rarely heard a nice word said about her among the women. I chalked it up to jealousy. We all wanted a piece of what Vivian had, if only we could articulate what it was exactly. I was prepared to befriend her, to be different from the other actresses who kept their distance from her out of fear or whatever it is that compels women to treat other women badly for no good reason.

The first day she walked onto the set of *London Town*, I got to see her mystique firsthand as our producer, director and cinematographer were rendered speechless and stupid by her mere presence. I noted the annoyed expression on her flawless face as they fumbled and stumbled to welcome her, as if she wanted to say, *Knock it off already. I'm not going to sleep with any of you, so quit acting like fools.*

I watched as she was introduced to Jonah, who played it differently than the other guys, giving her cool indifference rather than fawning adoration as he shook her hand and welcomed her to the set.

I saw it happen right in front of me... the awareness, the curiosity, the pique of a well-crafted eyebrow.

Her power was like a punch to the gut he'd worked so hard to hone into rippling muscles.

We'd been together a year by then—a lifetime by young Hollywood standards of that time—and were all but living together in his apartment, which he had to himself, whereas I had roommates to help pay the bills. He'd proposed to me three weeks earlier on the beach at sunset in Santa Monica. He was romantic, loving and committed. Until he wasn't.

At first, I chalked it up to the predictable male reaction, and while I was disappointed to realize he was just like all the other men who couldn't resist the siren-like temptation she posed, I tried to understand that he was only human after all. He and I had made a commitment to each other to resist the temptation we encountered every day, and I believed in him.

Then he became remote and withdrawn when we were at home. At work, he began to disappear between takes rather than spending the downtime with me the way he had only a week earlier. It took a day or two for me to put together that when he was missing, so was she.

On the fourth day, I followed her from the set to the trailers on the back lot. I stayed out of sight as I watched her approach Jonah's trailer, casting glances over each shoulder before she went up the stairs and let herself in. I held my breath, waiting for the door to open, for Jonah—*my* Jonah—to show her out, to tell her he was engaged, that he loved me and wouldn't betray me this way.

The door never opened.

Armed with the information I'd come for, I returned to the set and waited for my call. I'm not sure how I got through that scene or the next one, but I did the job and then went to Jonah's to pack my things. I returned to the apartment I hadn't slept at in months and waited all night for him to call me.

He never called.

The next day, I returned to the set, bringing outrage and fury with me. I'm not proud of the way I confronted them with the whole cast and crew watching, agape at my utter loss of control as I called them out—him for cheating and her for being the kind of woman who goes after someone else's man.

"If he was really your man, he wouldn't have been so easily taken," she said, "now would he?"

"I'd rather be cheated on," I replied, "than be known as nothing more than a whore who'd steal another woman's fiancé."

"Stella." Jonah stepped in before we came to blows. "That's enough."

I pulled off the gorgeous ring I'd loved so much and threw it at him, hitting him in the forehead. "Go to hell. You two deserve each other. Enjoy your whore."

I stormed off to my trailer and refused to come out until they'd both left.

Our blowup disturbed the filming schedule, and who do you think got the blame for that? Yeah, it wasn't them. From that moment on, everything changed for me. Word got out that I'd called Vivian a whore—twice—and I got tagged with the dreaded "difficult to work with" label, even if that wasn't at all true.

Who cared about the truth when there was a juicy Hollywood scandal for everyone to sink their teeth into?

I went from on the rise in my career to dead on arrival overnight.

My management firm dropped me. "Friends" I'd worked with on past productions suddenly didn't take my calls. I became persona non grata so fast, my head spun. I figured the storm would pass in a month or two, and I'd get back on track.

Six months passed without a single offer, and I began to panic about eventually running out of money.

When *London Town* was released, I wasn't invited to the premiere or any of the events associated with the release.

That was a low point, especially when Vivian was given star treatment for a supporting role, while I was frozen out as one of the leads. Things became even darker after that massive snub, which was relentlessly picked apart in the media.

I'd become truly desperate and was thinking I might have to get a waitressing job—or, God forbid, go home to Iowa—when my former manager, Dabney Richards, called out of the blue on a Tuesday in November. I was so shocked to hear his voice that at first I thought it was someone playing a joke on me. Until he called me by the nickname he'd given me—Stelly Belly—and I broke down into heartbroken sobs.

"Aw, honey," he said. "Don't cry. We're gonna fix it."

"How? Your firm dumped me. You're not even allowed to talk to me."

"I didn't agree with them dumping *my* client, so I left the firm and started my own."

"Because of me?"

"Among other things, but mostly because of you."

"Dabney... Why would you do that?"

"I see something in you, Stelly. You're destined for bigger things than a two-bit movie with that bitch Vivian. You're not the only one who sees her for what she really is. Believe me."

His words filled the cold, dark spaces inside me with warmth and compassion and the first spark of hope I'd felt in weeks.

"What am I going to do, Dabney?"

"You're going to *sing*, Stelly. You're going to sing your way straight to the top."

True to his word, he had me booked on *The Merv Griffin Show* a month later. That appearance changed my life in every possible way.

I smile at the memory of my beloved Dabney, who pulled me from the ashes, dusted me off and sent me in a whole new direction I never would've pursued without his support and encouragement. When Dabney, who never married or had children, became unable to care for himself at home alone, I paid for round-the-clock care for him and visited him weekly. I was by his side when he passed.

He was—and is—family to me.

I didn't plan on a singing career, but as Dabney used to say— when life gives you lemons, kick them in the ass and make a vodka with lemonade.

I dab at tears that suddenly appear as I think of him and the way he fought for me when everyone else had deserted me. And he indirectly led me to the rest of my life with that booking on Merv, where I met a handsome young actor with kind eyes and a smile that lit up my world.

While Max and I are still very much in the game in this town, I haven't heard a word about Jonah in ages, and Vivian hasn't worked in years. Her looks gave out on her, and all the plastic surgery in the world couldn't undo the ravages of time. That happens all too often, of course only to women. Old men can look like the back end of a cow and still get work. Women are held to a different standard. If she were anyone else, I'd feel sorry for her, but she doesn't deserve my sympathy.

I've never held a grudge like this for anyone else. I'm not proud of it, believe me. But some things just *are*, and my feelings for her are among those things for me.

Speaking of things that just are, Max emerges from the hallway into the kitchen, smiling when he sees me sitting in my spot at the table.

"You were a million miles away. What're you thinking about?"

"Things that happened ages ago."

He frowns as he slides into his chair. "You want to talk about it?"

"Not really."

"I hate that I've got you thinking about things that hurt you."

"That's not all I'm thinking about. There were good things, too, like Dabney and Merv and you."

"So many good things. You may not believe me, but when I think back over all the years, I can barely remember anything before Merv's Green Room."

I give him a skeptical look.

"No, really. I remember bits and pieces from childhood, things with my brother and sister, my parents, that kind of stuff. I remember my first acting roles and people I knew back then, but it's a fuzzy black-and-white reel. After the Green Room, everything is bright and colorful, as if someone turned a switch that day, and my real life began."

I fan my face as tears pool in my eyes. "That might be the loveliest thing you've ever said to me, and that's saying something."

He smiles, and my heart goes soft the way it always does around him. He's my kryptonite. He has been from the start. Whenever we've argued about something, which has been rare, I've found the strain between us so unbearable that I try to make it right as fast as I can without giving up my position on the matter. He does the same. We can't stand being at odds, and this is no different from any other time.

"I mean it, sweetheart. You brought all the color to my life, and when I tell you I rarely gave her a thought over all these years, I mean it. It's like the thing with her never happened, as far as I'm concerned. By the time I met you, she was so far in the past, she barely existed in my consciousness. I can't bear the idea of you thinking otherwise."

"I believe you."

"You do? Really?"

I nod. "Don't forget, I've been right here with you for all this time. If you were pining for someone else, I would've seen it."

"I've never pined for anyone but you, and you know that."

"I do."

"I'm supposed to be sorry for keeping such an important thing from you, but a very big part of me isn't sorry at all."

I raise a brow at his defiant tone. "Is that right?"

"Yep. Think about the day we met." He sits next to me and takes hold of my hand. "Close your eyes and put yourself back in that Green Room, where everything was on the line for you. If you had any prayer of a comeback, you'd know it after that appearance."

With my eyes closed, I travel back in time to that momentous day. Other than our wedding day and the births of our children and grandchildren, that day stands out in a sea of regular days, with a bright shining light on top of it to indicate its importance to the story of my life—and Max's.

"Are you there?"

Nodding, I say, "I want one of those pastries."

Max laughs. "They were good."

"The best. I always thought it was funny that he served such fat bombs to people obsessed with their weight."

"We couldn't resist them."

"I sure as hell couldn't."

"Me either. Do you remember how anxious you were that day? And how much was riding on it?"

"I can feel it right here." I place my free hand on my chest, which feels tight and achy, the way it did then.

"You were a ball of stress while we waited. I could feel it rolling off you. Of course, I knew the story of what'd happened to you and why. Everyone knew. And what I couldn't tell you then was that I understood better than anyone else why you would've called her out the way you did. I knew her. I knew what she was capable of and the lengths she'd go to feed her voracious thirst for fame and glory. I'd seen it with my own two eyes, and I admired you for having the moxie to call her on it."

"You did? You never told me that."

"I studiously avoided the topic of her with you."

The way he says that makes me snort with laughter. "Probably a good idea."

"I knew it right away, Stel. If I told you I had a past with her, I never would've had a future with you."

I open my eyes to look at him. "That's probably true."

"It's definitely true. And from the moment I met you, all I wanted was more of you. I put my own selfish desire for you ahead of telling you the truth, but I still say I did the right thing."

"One of the things I'm struggling with is how I could've heard about it from someone else. That you let me go through my life with that possibility out there..."

"No one who knew was ever going to talk about it. I was confident about that."

"How has it never come up between us in all these years?"

"I never think of her. *Ever.* That's how it didn't come up. She ceased to exist for me long before I met you. Not to mention you still see red any time her name is mentioned."

I can't deny that, so I don't try. "Will you tell me how you came to be married to her?"

"Ugh. Do I have to?"

"I can't help having questions."

"I know, but what does it matter now?"

I shrug. "I wish it didn't, but I'd like to fill in some of the blanks."

"I'd rather talk to you about anything other than her."

"I understand that."

"But you still want to know."

"I do."

"All right, then," he says on a deep sigh.

CHAPTER 18

Olivia

The kids are in bed and finally asleep. Candace and I are settling in to finally watch *Wicked* when my phone chimes with a text from Liza, Quantum's publicity manager, who's now mine, as well.

People mag wants you for their cover, too.

I gasp.

"What?"

I show her the text.

"Holy. Shit. Liv."

"I can't believe all this."

"It's really happening. How do you feel?"

"Excited, nervous, scared of what it'll be like to lose my anonymity."

"You get recognized all the time."

"This'll be a whole other level."

"Yeah, you're right."

"I mean, Flynn's parents were just on the cover of *People* for their fiftieth anniversary, and now I'm going to be, too? How's that even possible?"

"You've worked your ass off for years to get to this moment. You deserve it."

"Someone on Insta called me a nepo baby the other day. They said I never would've gotten the part if I wasn't playing my sister in my superstar brother-in-law's passion project."

"That's a revolting thing to say."

"It's true, though."

"So what? You still had to deliver on the performance, or they would've replaced you. As much as Flynn loves you, and he loves you a lot, he wouldn't have risked the success of such an important project if the actress playing Natalie didn't nail it. You *totally* nailed it."

"You really think so?"

"I was there every day. I know so—and so do Flynn, Hayden, Kristian, Jasper and everyone else who worked on the film. You dazzled them. Flynn used that word. Repeatedly."

"I sorta felt like he had to say that because of who I am to him."

"He could've said you were good, great, excellent even. He used the word '*dazzling*' because that's what you are. And before you tell me I have to say that, too, I don't. If I didn't think you were amazing, I would've said so a long-ass time ago. Flynn would have, too."

"He promised me he'd keep it real with me."

"And he did, the whole way. You saw him in tears several times during the filming as you brought to life scenes from his life and did it so beautifully. Please stop with the crisis of confidence. You're going to get all the awards for this movie because you *slayed*."

"Thank you."

"Can we watch *Wicked* now?" We've been trying to get to it for months and promised each other we'd finally watch it tonight.

My phone buzzes with a new text that has me sitting up from the slouch I was in.

"What now?"

"Teddy Abrams."

"What about him?"

"He... He just texted me."

"How in the hell did he get your number?"

"Who cares? He texted me!"

"What did he say?"

"That he's been following my career with interest and would love to hang out sometime."

Candace does this weird twisting thing with her mouth.

"Say something!"

"Eh, he doesn't impress me."

"Come on! He's one of the hottest guys in the world." I appreciate him reaching out to me. I needed that after nursing a fierce crush on Larkin Wilder, the actor who played Flynn in *Valiant*. The chemistry between us was unbelievable, so much so that Hayden said once that we reminded him of Flynn and Nat at the beginning. I know Larkin felt it every bit as much as I did, but he's engaged to his childhood love, so that's not going to happen.

"But is he a nice guy?" Candace asks. "You don't even know him. Before you reply to him, find someone who knows him and get the lowdown."

I tune back in to realize she's talking about Teddy while I'm thinking about Larkin. Nothing new there. "Who do I know who knows him?"

"If you don't know someone, Flynn will."

"I'm not bothering him with this."

"He'd want you to."

I start typing my reply. "It's just a text. I'm not about to marry the guy or anything."

"What are you saying?"

"Just, 'Hey, thanks for getting in touch. Nice to "meet" you.' That kind of thing."

The phone buzzes with a new text.

What're you doing tonight?

"What'd he say?"

"He asked what I'm doing tonight."

"Tell him you're busy and you'll get in touch another time. I want to watch the damned movie."

Busy tonight. I'll text another time.

I'll look forward to that.

What does that even mean?

Candace starts the movie and snuggles under the blanket we're sharing to get comfortable. "Are you paying attention?"

"Yeah."

Almost every aspect of my life feels a little out of control all of a sudden. I shot *Valiant* last year and have done several other smaller projects since then while feeling as if I'm in the calm before a storm that I lack the imagination to properly anticipate. Before I was cast in the film, Flynn and Hayden sat me down to talk about this. They wanted me to be sure, really, really sure, before they moved forward with me as their lead actress.

"It's going to be insane," Flynn said at that meeting. "I wish there was a way for me to fully explain to you what it's like to go from low-key celebrity to world famous overnight, but there's no way I can do it justice. It's something you have to experience to fully understand."

I could tell he was holding back somewhat because he didn't want to scare the shit out of me.

But I'm scared anyway.

Of the attention, the crazies, the demands on my time, the way everything will change, even things I don't want to change, such as my relationship with my sisters, nieces and nephews.

I told them at the meeting that it was what I wanted, and it was. It is. At least, I think it is... How in the hell do I know if it's what I want when my own superstar brother-in-law couldn't find the words to properly explain the reality of that kind of fame to me?

The covers of *Variety* and *People* and a text from Teddy Abrams, all in the same day... I have a feeling that's the least of what'll happen after the movie is released. I'll be on the road promoting it for six weeks, beginning in early March. While Flynn, Natalie and Bennett will be with me for some of it, the other three kids won't be. Six weeks without snuggles from my babies. They'll grow a foot while I'm gone. Will they even remember me?

Candace looks over at me and presses Pause on the remote. "Why're you crying?"

I wipe the tears from my face. "I'm feeling a little overwhelmed all of a sudden. It's starting to get real."

"You're ready for it."

"Am I?"

"You've got the best possible team supporting you and showing you the way. What other young actresses have the likes of Flynn Godfrey, Max Godfrey, Stella Flynn, Marlowe Sloane, Hayden Roth and their whole crew standing behind them? They'll protect you and stand by you through every step of this journey. You know that. Remember when we were discussing this role and whether you should do it?"

"Yeah, I do." I wipe away more tears. "That was the number one reason we decided to go for it. Because of them."

"Flynn and the others have your back. He'd never let anything bad happen to either of us."

"Even he can't stop some of it."

"True, but we've learned a few things in the years we've worked in this industry. We can take care of ourselves, if need be." She reaches out to take my hand. "You'll never be alone with any of it. We're ride or die, girl."

"That gives me tremendous comfort. Thank you for the reminders."

"We've got this. Now, can we *please* watch *Wicked*?"

I laugh at the face she makes as she says that. "Let's do it."

Max

WHEN I SAY MY MARRIAGE TO VIVIAN IS THE LAST THING I WANT TO talk about, I mean it. Revisiting my tumultuous relationship with her has never been on my to-do list, and talking about it with Stella is like pouring acid on an open wound. But because I'm so thankful to still be talking to her at all, and because she wants to know, I'll tell her.

"I met her at a party at Bobby Scott's house. It would've been about three years before I met you. I was about to turn twenty-three and had just had my first big hit with *Sandman*. I had work lined up for the next two years, which made me a success in the eyes of many of the guys I'd come up with who were still hustling, hoping for a break.

"A friend said, 'Bobby wants to meet you and asked that you stop by his place Friday night.' When one of the top producers in the business wants to meet you, you change your plans for Friday night, especially after your management has dropped you for acting like a dick. Bobby's place was up in the Hills, not far from Flynn's. I remember it being hard to find and thinking I was going to miss the whole thing because I couldn't follow basic directions."

"GPS was the best thing to ever happen to you."

I bark out a laugh. "That's a fact. Anyway, the party was in full swing when I arrived to valet parking and tuxedoed waiters with trays of champagne and some of the fanciest food I'd ever encountered. The house was unbelievable. It was all glass, one of the first truly modern contemporaries. I'd never seen anything like it or the views of LA. I remember thinking I'd never want to live in a glass house because everyone could see inside. Not to mention, people in glass houses..."

"Shouldn't throw stones."

"Right. It was just too weird for me. Bobby spotted me right away and came over, made a big fuss about how he'd been dying to meet me for ages and how he loved me in *Sandman* and wanted to work with me. You knew him, right?"

"I did, but not well until I met you."

"He had a powerhouse personality. You couldn't help but be sucked into his orbit. He was like the sun. If you were lucky enough to be one of the planets circling him, you felt like you were on top of the world. I was still new enough to be truly blown away by him. It took a while to see the rot beneath the glitzy surface."

Bobby Scott was sued for sexual harassment by thirty actresses in a class-action lawsuit that rocked our industry twelve years ago. He went from being one of the most powerful people in our business to persona non grata overnight.

"Bobby introduced me to Vivian. He said he wanted us together on camera as soon as he could find the perfect vehicle for us. We were both new enough to be taken in by his enthusiasm, not to mention his star-making reputation. If Bobby Scott saw something in you, that meant big things."

"I remember. He wielded outsized power, which is how he got away with the things he did for so long."

"I never saw any of that, and I was around him a lot."

"He saved his worst behavior for when he was alone with a young actress looking to him to make her a star. He preyed on their dreams and their vulnerability."

"Men like him give us all a bad name, but we were years from seeing his true colors then. He wanted to pair me with Vivian Stevens, and I was all in on that. She was the hottest new commodity in town, and everyone wanted to work with her. What surprised me when I got to know her was the naïveté I found beneath the confident, polished exterior."

Stella gives me a skeptical look. "Naïveté? For real?"

"You wouldn't have seen it. She kept it very well hidden when she was working, but it was there, even if she'd grown some sharper edges by the time you met her. She'd had a very coddled upbringing. She wasn't street-smart the way you need to be in this town. When I first knew her, I used to worry about her ending up like Marilyn, chewed up and spit out by people who used her to advance themselves."

"And you don't think she was playing you a bit by making you think she was naïve?"

"No, not at all. For all her exterior sophistication, she was very different when she put down the mask she wore in public."

"How so?"

"You know how I always say there're people who *get it* and people who don't?"

"Uh-huh."

"She didn't get it. The world was baffling to her. The simplest things were too much for her. She didn't understand how things worked or how people manipulated others to get what they wanted. She was like a butterfly without wings."

"How could you stand that? You can't tolerate stupid people."

"She wasn't stupid. She was innocent, unprepared for the world in which she lived and worked. Did you know she was more or less raised in a convent? Her mother got pregnant as a teenager, and the nuns took her in. They helped to raise Vivian."

"No way."

"It's true. That explained a lot about her."

"So how does she go from being cloistered in a convent to the sexpot of stage and screen?"

"She got noticed by someone like Bobby Scott, who had the means to remake her in his image, and that's exactly what he did. He turned her into the woman the public knows, but underneath the veneer, at least when I knew her, was a girl who was in way over her head in every part of her new life."

"You would've felt protective of her."

"That was the first thing I felt toward her when I realized the veneer was a façade."

"I'm trying to reconcile the woman you describe with the one who strolled onto our set and walked away with my fiancé without so much as a care."

"By the time you met her, she'd begun to understand her power and how to use it to get what she wanted."

"Awesome."

I smile at the sarcasm dripping from that single word. "I'm sorry she hurt you. I hated the way that went down, even if I eventually benefited from it."

"She didn't hurt me so much as infuriate me. Women in our business stuck together in those days. We looked out for each other. We took care of each other. She was the antithesis to that. She steam-rolled right over me and my year-long relationship like it was noth-ing, and don't try to tell me she didn't know he was engaged. He was a bigger star than she was then. Everyone knew."

"Of course she did. She didn't care. She wanted him, and she took him. That's how she behaved for the next twenty years and ended up married six times."

"Seven."

"Shhh, that's a secret we're hoping to keep."

"I want to know what happened after you met her at Bobby's party."

"She tucked her hand into my arm and asked me to introduce her to people at the party. I took her around the room, and I liked the way the other guys looked at me when I had her on my arm. They were jealous, and I was young enough to get a kick out of that."

She gets up to make another cup of tea. "Men. You're all the same."

"In some ways, we are. In others, we're very different."

"And I know that." She smiles at me over her shoulder. "You're better than most."

"I'd like to think so. At that time, though… I was young and dumb—"

"And full of cum," we say together, laughing at one of Hayden's favorite sayings.

"That's so gross," Stella says, laughing.

"Good old Hayden."

"He does have a way with words."

"I wanted her as much as the other guys did, and that she seemed to want me, too, was a heady thing when she could've had anyone. I was instantly smitten. We were pretty much together from that night on. As hard as Bobby tried, though, he never did come up with a project for us to star in together, and he was adamant that we keep our personal relationship off the radar. He said we were both far more bankable single than we were in a relationship, and he more or less said he'd walk away from us if the word got out that we were together."

"He wouldn't have done that. You were both hot commodities then."

"I know that now. At the time, we were intimidated enough that we went deep underground with the personal stuff. He was outraged when we told him we'd gotten married. He said we were stupid idiots to get married so young when our careers were taking off the way they were. His adamant disapproval took the blush off the rose pretty quickly. We went from being blissfully happy to fighting about everything. Safe to say, we ruined it by getting married."

She returns to the table with a perfectly steeped cup of tea and a mug of fresh coffee for me.

"Thanks, hon."

"As upsetting as this has been, I don't like to think of you as being unhappy, even if it was before I knew you."

"It was a difficult time, to be sure. Especially after I pushed the boundaries in the bedroom."

Stella props her chin on her upturned fist. "Tell me about that."

"Do I hafta?"

"Yeah, you do."

Sighing, I resign myself to talking about something I'd much rather forget. "I told you how I'd gotten into the scene with some friends."

"Tell me more about what you liked about it."

"Everything. The way we talked openly about things people never talked about. The talking was almost as hot as the doing. Remember how it was then? Women were taking command of their lives and their sexuality and exerting their power. It was an exciting time. They were as into it as we were. You could have this intense scene with someone and never see them again. No commitments, no expectations. I loved it."

"Why didn't you tell me about that when we met?"

"You weren't like the other women of that time. You were elegant and refined and captivating. It never occurred to me to bring that up with you, especially after it was such a disaster with Vivian."

"How so?"

"She was furious about it. She told me I'd deceived her, hidden a big part of myself from her and made a fool of her by wanting things she thought were abhorrent. Remember, she was raised in a convent. As much as she portrayed herself as a sexpot, she was a virgin when I met her."

"*What?* No!"

"She was. I was her first." I'm not sure I should've told her that, but I promised to be honest.

She goes completely silent on me, which has me breaking into a cold sweat.

"What're you thinking?"

"That I still can't believe you were married to her, slept with her. I can't wrap my head around it."

"I'm sorry. This is a terrible thing to drop on you at this point in our lives."

"It's just another reason to despise her."

I didn't expect to laugh just then but leave it to her.

"What'll we do if we can't stop the book?" she asks.

"We'll do like Marlowe said and laugh it off, make light of it. Like that was so long ago, we don't even remember it."

"There's no way we'll let her think it's upset us in any way. That'd be the ultimate revenge."

"Is my love feeling a bit vindictive?"

"If she plans to run you—and us—through the wringer, I'll make her sorry she was ever born."

CHAPTER 19

Ellie

$\mathcal{I}$ wake up before the kids, which is rare. They're usually up long before I'm ready to be alert. Jasper and I take turns sleeping in, but when I turn over, I see that he's awake before dawn, too.

"Why are your eyes open at this ungodly hour?" he asks as he turns to wrap his arm around me.

"I was about to ask you the same thing."

"I'm thinking about your parents and hoping they're okay."

"They seemed good last night."

"They did, but who knows what's really going on behind the scenes?"

Sighing, I say, "I can't bear to think of them as anything other than blissfully happy together."

"Same. It's hard to fathom that they could be dealing with something like this."

"I keep putting myself in her place and asking how I'd feel about it."

"I can see both sides. Can you?"

"Definitely. Daddy would've wanted to protect her from something that could hurt her, but keeping an earlier marriage from your wife is a big deal."

"He did it for all the right reasons. She'll see that once she has a minute to process it."

"I hope so. Maybe we can take the kids over to visit them today."

"They might want a minute alone."

"I'll ask them what they prefer."

"In the meantime, it's a rare moment we have here, awake before the kiddos."

Those words, said in that accent, still do it for me after years of waking up to him next to me, of listening to him say the most mundane things in the most beautiful way... It never, ever gets old.

"What?" he asks, puzzled by the way I'm looking at him.

"I'm thinking of how lucky I am to get to listen to you say... well... *everything* in that accent."

"My love is such a slut for the British accent."

I laugh because that's entirely true. All he has to do to get my motor running is to whisper something filthy in my ear—or even something as simple as the grocery list—and I'm a goner. "I'm a slut for *your* accent and yours alone. It does it for me. *You* do it for me."

"Likewise, my darling."

"Nice how that worked out, huh?"

"Nicest thing in my whole damned life. You and our sweet babies."

He kisses me, and I quickly pull back. "I should brush my teeth."

"Let's not risk missing our moment, darling."

He's right... That moment is fleeting at best. My husband is excellent about moving things along, especially since we sleep in only enough clothing to be decent if our kids need us during the night. Which means not much.

"Remember when we used to spend hours doing this?" he asks as he slides into me and takes my breath away as usual.

"Hmmm, vaguely. It's been a while."

"We need a getaway by ourselves one of these days."

"Whenever we do that, we come home early because we miss them."

"We have to get over that."

"Not there yet. You?"

Laughing, he leaves a trail of fire on my neck and then bites down on my earlobe. "Nope."

"They say we'll have time to ourselves again when they move out."

"How many years will that be?"

"Matilda is almost three, so fifteen?"

His grunt of annoyance makes me giggle. "I'll be old and impotent by then."

"Don't even say that! I need you to service me until we're old and gray and too feeble to care."

"I'll service you, my darling, as often as I possibly can."

"And if you could say stuff like that every single day, that's all I need to be happy."

"You're easy to please."

"Only because I get to listen to you for the rest of my life."

"Most women can't stand the sound of their husband's voice."

"I'm not most women, and you're definitely not most men. All my friends are jealous that I get to listen to my life in a sexy British accent."

He rolls his eyes, slides deeper into me and holds still, which drives me nuts—as he knows all too well.

I moan with frustration and push against him, urging him to move things along.

The monitor on the bedside table sparks to life with a squeak from our little girl.

Jasper shifts into high gear and gets us both to the finish line just as we hear a rumbling from Harry.

"Well done, my love," I whisper as we hear giggling down the hall. The first thing they do each morning is find each other. Then they come for us.

He gives me one last tight squeeze before we disentangle. "If I forget to tell you later, this is already the best day of my life."

Even though he says that every day, the words go straight to my heart like always. He's so thankful for the life we have together, the life he fought to have when he stood up to his father's blackmail and cruelty. That seems like a long time ago now, but neither of us will ever forget the epic battle we waged, with the support of my family and our friends, to have this life.

"It's the best day ever because I get to spend it with you and our babies."

He leans back to kiss me, and we have all the important parts covered when the kids come blasting into the room with our dog, Randy, in hot pursuit. The minute Harry was born, Randy threw me over for my son. They're best friends forever. Randy is so protective of both kids that I don't mind losing him to them.

Both kids and the dog bomb into bed with us, bringing hugs, kisses, sharp elbows and dog breath to our morning.

I look over at Jasper, who has Matilda in his arms, and catch the smile he directs my way.

Despite my ongoing concern about my parents and the state of their marriage, I settle into another best day ever with my beloved husband, our precious kids and our fiercely loyal Randy.

Flynn

WE'RE TREATED TO AN EARLY WAKEUP BY BENNETT, WHO COMES TO WITH a squeak that ranks right up there with the cutest things I've ever heard. He rarely screams or cries the way his siblings did as babies. Rather, he uses that delightful little noise to let us know he's awake, wet and hungry.

"Let me," I tell Nat as I give her a kiss and leave her to sleep for another ten minutes while I get him up from the portable crib and changed so she can provide the breakfast portion of the program.

After being up far too late making love to my wife, I yawn my way through the whole thing, while he's bright-eyed and grinning, his legs moving as if he's running a marathon or some such thing. "Someone is full of beans today."

He smiles, gurgles, squeaks and kicks with a determination that cracks me up. If he doesn't turn out to be a star soccer player or football kicker, I can't imagine what they're like as babies.

I'm still surprised by how natural fatherhood feels to me. When we were expecting Cece, I was afraid I'd be more of a liability than an asset to Nat due to the pampered, privileged life I'd led up to that point. I was the youngest kid with three older sisters who doted on me as much as my mom and Ada did.

Those worries turned out to be pre-fatherhood jitters. When that baby girl needed something that only her mother or I could provide, I found a deep reservoir of capability I never knew was there. She also brought the kind of joy that made all my previous life accomplishments seem insignificant by comparison.

Fatherhood is my favorite thing yet, other than being Natalie's husband, that is.

"Are you ready to conquer the day, Benny Boy?"

Gurgles, kicks and squeals are his answer to my question.

I pick him up and carry him to his mother, kissing her bare shoulder. I'm not sure if it's the kiss or the squeak that rouses her, but she comes to with a startle, pushing her glorious hair back from her lovely face and smiling at us, happy to see us even after sleeping about three hours in total.

We'd both tell you it was worth it to have that time alone.

At least I hope she thinks so. We'll be dragging ass at Marlowe's party later.

She reaches out to take the baby from me. "Is my little man hungry?"

"He's hungry and full of energy this morning."

"How did the two of us give birth to four morning people?"

"I hear they'll become more like us around twelve or thirteen."

She guides Bennett's little mouth to her breast. "Will we survive until then?"

I'm endlessly fascinated—and aroused—by the sight of my wife feeding our babies. Hayden and I have talked about how it's the most amazing thing we've ever seen and that we never get tired of watching, even when our wives tell us to get another hobby.

"What's so funny?"

I stretch out in bed next to them. "How much Hayden and I love watching the breastfeeding and how you and Addie tell us to get another hobby."

"Four babies each, and the two of you are still perving on the breastfeeding."

"It never gets old to us."

"Believe me, we know. Addie and I have talked about you weirdos."

"Sticks and stones, babe. We're crazy in love with our wives and watching them mother our babies is hot as fuck."

"Don't swear in front of your son."

"He has no idea what that means."

"He's learning every minute of every day, and we want him to learn the right things. I believe this is the fourth time we've had this same conversation."

I fan my face. "And when you chastise me..."

"Don't you have somewhere to be?"

"Not for four more hours. Want me to order breakfast?"

"Yes, please, and coffee." She allows herself one cup a day when breastfeeding.

"Coming right up."

When I return to the bed, Natalie shows me her phone so I can watch the video Candace sent of what's going on at home. All three kids are piled on top of Olivia in the middle of the playroom floor, and my sister-in-law is loving every minute of it. "Looks like business as usual at home."

"Yep, only you're not the one at the bottom of the pile."

"Is it weird that I miss being at the bottom of their pile?"

"I think it's normal, even if it's weird, too."

"How can we yearn for a break from them and miss them so much, too?"

"That's parenthood for ya."

We enjoy breakfast in bed, playtime and then a nap when Bennett falls back to sleep between us. Last night, I set an alarm for eleven, just in case I needed it, and when it goes off, I quickly silence it and head for the shower.

I'm determined to take care of this business with Vivian for my parents and get home in time for the Christmas party at Marlowe and Sebastian's later on. We take turns hosting an annual before-Christmas gathering so we can exchange presents with the kids ahead of our trip. Only the Santa gifts get shipped to St. George, which simplifies things a bit.

As I shower, shave and get dressed, I'd much rather think about the traditions our "family" has established over the years and how much I enjoy them than ponder the stakes of this meeting with Vivian Stevens.

In my nearly twenty years in the business, we've never crossed paths, which is unusual in this town. Perhaps that was intentional on her part because of who my father is. Or maybe it was because my star was ascending while hers was on the way down.

I hate the way our business treats aging women, often discarding them for a younger, flashier version with a cruel ruthlessness. Some women, like my mother, manage to hold off the ravages of time and extend their careers later into their lives. Vivian wasn't one of those women. Time did a number on her once-flawless face, and when her looks caught up to her age, she was pushed aside like so many others before her. Until my father told me about her memoir the other day, I hadn't seen or heard anything about her in years and hadn't given her a thought in all that time.

I heard what Natalie said yesterday about being mean to an older woman, and I get where she's coming from. I won't let her think I want to work with her. But I'll do what's necessary to protect my parents. If that means threatening to destroy whatever comeback she thinks might happen because of her memoir, I'll do it.

Rarely do I feel the need to be ruthless to get what I want. That's not how I operate. My father would've kicked my ass from one end of Sunset Boulevard to the other if he'd heard I was behaving that way. It's never been my style. However, nothing has ever threatened my parents or their marriage the way this potential bombshell has and still could.

That means the gloves come off, if necessary.

I hope it doesn't come to that.

I call down to the valet to ask to have the car delivered to the main entrance.

"Right away, Mr. Godfrey."

"Thank you."

At eleven thirty, I grab the copy of the NDA, leave Nat and Ben sleeping and put the Do Not Disturb sign on the door. Natalie arranged for a late checkout, so they won't be bothered.

In the elevator, I send her a text. *Heading to Vivian's. Will text you when I'm on the way back. Last night was everything. I love you.*

As I come off the elevator, I see the car is already there, so I keep my head down, hoping I won't be recognized as I make my way to the door. I hear the usual buzzing that happens when people realize it's me, but I don't look up or deviate from my destination.

I slip a twenty into the hand of the valet who hands me my key and make a smooth getaway, releasing a sigh of relief as I pull away from the hotel. At a stoplight, I put Vivian's address into the GPS. I know the general location of where she lives, but the directions will save me some time.

With AC/DC's "You Shook Me All Night Long" playing on the Bluetooth, I turn up the volume while there're no young ears to protect. The song is a fitting anthem for the night I had with Natalie. I have a few aches and pains today that remind me I'm going to be forty in three days.

Forty.

Like, how in the actual fuck did that happen when I still feel like I'm twenty-five? Most of the time, anyway. After getting it on with my wife for half the night, I feel every minute of my forty years.

I'd much rather be the age I am now than go back to when I was younger. I'm happier today than I've ever been, married to the woman of my dreams, settled into a deeply satisfying family life and career. I can be choosy about the projects I take on and arrange the rest of my life around my wife and kids.

Life is good, better than it's ever been now that Bennett has joined us, and we have two daughters and two sons to watch grow up.

I honestly couldn't ask for anything more than I already have.

In that sense, turning forty isn't so bad. Besides, I'll be in good company. Hayden, Emmett, Marlowe and Kris are right there with me, Jasper's already forty-one, and my sisters are in their forties, too.

If anything, this milestone birthday is a reminder of how fast the time goes by and how important it is to live each day to the fullest. Thanks to my wonderful family and amazing friends, I do that most days.

Today feels oddly off, stressful in a way I haven't felt since Nat was in labor with Ben. Though my wife was a warrior all four times, I'd heard enough about what could go wrong to be riddled with anxiety until baby and mother were declared safe and healthy each time.

I don't want to be driving to Vivian Stevens's home to present her with an ultimatum. I'd rather be doing a lot of other things with a lot of other people. However, I'm glad my dad asked me to take care of this rather than trying to do it himself or sending Emmett, who would've happily taken care of it for him. It's better that I go, and that I'm alone, so it won't seem like we're ganging up on her.

That's not the goal here. The only thing I care about is protecting my parents and their hard-earned reputations. I'd be surprised if there's a bigger bombshell contained in her book than her marriage to Max Godfrey. That would've been a big enough story with them involved, but add me to the equation, and it becomes a much bigger deal.

And yes, I despise that aspect of celebrity. Each time one of our babies was born, we had to have an entire team of people fending off the media at the hospital and at home. The photo we released on Instagram of us holding the new baby's hand and announcing his or her name was never enough for them. They wanted more and were willing to stalk new parents to get it.

After Scarlett was born, Emmett sued one outfit for invasion of privacy and intentional infliction of emotional distress, not that it stopped them for long. With Bennett, they didn't even get the Instagram photo, and we still haven't publicly revealed his name. Let them wonder.

I pull up at the gate to Vivian's home and press the button, expecting to have to give my name, but the gate swings open to admit me.

Her home is a Spanish-style, two-story structure with a fountain in the middle of the circular driveway. By the rusty look of the fountain, it hasn't worked in quite some time. As I approach the front steps, the door opens, and Vivian herself is there to greet me, wearing a flowing floral caftan. Her dark hair is fully styled, and her makeup is artfully done but can't hide the truth. Her skin looks like tissue paper that was wadded up and then smoothed over.

"What a pleasure to have such a delightful visitor."

"Thank you for seeing me."

CHAPTER 20

Flynn

 *V*ivian shakes my hand and steps aside to admit me.
"Please come in. I thought we could sit outside and take advantage of this warm day."

She tucks her hand into my arm and escorts me down a hallway lined with photos of her with everyone who was anyone back in the day, through an outdated kitchen to a table with an umbrella on the back patio. A tray containing a pitcher of lemonade, glasses and cookies is on the table. "Please make yourself comfortable."

"Thank you." The yard is an overgrown jungle, the pool is empty, and an overall aura of neglect clings to the place.

Vivian pours lemonade for both of us and offers me a cookie.

I take one to be polite.

She sits next to me and takes a sip of lemonade. "I've so admired your career. *Camouflage* and *Insidious* are two of the best films I've ever seen."

"That's very kind of you to say."

"It's the truth, and you've got the awards to prove it."

"We've had a nice run at Quantum."

The look she gives me has probably brought many a man to his knees over the years. "Handsome as sin and modest, too. That's a deadly combination."

"Is it?"

"Oh yes. I've followed your romance with your pretty wife. I understand a film about her is in the making."

"Yes, *Valiant* is out in March."

"I can't wait to see it."

"It's been a labor of love that's taken years to get to this point."

"The best things take the longest to come to fruition, or so it seems." She sits back and eyes me shrewdly. "I'll admit to being curious about why you wanted to see me."

"I figured you might've guessed."

"I'm afraid you have me at a disadvantage."

I remove the NDA from my pocket and hand it to her.

She reaches for reading glasses that I hadn't noticed on the table and props them on her nose to read the document, glancing up at me and then back at the paper. When she's finished, she folds it into threes and places it on the table. "I assume this is a copy for me to keep."

"It is."

"You remind me of him," she says softly. "Handsome as can be, with kind eyes and a sweet disposition."

"I never get tired of being compared to him. He's the best man I've ever known."

"He's the best man I've ever known, too."

I'm surprised to see tears in her eyes.

"He's my greatest regret."

She removes the reading glasses, folds them, places them on the table and dabs at her eyes with a napkin. "I can see I've taken you by surprise."

"A little."

"You don't let a man like Max Godfrey get away and not live to regret it."

Dad would be shocked to hear that. He's under the assumption that she has no love lost for him.

"I spent most of my adult life trying to find what I had with him, and as you and the rest of the world know, that didn't work out so well."

"I'm sorry." I didn't expect to like her or to feel sorry for her.

"I'm sure your mother has nothing nice to say about me."

"Well..."

"It's okay. I did her dirty, as the kids say. I've made a lot of mistakes in my life, and that was another I deeply regret. She was—and is—a nice person, and I'm sorry I hurt her the way I did. I chalk it up to immaturity, an overinflated ego and the feeling of invincibility that we all eventually outgrow, hopefully before too much damage is done. Sadly, I left some destruction in my wake, and I own that."

"Do you own it in your book?"

"I discuss the mistakes I made and that I regret hurting others."

"Do you name my parents?"

"I do."

"Including your marriage to my father?"

"Yes."

"Per the terms of the NDA, you're not legally permitted to discuss him or the marriage."

"I figured that document was long gone into the dustbin of history."

"Now you know it's not. In consultation with our attorneys, my father is fully prepared to enforce the terms of the NDA."

She releases a deep sigh and looks down at her folded hands. "I was hoping you'd come to offer me a part in your next film."

"I'm sorry to be the bearer of bad news."

"It's devastating news."

I begin to feel as uncomfortable as I've been in a long time.

"I'm sure you can tell that I've fallen on hard times. Divorce is expensive business in a community property state, and I haven't worked in quite some time. The memoir is my lifeline." She glances my way. "I understand that your parents want to protect their privacy, and they certainly have a right to that. But... I'm not sure what I'll do if the book isn't published. M-my home is mortgaged to the hilt, and I'm behind on the payments... I won't receive the bulk of the advance until the book is published." All at once, she seems to realize she's oversharing and shakes her head, forcing a smile. "Of course, none of that is your problem or your parents'."

"Do you have any family?"

"Not anymore. My precious son, Tommy, passed about a year ago from cancer. He was dreadfully ill for about five years before I lost him. Terrible disease."

"Yes, it is. I'm so sorry for your loss." I ache at the thought of losing either of my sons.

"Thank you. He was the light of my life, to be sure, and he wanted his illness kept private, which was his right." She reaches over, puts her hand on top of mine. "I want you to know... Your father is within his rights to insist that NDA be upheld. I wouldn't blame him if he did that. But if there's any way..."

"What do you say about him and my mother in the book?"

"I could show you the actual passages if that would help."

"It would."

"I'll be right back."

I'm left feeling sympathetic toward someone I expected to revile. What the hell do I do now? My phone chimes with a text from my dad. *Are you still at Vivian's?*

I am. Interesting woman. I'll call you when I leave.

Pins and needles.

I understand.

She returns to the patio, holding a hardcover book that she hands to me. There's a photo of her in her prime on the cover, and the title is *My Life and Times* by Vivian Stevens. I notice there're sticky notes marking the sections of interest to me.

I flip it open to the first passage and read about how she met my father through now-disgraced producer Bobby Scott (more to come on him, she promises) and quickly fell madly in love with the handsome young actor.

This news will take the world by surprise, as Max and I were urged to keep our relationship—and our eventual brief marriage—private, lest we hurt careers that were just getting started. In those days, you see, it was a liability to be "off the market" or, God forbid, married. *We were told our fans needed to be able to imagine the fantasy of themselves with us, or some such nonsense. At any rate, we were told to keep quiet about it, so we did. We weren't together long due to the relentless pressures of two busy careers, months apart on location and endless demands on our time.*

In the more than fifty years since, I've thought of him often and wished we could've made it work because I never met another man quite like him. Honorable, kind, caring, compassionate, grounded, not at all caught up in the madness that was his life—and mine—at the time. I wish I could say the same about myself. I was young and foolish enough to believe that another Max Godfrey would come along one day, but that never happened. Instead, there was a series of poor substitutes, while Max went on to have a long and successful marriage with Stella Flynn, a woman who rightfully despises me.

I glance up at Vivian, surprised by the raw emotions she conveys through her words.

I met Stella on the set of London Town. *She'd recently become engaged to Jonah Street, a man I'd long admired from afar. I'm not proud of how I behaved when I met him in person. I was instantly taken in by his easy charm and sexy smile, swept away on a sea of inevitability, or at least that's how it seemed at the time. Looking back at it with the perspective of fifty-plus years, I cringe at how I behaved. My disrespect for Stella is something I regret to this day. She was always a classy person, the kind who took the high road, except for when someone walked onto her set and made off with her man.*

In front of the entire cast and crew, she called me a whore.

Her words cut me to the quick. Not because I didn't deserve them, but because I did. I'd become someone I barely recognized and was ashamed of the pain I'd caused another young actress. In this brutal town, women had to stick together, and I'd broken the code of sisterhood we relied upon to survive in a man's world.

Stella paid a big—and unfair—price for that episode, with her career temporarily derailed as people took sides. Most of them took my side, even if I didn't deserve their loyalty. I want to be clear that I never asked anyone to blacklist her. That happened anyway. The nastiness directed at her was one hundred percent my fault. I own it, not that it matters now, but I regret that it happened in the first place. In the end, despite his undeniable charm and handsome face, Jonah wasn't worth the price either of us paid for the mistake of caring for him.

It's made me happy to know that she and Max found each other, built a beautiful family and produced a movie star named for both of them in their talented, charismatic son, Flynn. That they also continue to enjoy block-buster careers is a testament to their talent and perseverance in this dog-eat-dog business.

A life well lived doesn't come without its share of regrets. I've gotten to watch the woman I once wrongly considered an enemy be loved by the man I let get away. Only in Hollywood!

I look up at her, oddly moved by her words and the frank way she owns her mistakes.

She smiles warmly. "Other than the surprise revelation that your father and I were once married, hopefully you didn't see anything too egregious."

"No, I don't, but I can't speak for my parents. May I have this copy to share with them?"

"Only if you promise to keep it confidential. The publisher has been adamant about that. They feel the revelation of my marriage to Max will make the book a runaway bestseller, which would change my circumstances dramatically. Not that that's your problem or your parents'..."

"I understand the need for confidentiality, and no one will hear about the contents of your book from us. You have my word on that."

"Then you may take that copy with you." She glances toward her unruly backyard, which I'm sure was once glorious. "As you can imagine, I'll need to know fairly quickly if your father plans to enforce the NDA. The book is due to be released next month."

"We'll be in touch as soon as possible."

"Thank you."

"Thank you for seeing me."

She flashes the smile that made her a star. "Oh, honey, that's been entirely my pleasure."

Flynn

BEFORE I LEAVE VIVIAN'S, I TEXT NATALIE TO LET HER KNOW I'M ON MY way back to the hotel to pick up her and Bennett.

We'll be ready, she replies.

As I head through Vivian's gates, I call my dad.

He picks up on the first ring. "Hey. You've got both of us. How'd it go?"

"Surprisingly well. She was very nice and welcoming."

"What did she say about the NDA?"

"I think she was caught off-guard by it. She said she figured it'd been relegated to the dustbin of history."

"That's convenient," Mom says. "Sounds like her."

"I don't think she's the same person you knew back then, Mom."

"Don't tell me she got to you, too."

"It wasn't so much that she got to me as she shared some things I didn't know. For one thing, she's out of money and in danger of losing her home."

"A likely story." Mom's tone is full of disdain.

"It's true. The place is a wreck. It hasn't seen a maintenance worker or gardener in years. Did you know she lost her only child to cancer a year ago?"

"Not Tommy," Dad says. "Good Lord. Everyone knew he was her pride and joy."

"She said he fought the disease for years before he passed."

"I'm so sorry to hear that," Mom says. "No one deserves that kind of pain."

"Are we mentioned in the book?" Dad asks.

"Yes, and she showed me the passages. She divulges that you two were briefly married at a time when young, hot stars were encouraged to stay single to keep the fantasy alive for their fans. She says she was foolish enough to believe that another Max Godfrey would come along one day, but that never happened."

"Why does it please me to know that she regrets letting him go?" Mom asks.

Dad chuckles.

"And, Mom, she totally owns that she did you dirty with Jonah. She regrets hurting you."

"Well... I certainly didn't expect that."

"I've got a copy of the book for you to read for yourselves, but I didn't see anything in the parts about you that would harm either of you other than some increased publicity due to the revelation of her marriage to Dad."

"Which could be good for business," Dad says.

"Honestly, Max."

"What? I'm just saying..."

Their exchange makes me laugh. "You guys are coming to Marlowe's this afternoon, right?"

"We'll be there."

"I'll bring the book with me. You can take it home, read it and decide how you feel, but here's the thing... She needs the money from the book—and she needs it badly. She's behind on her mortgage, and the place is falling down around her. She understands that if you choose to enforce the NDA, we could probably stop the publication of the book, but that'd be the end of her financially since her acting career is over. She gets the bulk of the money for the book after it's published."

"So she put a guilt trip on you, then," Mom says.

"It wasn't like that. She was very matter-of-fact about what's at stake for her."

"You liked her," Dad says.

"I really did. I went in there expecting to despise her, but she was warm and welcoming and fully owned her bullshit from the past. I found myself admiring her by the time I left."

"And of course you want to help her," Mom says.

"I'll be sending my gardener over there after the holidays."

"Oh, Flynn!" Mom says. "You don't have to do that."

"I know I don't, but I will anyway."

"You're a good man, son," Dad says gruffly.

"I learned from the best." I pause before I add, "Listen, it's totally up to you guys to decide what you want to do next, but it's very clear to me that if there was any kind of contest, so to speak, you two won by a mile. Your lives have been blessed beyond belief compared to hers. She's alone in the world, while you're surrounded by a big, loving family, and yes, I know she made her bed and now she has to lie in it, and I get not wanting your past history with her put on blast... Anyway, we can talk about it after you read the passages that involve you, but in my opinion, there's nothing awful. If anything, you both come off looking like the wonderful people you are."

"And you're not at all biased," Mom says with a laugh.

"I'm extremely biased, and you know I'd move heaven and earth to put a stop to this thing if I thought it would hurt either of you in any way. But after meeting her and talking with her and reading the part of the book that involves you... In my opinion, there's no *there* there."

"As you know, your opinion means the world to us," Dad says. "We appreciate you taking this meeting and your insight."

"Happy to take one for the team. I'll see you later on."

"See you then," Dad says. "We love you."

"Love you, too."

I end the call about two minutes before I pull up to the hotel. Natalie and Ben are outside with a bellman, awaiting my arrival. I put the SUV in Park and jump out to help her with the baby and the bags.

She smoothly tips the bellman, thanks him for his help and then turns to me. "How'd it go?"

I lean in to kiss her without a care as to the photographers that could be lurking nearby, hoping for a celebrity sighting. "Better than expected." I hold the passenger door for her and wait for her to get settled before closing it. As I'm rounding the front of the car on the way to the driver's seat, someone calls out to me. I give a wave and continue on my way, not interested in being waylaid by a fan right now.

We pull away from the hotel and head for the Hollywood Hills.

"How're things at home?"

"All good. Olivia made pancakes shaped like Mickey Mouse that were a big hit."

"How are they better at this than we are?"

"They're younger and more energetic, not to mention endlessly creative."

"We used to be energetic."

"We were pretty energetic last night."

"Yes, we were." I bring her hand to my lips. "Thank you for a great night. I needed the time alone with you."

"I needed it just as much."

Bennett lets out a squeak to remind us that we're not completely alone.

I glance at him in the mirror. "Hey, buddy. We hear you. You're here, too."

"Tell me about Vivian."

I relay the same story I told my parents, giving her the highlights.

"That's so sad about her son."

"Is terrible. She's all alone in the world and out of money after all the divorces."

"What did your parents say about it?"

"They're reserving judgment until they read the book." At a stoplight, I grab the book I stashed behind the passenger seat and hand it to her.

"Beautiful photo of her," Natalie says of the cover image.

"It is. She doesn't look like that anymore."

"Which would be another in a string of painful losses for a woman who traded on her looks to make a living."

"I suppose so."

"Can I say something else?"

I glance at her, surprised she'd ask for permission to speak her mind. "Whatever you want."

"I'm really proud of you for how you handled the meeting with her."

"You are? Why?"

"Because you didn't go in there like a battering ram to defend your parents. You listened to her and came away with a feeling of compassion toward her, when it would've been easier not to notice her suffering."

"I'd have to be a robot not to notice the suffering."

"Some people wouldn't have seen it, even if it was smacking them in the face. I like that you're planning to clean up her yard and that you want to help her, even if you didn't expect that going in."

"Thank you for your input yesterday. You were right that there was no place for deliberate unkindness."

"There's never a place for that."

"Sometimes I need a reminder."

"If we'd never had that conversation, you would've taken one look at her situation and backed off that plan. I'm sure of it."

"I wish I was."

"You would have. At the end of the day, she's an old woman with no real power in this world."

"Except to expose something my father would rather keep private, not to mention a rehash of the scene with my mother."

"They're strong enough to withstand that storm, and like Marlowe said, they could act like it's nothing new to them. That would take the steam out of the story."

"Right."

"Do you think your dad will enforce the NDA after they read what she wrote about them?"

"I doubt it. There's nothing in there that can truly hurt them."

"I really hope they let her publish her book, so she'll get the money she needs to live out the rest of her life in comfort."

"I do, too, and I wouldn't have expected to feel that way when I left the hotel earlier."

"And that is why I'm proud of you."

I give her hand a squeeze. "I always want you to be proud of me."

"I'm the proudest—and luckiest—wife ever."

"I'm the luckiest. No contest."

"Luckiest wife?" she asks with a saucy grin.

"Luckiest *person* in the whole world because your old dog chose me for you."

"Fluff knew what she was doing."

"I'm thankful for her every day of my life."

"Me, too."

CHAPTER 21

Marlowe

G etting anything done with two three-year-olds underfoot is close to impossible. I feel like they undo things as fast as I do them, but with more than forty of our closest friends due to our house in a couple of hours, it's time for drastic measures.

"Seb!"

He pokes his head out of the guest bathroom he's been cleaning. "Yes, dear?"

"I need help."

"I'm helping."

I point to the whirling dervishes as they chase each other around the living room, and around me, nearly knocking me over with their combined energy.

"Ah," he says, dark eyes twinkling with amusement. "I see the problem."

"Help!"

"Dad to the rescue." He pulls off the rubber gloves he wears to clean—which I ridicule him for endlessly—and assesses the situation in the living room that now has to be straightened for the third time today. He's wearing a tank-style T-shirt that puts his ridiculously impressive muscles and sleeve tattoos on full display. As usual, I'm distracted by the sight of my sexy man.

I look up at him. "We're never going to be ready in time."

"Who cares? It's just the family. They don't expect us to be perfect."

"Addie's house is always immaculate when she has us over. So are Natalie's and Aileen's."

"Do you think they're going to come in here and think, 'Marlowe is a mess'?"

"No, but—"

He kisses me. "No buts. It'll all be fine. The whole point of this occasion is for the kids to turn the place upside down. So here's a big idea. Why don't we clean *after* the party rather than before?"

"Are you insane?"

The kids have taken their screaming chase down the hallway to their bedrooms, giving us a moment's reprieve before they return.

"It's a fool's errand to clean up before a bunch of young kids come to open presents and cause chaos."

If I tell him he's right, I'll never get him to clean before a party again.

"I know what you're thinking."

I love the way his eyes get even darker when something makes him laugh. "You do *not* know what I'm thinking."

"Yes, I do."

"Okay, hotshot. Lay it on me."

He steps closer, wraps his arms around me and kisses me. "You think if you admit I'm right and call off the cleaning crew that you'll never get me to clean again before a gathering."

I glare at him.

His howl of laughter is super annoying. "You're so cute when you're pissed."

"I must be freaking adorable right now, then."

He kisses me again. "You're freaking adorable all the time, but especially when you get mad at how right I am."

I try to squirm free of his embrace, but he's not having it. "Don't go. The hooligans have left the room. We have one whole minute to ourselves."

"While they dismantle the drywall or some such thing."

"Eh, drywall can be fixed."

"What if they eat it?"

"Good point." He gives me another kiss and releases me. "Put down the mop. It's pointless, and no one cares. I'll go see what your children are doing."

"If they're eating the drywall, they're *your* children."

"So noted," he calls over his shoulder.

Because I can't resist the need, I go around the living room and return pillows to the sofa and toys to bins while I listen to Sebastian talking to our babies with the love, patience and humor that make him the far better parent—in my opinion, anyway. I get the love and humor part right most of the time but tend to fall apart in the patience department.

That's what I get for waiting until my late thirties to have children —and then getting two for the price of one. I'm still mad at Sebastian for knocking me up with twins. They are, however, the greatest joy in our lives, and I wouldn't trade them for anything, not even a moment or two of quiet every now and then.

Seb says we can sleep in when they're surly teenagers who ignore us. Is it wrong of me to look forward to that stage a teeny, tiny bit? Toddlerhood is *insane*, especially times two.

He comes back to the living room with a kid tucked under each arm, squealing with laughter the way they always do with him. He's a much more natural parent than I am, which he says isn't true. But it is. I get overwhelmed a lot faster than he does, whereas they're never too much for him.

We each got a mini-me. Delaney is me all over again, with strawberry-blonde hair and blue eyes, while Domenic is his daddy's doppelgänger, with dark hair and eyes.

He swings them around. "Mommy cleaned up the living room

again. It has to stay this way until our friends come, or Domenic and Delaney will have to go to time-out. Got me?"

"Yes," they say, laughing.

"What did I just say?"

Delaney answers for both of them, as usual. "Don't mess up the living room. Again."

Her baby voice is beginning to mature a bit, which makes me ache for the passage of time that I just said I couldn't wait for. My friends tell me that's motherhood for you. While you yearn for things to get easier, you hate to see the baby years come to an end.

"Is it safe for me to put you down?" Seb asks them.

"No!" They shriek with laughter when he spins them around.

"How about now?"

"No!"

More spinning.

"If they puke, I'll kill you."

"Mommy gonna get you, Daddy," Dom says.

"We better calm down, then." He puts them down, laughing at the way they wobble with dizziness and then sends them off to play in their rooms.

"We make a mess in there," Delaney says as she leads the charge.

Sebastian rubs his hands together. "I think we've reached an understanding."

I crook my finger to bring him over to me.

"You beckoned?"

I go up on tiptoes to kiss him. "You're great with them, and I love you."

"You're great with them, too, and I love you."

"You're better."

He shakes his head. "We bring different skills to the table that make us an awesome team."

"We're a damned good team."

"You know it. No one else I'd rather team up with than you, babe."

"Even when I'm grumpy?"

He wraps me up in his warm embrace, and I rest my head against his chest. "Especially then."

With the Christmas tree sparkling in the corner of the big room, I'm feeling peaceful, centered and excited to celebrate my favorite holiday with my favorite people.

Until a loud crash sounds from the other end of the hallway.

"What the hell was that?"

"Daddy's on it. Nothing to see here."

As I watch him go, all I can do is laugh at the madness that is my life.

Max

THE PARTY AT MARLOWE'S HOME IN BRENTWOOD IS A THREE-RING circus of screaming kids, stressed-out parents and enough love and laughter that we barely notice the commotion. Stella and I have learned to premedicate ahead of these events with Advil and Bloody Marys.

She's seated across the room with Natalie, Ellie, Aimee, Annie, Addie, Leah, Aileen and Marlowe, fawning over Holt and Bennett. As the newest babies in the crew, they're getting most of the attention from the moms, all of whom say they're done having babies. Stella and I have a bet that there'll be at least one more for the Burkes and possibly another for Kris and Aileen.

Addie is weepy as she rocks Holt. "We could have *one more*, couldn't we?" she asks no one in particular.

"I heard that!" Hayden calls from the corner where the guys have gathered. "And the answer is *no*! I'll end up with a fifth daughter to make me her bitch, and I'm already fully bitched by the four we have."

"Hayden!" Jan says. "Language."

"Are you still fighting that battle, Jan?" Flynn asks, laughing. "I hate to tell you it might be a lost cause."

"We have to try for the sake of the children," Jan replies.

Ever since little Bella Roth's first word was *fuck*, Addie and Jan have been on a mission to clean up Hayden's language. So far, it's not going so well, which cracks me up. Not that I'd tell the ladies that.

Bella saying *fuck* as her first word is one of the funniest things I've ever heard. Most of the others agree with me, but we keep that to ourselves. Addie was extremely *un*amused by the whole thing.

When "Santa," memorably played each year by Simon York, arrives to deliver a massive pile of presents, the kids go nuts, the wrapping paper flies through the air, and new toys are assembled by devoted parents with the help of my eldest grandchildren, who are great with the little ones.

Marlowe serves a delicious meal of spaghetti, meatballs, chicken parm, eggplant parm, garlic bread and salad, along with chicken tenders and mac 'n' cheese for the kids who won't eat anything with tomatoes. Dessert is a towering platter of Christmas cupcakes and another full of cookies that Natalie made with the "help" of Cece and Scarlett.

This event has become one of my favorite annual traditions, but even as I enjoy the holiday revelry, I'm anxious to get my hands on Vivian's book to see for myself what she wrote about me. Flynn says it's no big deal, and I believe him, but until I read the words, I can't be certain how I'll feel about them.

Emmett brings me a glass of whiskey. "Figured you might need this by now."

"Stella and I have learned to pregame, but I won't say no to reinforcements."

"Pregaming is a smart strategy in this crowd."

"It's all about the survival."

"Flynn told me he's seen the book, and the bombshell isn't as bad as it could be."

"Yes."

"You can demand that the NDA be enforced if that's what you want to do. You have every right to protect your privacy."

"Thank you for the reminder. I'll let you know later after I read it."

"Whatever you need. I'm here."

"That means a lot to me—and to Stella. We appreciate you."

"We love you guys. We all do. There's nothing any of us wouldn't do for you after you've given many of us the first real family we've ever had."

"You guys have created this incredible family. We can't take any credit for that."

"Max... Come on. You and Stella have shown us how it's done. I know I'm not the only one who feels that way."

I'm ridiculously moved by his heartfelt words. "It's very kind of you to say so."

"Just stating the truth." He squeezes my shoulder and then goes to check on his wife and son.

"Everything okay?" Flynn asks when he joins me.

"Everything's great. Who could have a problem in the world surrounded by all these happy kids?"

"I'm relieved after seeing Vivian. I'm sure you must be, too, to know it's not a smear job."

"I am."

"She said she spent the rest of her life looking for another guy as good as you and never found one."

"That was very surprising to me when you told us that earlier. I never would've guessed she felt that way."

"Sometimes you don't realize what you have until it's gone."

"I suppose so. I'm sorry her life has been difficult. I wouldn't wish the loss of a child on anyone."

"It's terribly sad."

"Indeed." I glance at him, noting a little more silver in his dark hair these days. I can't believe my "baby" will be forty in a couple of days. "I thought about what you said about how we won the game of life, and it's true. Not that I ever thought of it as a competition, but if it was... Well, we've had it all, and Vivian has had it rough. Some of that is her own fault, but a lot of it wasn't."

"I can't say for certain, but I think you and Mom would both like who she is today."

"Maybe so."

"I put the book under the driver's seat in your car. Will you let me know as soon as you've had a chance to read it? I don't want to leave her hanging indefinitely."

"She really got to you, didn't she?"

"Yeah, I guess. I mean... She's the definition of a faded star. Add to it all the losses, divorces and the accompanying financial ruin... It was hard to see."

"I love your big heart, son."

"It came right from you."

I put an arm around him and give him a squeeze.

"I'd better help Natalie round up the troops and get them home to bed. We've got a big couple of weeks ahead."

"I can't wait for every minute of it."

"Same. Been looking forward to it for months. I'm glad you and Mom seem to have worked things out in time for the holidays and the trip."

"We're getting there." I can't even think of what she's asked of me without feeling like I might die of mortification, but I'll do whatever it takes to make things right with my love, even if it means embarrassing the hell out of both of us.

Stella

MAX DRIVES US HOME A LITTLE AFTER EIGHT. WITH SO MANY YOUNG kids, the parties start and end early these days, which is fine with us.

We're both tense now that the hour is upon us in which we'll get to read Vivian's book. It's a bit unnerving to think about being "talked about" in another celebrity's memoir, especially someone with whom you have a less-than-positive history. Even knowing Flynn's take on it, neither of us will rest easy until we read it ourselves.

"That was a fun time, as always," he says.

"My favorite holiday party, even if it's a lot of work ahead of time."

The "kids" have told us we don't have to buy for all the children, but we wouldn't think of not having something for them at Christmas and on their birthdays. Each of them has become like an extra grandchild to us, and we love them dearly.

"Thank you for handling that for us," he says.

"It's better for everyone if you don't do it."

"Haha, very true."

Max hates to shop. One of the best things that ever happened to him was a son-in-law in the jewelry business. Neither of us needs a thing, so some years, we don't even bother with gifts. This is one of those years, thank goodness.

"Are you thinking about the book?" I ask when we get close to home.

"Hard to think about anything else."

"I'm trying to focus on what Flynn said, but..."

"Yeah, same."

"Let's get it over with," I tell him when we arrive at home. "I'll get the nightcaps."

"Sounds good." He retrieves the book from under his seat and brings it inside.

"Let me see it." I take a close look at the image on the cover. Just yesterday, the sight of her flawless face would've infuriated me. Now I feel nothing when I look at the photo on the jacket.

At some point in the last few days, Vivian Stevens has lost the power to upset me, which is an interesting realization. I pour us each a drink and bring them with me to our sitting room, where we spend most of our time together.

"You want to go first?" he asks.

"Read it to me."

He props reading glasses on his nose, takes a sip of whiskey and begins to read.

I close my eyes and listen intently. If Flynn hadn't read it before us, my stomach would be knotted in dread. I'm thankful for his advance take on it and to know there's nothing too terrible coming.

"I was young and foolish enough to believe that another Max Godfrey would come along one day, but that never happened.

Instead, there was a series of poor substitutes, while Max went on to have a long and successful marriage with Stella Flynn, a woman who rightfully despises me."

I certainly didn't expect her to say that.

"My disrespect for Stella is something I regret to this day. She was always a classy person, the kind who took the high road, except for when someone walked onto her set and made off with her man.

"In front of the entire cast and crew, she called me a whore.

"Her words cut me to the quick. Not because I didn't deserve them, but because I did."

I'm stunned by these and the other things she says about me and Max and how she pulls no punches about her own behavior.

"A life well lived doesn't come without its share of regrets. I've gotten to watch the woman I once wrongly considered an enemy be loved by the man I let get away. Only in Hollywood!"

Max closes the book. "That's all of it about us."

CHAPTER 22

Stella

"*J* have to admit," I tell him, "I didn't expect her to fully own it the way she does."

"Me either."

"And that she knows what she lost when she let you get away takes some of the sting out of it."

"I'm one of a kind."

That makes me laugh as hard as I have in days. "Yes, you are. What do you think of it?"

"Like you, I'm impressed by the way she owns it. No hedging, no excuses. Just the truth of the matter. It could've been much worse, I suppose."

"*Much* worse. At least she didn't bring the sex stuff into it."

"Small favors."

"What happens now?" I ask him.

"We need to let Vivian know whether I intend to enforce the terms of the NDA. If we pursue it, Emmett feels we could stop the publication of the book."

"Wouldn't it look like we have something to hide if that got out?"

"I suppose it would."

"Do we have anything to hide?"

He glances at me over the top of his glasses. "Not anymore."

"Do we care if people know you were once married to her or that I called her a whore and that it cost me my career for a time?"

"I don't much care, but I bet Jonah will."

That makes us both laugh.

"He doesn't come off looking so great."

Max chuckles. "He's not worth the bother."

"That's something Vivian and I agree on. You know… A funny thing has happened on the way to this memoir being published."

"What's that?"

"I don't care about any of it anymore. I don't feel a single thing when I see her gorgeous photo on the cover of that book. My outrage has left the building."

"That's a nice side effect of all this upset. Flynn says she doesn't look like that anymore."

"Who among us looks like we did back in the day?"

"You do."

"Oh please. Do you need stronger glasses?"

"I do not," he says indignantly. "My wife is as gorgeous today as she was the day I met her."

"You're a damned liar, but I'll allow it in this case."

We share another laugh.

"If it's all right with you, I'll tell Flynn we have no objection to the publication of the book. But I want us to agree that *when* we're asked —not if—we'll say of course you always knew about my first marriage. It was a blip in time before we ever knew each other."

"Yes, that's what we'll say."

"I'm sorry again that I didn't tell you a long time ago."

"I understand why you didn't. I could be a bit unreasonable about her."

He raises a dark brow. "A *bit*?"

"Don't push your luck, mister."

"Yes, dear." He gets out his phone and sends a text to Flynn, who responds right away. "He says, 'Thanks for letting me know. She'll be relieved to hear the news.'"

"I'm sure she will."

"I hate to hear that she's fallen on such hard times and that she's so alone in the world."

I glance at him tentatively. "Are you going to want to do something about that?"

"Like what?"

"I don't know. *Something.*"

"Nah. I mean, she's still the woman who stole your fiancé once upon a time."

"Thank goodness she did, or I might've been married to Jonah Street when Max Godfrey came along."

"Lord, I hadn't even thought of it that way."

"I have. Many times over the years. Not that it took away my disdain for her and what she did—what they *both* did—but I've always been grateful that I didn't marry him, that I was free to fall madly in love with you."

"I guess things happen the way they're meant to, even if we can't see that at the time."

"Yes, for sure."

He glances at me. "So if I wanted to do *something* for her..."

"I wouldn't object. I might even participate."

"Wow, look at you coasting down the high road."

"I like to think I can still learn at my advanced age."

"There's nothing advanced about your age except in the area of wisdom."

I snort with laughter. "You have to say that. You're older than me."

"Don't remind me that I robbed the cradle."

"Three years is not a robbery, old man."

"Who you calling old?"

I can tell that I surprise him when I get up from my chair and go to him, sliding onto his lap.

"To what do I owe the pleasure?" he asks as he wraps his arms around me.

"I want you to know that even though I don't condone secrets or lies, I'm sort of glad this happened because it gave us a good shaking, a reminder that for all our years together, we can still be vulnerable to trouble unless we stay vigilant."

"I've never not been vigilant where the most important person in my life is concerned."

"You know what I mean. Neither of us would've thought something like this was possible at this stage of the game."

"Your point is well taken. I'll always be sorry you were hurt by the secret I kept."

"I'm over it, and in the process, I've let go of decades' worth of animosity toward someone who got over the whole incident years ago. I ended up with the husband, the family—and the career—I was meant to have."

"Yes, you certainly did."

"The acting career was never going to be what the music became."

"I don't know about that."

"I do. The incident with Vivian forced me to pivot sooner than I might have otherwise. I could've spent years chasing the wrong dream."

"I think you could've been just as great of an actress as you are a singer."

"You have to say that. You're my husband."

He pats my backside. "I don't gotta say nothing but the truth."

"You know what I want to do?"

"What's that?"

"Get in bed and talk about the day we met."

"That was one hell of a day."

"Let's relive it, shall we?" We usually do that on our anniversary but haven't gotten to it yet this year.

"I'd love to."

Max

WHEN WE'RE SNUGGLED UP TO EACH OTHER IN BED, I LET MY MIND wander back in time to the most consequential day ever. This is my favorite story of them all, the day I met the love of my life.

"The very first thing I remember is how uncertain you were, how nervous about performing on Merv."

"There was *so* much at stake. I can barely stand to think about the spot I was in, a heartbeat away from having to go home to Iowa a failure."

"You were never going home to Iowa."

"I didn't know that then! What if I'd bombed on Merv?"

"You were never going to bomb either. You were—and are—far too talented to bomb."

"It was by no means a sure thing back then."

"I found it refreshing that you were so nervous. I was far more accustomed to meeting cocky young blowhards who had a fraction of your talent. I watched you from backstage while you performed. I caught Merv's eye across the stage and saw he was as blown away by you as I was. During the commercial break, he said to me, 'That young lady is going to be a big star.'"

"You never told me that!"

"I did, too."

"I would've remembered that. How is it that I'm still hearing new details about that day fifty-two years later?"

"I swear I told you."

"Maybe you did, and I forgot. That's entirely possible."

We share a laugh, as we often do, over the relentless march of time and how stupid we feel when we can't recall things. I tell her it's because our hard drives are full.

"After the show, I was so afraid you'd leave before I could ask you..."

"What did you want to ask me?"

We both know the answers to all these questions, but it's still fun to ask them. "I wanted to ask you to spend the rest of your life with me, but I feared that might be too much too soon."

Her laughter is the sound of joy to me. "Perhaps a bit too much. Not that we took our time or anything. I still cringe when I think about how I behaved that night."

"Tell me how you behaved..."

"I can't. It's too embarrassing."

I poke her ribs, which makes her gasp and then laugh. "Come on... You know it's my favorite story ever."

She turns her face into my chest. "I can't."

"Remember how *immediate* it all was? Like there she is, and now we're together forever?"

"I do. It was like a force bigger than us, or something equally dramatic."

"Which is why what you did that night shouldn't embarrass you after all this time."

"It does. I would've smacked my girls around if they'd done that."

"Um, I hate to tell you, but I bet they have..."

"Stop it. My girls would never sleep with a new guy the night they met him."

"If you say so, dear."

"Let me have my illusions, will you? I still can't believe you got me into bed that night."

"It was more like the next morning..."

"The three-day first date."

"It was the last first date of our lives, so we had to make it memorable."

"We sure did that."

"By the time we came up for air, your career had been fully resurrected."

"Dabney was *so* mad at me," she says with a laugh. "'Where the hell ya been, Stelly Belly? Everyone wants to book Stella Flynn!'"

"I've always loved your impressions of him."

"He was the best, but oh, he was mad that I disappeared for three days after Merv."

"Was it worth it?"

"You have to ask?"

"Just checking."

"You know I've never regretted a moment I spent with you. Except for how easy I was that first night."

That cracks me up. "We were both easy that night."

"I decided I had to marry you so I could live with myself."

"Haha. You were such a good girl until you met me."

"I fell into a fast crowd."

"It's amazing when you think about how after that we never spent another night apart, except when we were working."

"Until this week…"

I wince. "I hate that I caused it."

"We're not talking about that. We're talking about fifty-two years ago."

"Right."

"Stay on topic."

"Yes, dear. So we left Merv's studio and then what?"

"You were starving, so we went to get something to eat."

"I took you to Frankie's, where my buddies were playing poker. They never let me forget that I chose you over them that night."

"They got over it eventually. That was the best meal I'd had in years."

"You still love Frankie's filet and scalloped potatoes."

"Yum, and the creamed spinach. To *die* for. Is it too late to call for takeout?"

"I think it might be. We'll stop by for dinner after the trip."

"How many dinners have we had there since that first night?"

"Oh God, hundreds. Sometimes I think he keeps the place open just for us."

"No way."

"He gets offers to sell all the time, but he declines out of fear of new owners changing it."

"Some things should never be changed, and Frankie's is one of them."

"Right you are, love. That was the first time you had crème brûlée, remember?"

"I'll never forget it. Best thing I'd ever tasted."

"We drank a lot of wine at that dinner."

"That's how you got me into your bed."

"I don't recall much arm-twisting..."

"Hush. I was coerced. That's my story, and I'm sticking to it."

After all these years, she still makes me laugh like no one else ever has.

"It's not funny!"

"Yes, it is."

"How did we get from Frankie's to your place, anyway?"

"I believe it was a taxi that conveyed us."

"And the driver was a big fan of yours! He didn't want to charge you for the ride."

"I insisted, and he became a friend. I told him to come into Frankie's, and I'd buy him a drink. He ended up joining the poker game for a while before he moved back to New York."

"What was his name again?"

"Henry Douglas."

"Ah, right. I remember now. He was a good guy."

"The best. We all loved him until he wiped the table clean with us."

She laughs. "He was a New York card shark posing as an LA cab driver. Is he still with us?"

"Nah, he died about ten years ago or so."

"That's right. Cancer, right?"

"Lung cancer. He loved his smokes and refused to give them up. So now we're at my place... What happens next?"

"I believe there was more wine, and you fired up the record player."

"That was the first time we danced to our wedding song. I already knew it then, that you were my first, my last, my everything."

"You couldn't have already known that!"

"I knew it in Merv's Green Room. I'd never reacted to anyone the way I did to you."

"Same," she says with a sigh. "That's why I was so easy. The first time you kissed me..." She shivers. "It was... Well... I've never forgotten it."

"Tell me more."

"One minute we were dancing, and the next..."

"Yes?"

"You pulled back, ever so slightly."

"I wanted to keep you close to me while I looked at your gorgeous face. I couldn't believe how lucky I felt to be there with you."

"*You* felt lucky! I was with *Max Godfrey*!"

"I felt like the luckiest guy alive that night and every night since."

"I wanted to pinch myself, thinking my friends would never believe where I was or who I was with. And then you kissed me, and it was like nothing else had ever happened to me before right then and there."

"I felt the same way, like hello, here she is. The one I didn't even know I was looking for until she arrived."

"You've always said the sweetest things."

"I have the best inspiration. What happened next?"

"Somehow, and I'm still not entirely sure how, we went from earth-shattering kisses to naked in bed together in the span of seconds."

"It was actually more like an hour."

"No way."

"I swear!"

"I don't believe it. Felt like seconds."

"It was an hour's worth of seconds."

"If you say so. An hour... Jeez. I really put up a fight, huh?"

"We were powerless to resist each other."

"'Powerless' is a good word to describe it. I'd never been so swept away by anything or anyone. I thought those things only happened in fiction, not in real life."

"You said that to me at some point during those first few days. You said you thought things like this only happened in fairy tales."

"It was like being in a dream or something."

"Except it was very, very real."

"That was the first time I ever showered with someone else."

"Mmm, remember that first time in the shower?"

"Uh, yes, because I didn't know *that* could be done in a shower!"

Laughing, I remind her, "*That* can be done in a lot of places, as we've discovered."

"Don't remind me of the many ways you've corrupted me."

"Or how often we nearly got caught."

"I can't even think about that without wanting to die. It was bad enough being hounded by the press when we were fully clothed..."

"You were always so afraid a photographer would pop out of the bushes."

"With good reason!"

"That was such an exciting time. Madly in love and in hot demand everywhere."

"It didn't matter what I had to do in a day," she says, "all I cared about was getting it done so I could get back home to you."

"Same for me. I was obsessed with my girlfriend and then my wife. I rushed through every commitment so I could get it over with."

"It's a wonder we weren't fired or sued or blacklisted during that stage."

"So true. Back to that three-day first date, though... Remember how I had to go out to get food so we wouldn't starve to death?"

"And more... protection."

"That, too. We'd burned through my whole condom supply by then."

She covers her face. "You just love to embarrass me."

"It's one of my favorite things."

"Believe me, I know. You turned me into a sex-crazed lunatic."

"How about what you did to me?"

"What did I do?"

"You made *me* into a sex-crazed lunatic. I'd never had so much sex in my life. Everything hurt, including Mr. Johnson."

She busts up laughing. "Oh God, I forgot how you used to call it that."

"When I look back over my whole life, those first three days with you are like a bright light over everything else."

"For me, too. I've never forgotten that magical interlude when we checked out of life and fell into love."

"I like how you said that. 'We checked out of life and fell into love.' We sure as hell did."

"I've been thinking…"

"About?"

"The condition I placed on forgiving you for not telling me about Vivian."

"I've thought of little else since you laid down the law about that."

"I did some reading about it."

"Oh my God… I'm trying to picture that…"

"You can imagine how red my face was."

I snort out a laugh. "Scarlet fever red?"

"Redder than that."

Chuckling, I ask, "What'd you think of it?"

"That I understand why people like it. There's a lot to be said for the open communication and all that, but… I just don't think it's something I'd enjoy." She caresses my bare chest as she talks. "I know I said it was my line in the sand but saying it and doing it are two different things."

"That's very true, and for what it's worth, I never got very far on that subject with Vivian. She wasn't into it at all, and in the end, it was just another reason for her to want out of the marriage. She chalked it up to me being deviant that way, when that wasn't at all the case."

"Why is anything different considered deviant?"

"Good question. Different strokes for different folks and all that."

"Or our old mantra: live and let live."

"Exactly. What works for one of us might not do it for someone else, but that doesn't make either way wrong if no one is getting hurt."

"What other reasons did she have for wanting to divorce you? I'm trying to imagine a scenario where I'm married to Max Godfrey and trying to get out of it."

"I did back-to-back films during the time we were married. I was in Tunisia for a big chunk of the six months we lived together, and when I got back, she'd already started up with Garrison, who was Tommy's father."

"While you two were still married?"

"That was the word on the street from reliable sources. I confronted her with what I'd heard. She denied it, but I didn't believe her. I moved out of her place and called Corbin's dad, who'd joined our poker game the year before. He got the divorce train moving. At some point, she had the marriage annulled, which I found out about after the fact. I didn't see her again for years and rarely gave her a thought. That's how I knew I'd married the wrong person. I didn't miss her when I was away and didn't care when I found out she was cheating on me."

"Funny how she doesn't mention in the book that she cheated on you."

"I noticed that."

"I guess she's not coming clean on everything."

"Eh, what does it matter now?"

"It doesn't. That's what I'm saying. I want to rescind my condition. What we have, what we've *always* had, has been more than enough for me."

"For me, too. I swear to God on the lives of everyone we love, Stel, I've never once been with you and wished for anything or anyone else. As long as I had you, I had everything I'd ever wanted."

"That's all I need to know."

"I will mention, however, that I had a few things sent to a PO box under Edwin's name."

"What kind of things?"

"Want to find out?"

Her face flames with color that makes me laugh.

"Stop laughing at me."

"I'm laughing *with* you."

"Except I'm not laughing!"

That makes me laugh harder. "What do you say I make a pickup at the post office before the trip, and we see what transpires?"

"I'd be okay with that," she says primly, which makes me smile.

"Very well, then. That's what we'll do."

CHAPTER 23

Flynn

On Christmas Eve, forty-six of us fly on a chartered plane to St. George, Utah, where we take over every room in the Castaway Inn. By now, the owners, Jed and Dana Cawthorne, are old friends and look forward to our arrival every year. We've packed for winter in Utah and the beach in Mexico. The minute we're settled at the Castaway, we open the adjoining doors to create long corridors for the kids to safely run and play.

And then we unpack the booze that'll get us through this chaotic holiday.

The dads are asked to take the kids out to play in the snow to burn off as much energy as possible. We bundle them up and go out to the lawn in front of the inn for a massive snowball fight.

The Cawthornes put up a ten-foot-tall Christmas tree in the great room at the center of the inn and keep a fire going in the stone fireplace that we use to toast marshmallows and make s'mores after a dinner prepared in the inn's kitchen. Addie, Natalie and Aileen are the chief organizers, making sure groceries are ordered and preparations made for us to hunker down at the inn and relax as much as we can with a squad of little kids running us ragged.

We take turns cooking, with everyone assigned meals and others pitching in as needed.

It's a freaking blast and one of my favorite annual traditions. We're about to sit down for Christmas Eve dinner when Kris lets out a shout that has us all wondering what's going on.

"Aileen got the results of her latest physical. The doc said, 'All clear. See you next year.'" Kris pumps his fist before he embraces his wife in a tearful hug while the rest of us breathe a big sigh of relief. Her annual tests are tough on all of us. We can't imagine what it must be like for them. I'm so glad they can now relax and fully enjoy themselves.

My parents are in good spirits, so much so that they snuck off to be alone for hours after we first arrived and returned all flushed and weird-looking. My sisters and I can't bear to think of what they might've been up to, but we have our suspicions that things are back on track between them in every possible way. Not that any of us wants the details about that. We gave the grandparents the rooms at the far end of the long hallways so they could shut their doors and keep the kids out if they need a break. Apparently, my parents will be taking a lot of breaks.

This year, our trip to Utah is a little extra special because my fortieth birthday falls in the middle of it, and despite my requests that no one make a big deal about me on Christmas Day when we should be focused on the kids, I'm sure they have something planned. The highlight of Christmas Eve is Jasper's annual reading of "'Twas the Night Before Christmas," with all the women fawning over his sexy British accent. I swear he plays it up even more than usual because they love it so much.

Christmas morning begins before dawn for the parents of the youngest kids. The doors to my sisters' rooms remain closed until after nine o'clock, which feels like noon to the rest of us.

The best part of having everyone together is that the kids have one another to keep themselves entertained while we make sure no one gets hurt. My older nieces and nephews, along with Logan and Maddie, are endlessly patient with the little ones, but they're ready to check out by noon to ski for a few hours at Brian Head, with Trent and Hugh leading the excursion in two of the SUVs we rented. They promise to be back for dinner.

Later that afternoon, I'm sitting next to my mom on the sofa when she gets a text that has her flushing and sitting up straight.

"What's wrong?"

"Oh, um, your dad needs me."

"For what?"

"Ah, nothing."

She gets up and scurries off to their room while I glance at Ellie for insight.

"I don't want to know," she says, "and neither do you."

Good point.

While the kids play with new toys and their parents nap on the sofas in the big great room, I take a minute to check my messages for the first time all day. I'm replying to an influx of birthday wishes and roasts from old friends when I look up to see Domenic tossing something into the air.

When I realize what he's playing with, I do a double take. "Mo! *Marlowe!* Come here!"

Hayden looks up, annoyed that my bellowing ruined his snooze. "What the hell, Flynn?"

"Look at Dom."

Hayden redirects his gaze toward the child and chokes out a laugh when he sees what I saw.

"*Marlowe!*"

Mo comes running from one of the adjoining rooms. "What's wrong?"

"What's your son playing with?"

She looks and then lets out a shriek. "*Sebastian Lowe, I'm going to kill you!*" Marlowe grabs the large butt plug out of the air after Domenic tosses it up. She runs from the room while Hayden and I laugh until we cry.

Domenic chases after his mother, wailing that she stole his toy.

"What's so funny?" Nat and Aileen ask when they join us.

Of course we tell them, and within seconds, the whole group is hysterically laughing.

"Do they honestly think there's gonna be time for such things on this trip?" Kris asks.

"Seb was probably hopeful," Jasper says with a chuckle. "Delusional, but hopeful."

I text Marlowe. *Come back so we can laugh to your face rather than behind your back.*

I quit this family.

I can't stop laughing as I convey her message to the others. We start a singsong request for Marlowe to come here. "*Mo! We* love *you. Come* here!"

Five minutes of singing later, she appears, her face beet red and twisted with mortification.

"Aw, there she is," I say, grinning at her.

She's not amused.

"Has anyone seen Sebastian?" Hayden asks.

"I just threw his dead carcass in the dumpster," Marlowe says. "What was he thinking bringing that stuff or leaving it where little hands could find it?"

"What was who thinking?" Sebastian asks when he comes into the room, unaware that he's caught up in a scandal.

"*You!* Your son was just juggling a plug."

"I've told him not to play with the electricity."

"Not that kind of plug!"

The rest of us are dying with laughter as he finally gets what she's telling him.

"*Oh.*"

"You were feeling pretty hopeful about this getaway, huh, pal?" Emmett says.

Seb shrugs, looking sheepish. "What can I say? A guy can dream."

"How in the hell did your son find it?" Marlowe asks.

I love how Domenic is suddenly his father's son.

"I don't know. It was buried in my suitcase with some other... *Oh shit!*"

He takes off running, with Marlowe in hot pursuit, while the rest of us laugh until we're weak. Best Christmas ever.

That night, after dinner, everyone I love best in the world sings "Happy Birthday" to me while my three oldest kids sit with me to blow out enough candles to set off the smoke alarm. Thankfully, that doesn't happen, but I'm sure it was a close call.

"Thank you, everyone, and especially Natalie and my girls for baking my cake."

"Daddy," Scarlett says, "is forty old?"

The question is met with an uproar of laughter.

"It's pretty old, pumpkin. Do you still love me?"

"I'll always love you."

Her sweetness nearly brings me to tears.

"Ahem," Aimee says when she stands, holding her wineglass. "I'd like to make a toast to my *baby* brother, who officially becomes an adult today—finally."

Everyone applauds while I roll my eyes at her.

"It's nice to have you join our ranks in the forties, where you'll soon find that everything hurts and sags, and nothing works the way it used to."

"My stuff works *just fine*, I'll have you know."

"Blowhard," Hayden says.

I shrug. "I'm just sayin'... Ask Natalie."

"Leave me out of this," Nat says, laughing.

"Anyway," Aimee says, "despite all the nonsense that goes on in this group, we do, in fact, love you very much, and we hope the forties are your favorite decade yet. Cheers to Flynn at forty!"

"Cheers to Flynn at forty!"

"What does it say about us that our baby is *forty*?" Dad asks Mom.

"That we're older than dirt."

"Speak for yourself!" Dad says to more laughter.

"Your dirt is older than mine," Mom reminds him.

"Now that's just rude."

Their loving banter is the best gift I could've received for my birthday. That they're back on track is a huge relief to all of us, even if we're asking no questions about where they keep disappearing to.

After all the little ones are put to bed for the night, exhausted after a long, busy day, the rest of us settle in for the other thing I wanted for my birthday—a viewing of the final cut of *Valiant*.

With Olivia seated next to Natalie, I reach across my wife to squeeze my sister-in-law's hand. "You ready for this, pal?"

"As ready as I'll ever be."

"You're brilliant, and soon, the whole world will know it."

"That's the part that scares me."

Natalie puts her arm around her sister and holds her close as the movie begins. She knows the first thirty minutes will be hard to watch as the attack perpetrated on her by former Nebraska Governor Oren Stone plays out on screen. Hayden and Jasper used every tool in their considerable arsenal to handle this part of the story with as much care and sensitivity as they possibly could.

Even still, it's devastating to watch the realization that the children fifteen-year-old Natalie came to babysit aren't there, and neither is their mother. Olivia does an amazing job of conveying the fear and horror as Natalie, known as April Genovese then, begins to understand she's in big trouble.

"Should we pause it?" I ask Nat, who has her face pressed to my chest.

"No, I'm okay. I knew what to expect."

"That doesn't make seeing it any easier."

"No, it doesn't."

After a days-long ordeal that's conveyed in a sequence of shots taken from a distance, Stone takes her by the face and says her family will be ruined if she tells anyone what went on there.

April leaves the governor's mansion, where she was held captive for an entire weekend, and goes straight to the police station to report the assault, the first in a number of brave moves. Next, we're in the hospital, where a shattered young woman awaits the arrival of her parents, only to realize they're not there to support her but to condemn her for daring to say such things about her father's boss and best friend.

They leave her alone and broken.

She's taken in by a kindly police officer and his family, who care for her through the trial, as she fearlessly testifies against the man who stole her innocence. He's convicted, sent to prison and later murdered by another inmate.

"You're so good, Livvy," Natalie whispers to her sister. "I'm so proud of you."

"I'm so proud of *you*," Olivia says softly.

Next, we see April in a lawyer's office, spending five thousand dollars, raised for her by people who supported her case against Oren Stone, to purchase a new identity.

April becomes Natalie Bryant, and the first thing she does under her new name is go to college.

I helped to write the screenplay and supervised every aspect of the project as an executive producer. And still... it's heart-wrenching to watch it play out on screen. I begin to fear a backslide for my precious wife, who'll be forced to relive the horrors of the past repeatedly in the coming months as the film is released to the public with a massive publicity campaign. What if I've made a big mistake pursuing this project? The thought of that makes me feel queasy even as I prepare to watch the best day of my life unfold onscreen.

We see Natalie graduate from college and move to New York City to become a teacher.

Olivia brings to life her sister's courage and moxie with such convincing skill. We see her in class with her kids, on walks in the city with her dog, Fluff, and in her cozy apartment with her roommate, Leah.

"There I am!" Leah says. "Let the games begin!"

That makes everyone laugh, which is a relief after the grueling first half of the film.

"This is where things get good," Natalie says, smiling at me as we see her and Fluff out for a walk on the frigid January morning when both our lives changed forever.

Fluff breaks loose and charges into the park where Hayden and I are filming. Natalie chases after her precious pup and ends up crashing into me and falling to the pavement. I'm played by Larkin Wilder, an exciting new actor making his debut in this film. I expect him to be a big star, too. He's almost as handsome as I was at that time, a funny thought I keep to myself, so I won't be ruthlessly mocked.

When I lean in to help her, the dog portraying Fluff latches on to my arm, biting me harder than she should be able to.

"Actor Flynn is way hotter than the real thing," Hayden says.

"Funny, I was just thinking the same thing about actor Hayden."

"Boys," Addie says, "be nice."

"That's us being nice," Hayden tells his wife.

"Hush," Natalie says. "This is the good part."

The actors stare at each other, *almost* capturing the magic of the first moments between me and Nat. I say "almost" because nothing can do justice to the reality. I can still remember the feeling of being struck by lightning and the absolute certainty that if I let her get away, I'd regret it forever.

My character chases after her, calling her name while Hayden's character shouts at me to get back to work. I keep running, fearing she'll slip away before I get the chance to know her. I remember that feeling of urgency, as if my whole life depended on whatever happened next with her, and Larkin does a great job of giving me a slightly frazzled, desperate appearance.

She's afraid I want to sue her because Fluff bit me.

That's the least of what I want from her.

We go to Gorman's coffee shop—everything from that day was filmed on location in Greenwich Village during a freezing January day last year. The coffee shop's owner, Cleo, plays herself when we come in and cause a stir with the staff and patrons, who immediately recognize me. I go through the motions with Cleo, take some photos and sign autographs, annoyed that it's cutting into my time with Natalie.

By the time we're seated at a table with everyone in the place watching us, I've used up most of the thirty minutes I told Hayden I needed.

I ask her to dinner.

She's skeptical of my motives.

"I won't sleep with you."

The room erupts into cheers for Natalie.

"Go, girl," Aimee says.

"I'm not asking you to," I reply.

She's embarrassed.

I persuade her to have dinner with me, get her address and phone number and leave her with promises to pick her up at seven.

Hayden is furious when I return to the park. He says she's an infant and I have no business messing with her. That's true for many reasons, the biggest of which—the BDSM—isn't part of this story, and even though he's right, I'm not going to change my plans. I need to see her again as soon as possible.

"This is truly outstanding, guys," Mom says when we take a bath-room-and-beverage-refill break. "Even though I know the story, I still can't wait to see what happens next."

"How're you doing?" I quietly ask Nat while the others are occupied.

"I'm okay. It brings it all back—the ugly and the wonderful."

I kiss the back of her hand. "I remember every second of the wonderful."

"Me, too. I still can't believe it actually happened."

"Believe it, and it's been a dream come true every day since then."

"*Almost* every day," she says, smiling.

"Right." The rest of the world doesn't know about the time we nearly ended things over the secrets I kept from her about my affinity for the BDSM lifestyle, and they never will. That part belongs only to us. "It all led to where we are now, and that's the best place ever."

She leans her head on my shoulder. "Yes, it is."

"Our Livvy is going to be a big star."

"I know. I'm not sure how to feel about that."

"We'll take good care of her. Don't worry."

The others return to the sectional sofa, eager to see the rest of the film. They get to see me pick her up in the Bugatti, our first date at my New York apartment, how we ordered the same food and watched *The Sound of Music.* It was all so sweet and innocent, which was so far removed from how I lived my life then. She's shocked when I ask her to be my date at the Golden Globes, where I'm nominated for my performance in *Camouflage,* before I take her home to think about whether she wants to come to LA with me if she can get the time off.

We get to see the moment where Hayden again tells me I've got no business messing with a sweet young school teacher, that I'm going to ruin her orderly life. I make the huge mistake of listening to him and decide to take a step back from her.

Until she calls me and asks for a favor. Will I visit her friend Aileen, who's sick with breast cancer and has a huge crush on me, according to Aileen's son, Logan, who's Natalie's student.

"Think about everything that came from that first meeting," Logan says in the deepening voice that still comes as such a surprise to me. His mom is now married to Kristian because of the friendship we formed with Aileen and her family that day.

"That story would make for another great movie," Kris says with a smile for his wife.

"I still can't believe someone is playing *me* in a movie," Aileen says with a giggle.

Natalie and I have our first kiss outside Aileen's apartment building. An hour with her has shown me that a lifetime without her would be unbearable. I don't care what I have to give up to be with her.

We go to LA for the Golden Globes. She meets my parents, played by Max and Stella, the Godfrey family and Marlowe, played by a stunning redheaded actress.

"I'm so hot," Marlowe says.

"You know it, babe," Seb replies. "Hottest babe on the planet."

"He has to say that," Hayden teases.

We see Natalie put her feet in the Pacific for the first time and enjoy being styled for the big night. Everything about her is dazzled by the things she sees and experiences on her first trip to LA.

"You captured the feeling of that weekend so perfectly, Liv," she tells her sister.

"Thanks to all the conversations we had about it."

After I win the Golden Globe, she's one of the people I thank, setting off a buzz about the woman Flynn Godfrey brought to the event. I'm notorious for saying I'd never marry again after the disaster that was my first marriage, and people can see that this new relationship is different. The media frenzy is far worse than expected.

I arrange for security for Natalie and Leah in New York when we return to the city.

She goes back to work, and the press finds her there.

It's out of control, and then...

The lawyer who arranged her new identity sells her out to the tabloids, and the whole sordid tale with Stone is made public.

While her nightmare plays out for all the world to see, she loses her job, and I'm plunged into the kind of rage I've rarely experienced as I do everything in my power to mitigate the damage.

But it's too late. The damage is done. Her life in New York is ruined, and I'm heartbroken to be the cause of that.

"Ugh, I can still remember every second of that day," I whisper to her. "I've never been that angry in my life."

"I remember the shock of it all and realizing that only one person could've done that to me—the only one who knew me by both names."

All that plays out on screen, as well as my famous friends posting #TeamNatalie hashtags and support for her and other assault survivors. It's a PR nightmare, but Nat... Once she recovers from the initial shock of her story going public, she's serene and resolved to get on with her life as it is now, and the most amazing part of it is that she doesn't blame me for what happened.

She's comforting me, rather than the other way around.

Leah brings Fluff to her at my apartment, and we hunker down there, until I decide we need to get her out of New York to protect her from the media camped out at my place and hers. I set up a dinner with her students so she can say goodbye to them in one of the most emotionally charged scenes in the film, the one I think could win Olivia an Oscar, and then we fly to LA to hide out at Hayden's place at the beach.

I'm as agitated as I've ever been watching her become tabloid fodder, while she seems to have found her Zen about it all. It's a relief, she says, that people know. She doesn't have to worry about it blowing up out of the blue when she's unprepared and without the support of me and my savvy team.

Her calm approach is a revelation to me. Whereas I expected her to leave me, she digs in and fights for the life she wants with me. The most beautiful thing to come from the turmoil is the longed-for reunion between Natalie and the two sisters she lost when her parents turned their backs on her.

I ask her to marry me because I can't imagine a single day without her, and she accepts. I want to get married right away. She thinks I'm crazy, as do my friends, who urge me to consider a prenup. There'll be no prenup in this marriage. Everything I have is hers.

"Aww," Addie says. "So romantic."

"And *so* delusional," Emmett adds, making everyone laugh.

"When you know, you know," I tell him.

We stun the world a few days later with the announcement that Flynn Godfrey married Natalie Bryant in Las Vegas.

I've never been happier in my life than I am with my new wife.

Love wins.

Fade to black.

An epilogue fills in the rest of the story—how her father murdered the lawyer who sold her out, not for betraying Natalie, but because the whole world now knew what a scumbag his precious Oren Stone really was. Martin Genovese was convicted of first-degree murder and sentenced to life in prison with no chance of parole.

Natalie Godfrey, along with her husband, Academy Award® winner Flynn Godfrey, are the founders and cochairs of the Flynn and Natalie Godfrey Foundation for Childhood Hunger. They live with their four children in Los Angeles.

"I love how Nat comes first there," Hayden says.

I insisted on that. "It's her story. I'm just a supporting character."

"Hardly," Nat says.

The name OLIVIA BRYANT appears on the screen, and we go wild, cheering and whistling. We're all in tears over the power of her performance. After their father was convicted, the "girls" changed their last name to the one Natalie chose for her new life.

"It's the best thing we've ever done," Hayden says bluntly. "No contest."

I wipe away tears that have taken me by surprise. I had no idea what it would feel like to relive the full story this way. Safe to say the impact of it all put together is beyond powerful.

"I hope you're ready for superstardom, Liv," Marlowe says. "You've got the goods, girlfriend."

"You're magic on film," Jasper adds.

"Y'all." Olivia contends with a flood of tears. "Thank you for the opportunity, the support, the encouragement... I couldn't have gotten through this without Candace and everyone in this room. And my courageous sister Natalie..." She shakes her head. "There simply are no words to convey my admiration and love for you."

We respond to that with a round of applause for my beautiful wife.

"Stawp it." She laughs as she wipes away tears. "Cheers to my amazing sisters and my brilliant, talented husband, as well as Hayden, Jasper, Kris and everyone at Quantum, who turned our story into a passion project that'll hopefully mean the world to our babies someday."

"There's no doubt they'll love it as much as the rest of us do," Aileen says. "Congrats to all of you, and Nat... My beautiful, brave, wonderful Natalie... I love you so much, and I'm so proud of you and of Olivia for her fearless performance. I know I speak for all of us when I say how honored I am to have been even a small part of such an incredible story."

"Me, too," Logan says. "Having Ms. Bryant for my teacher changed our lives."

"You're making Ms. Bryant cry!" Natalie says.

Logan grins at her. They continue to share a special bond.

"I'm proud of you all," Dad says gruffly. "Your story will be such an inspiration to other survivors, Natalie. Flynn, Hayden, Jasper, Kris, Ellie, everyone at Quantum, another incredible production. You'd better get your monkey suits out for awards season next year. I predict another wild ride."

"Here's hoping," Hayden says. "Thank you for letting us tell your story, Natalie. You and I got off to a rough start way back when, but I hope you know how much I love you and how much we all admire you."

"Right back atcha, friend," Nat says with a warm smile for my best friend.

"A toast," Mom says. "To love, family, friendship and all good things in the New Year."

That's something we can all drink to.

EPILOGUE

Olivia

$\mathcal{H}$ ours after everyone has gone to bed, I'm wide awake in the room I'm sharing with Candace, staring up at the dark ceiling, still processing how it felt to see the completed film for the first time. While we were shooting it last winter, everyone kept saying we were making something truly special, but I had no idea how incredible it would be until I saw the finished cut.

Hayden and Jasper have created magic on film, and that I got to be part of that still amazes me. And terrifies me. The thought of losing the ability to move freely through my life is overwhelming to the point of panic.

I've never had a panic attack before, but I had a friend in high school who used to get them. They're terrifying. My chest is tight, and my throat is closed around a lump of emotion that settled there at some point during the viewing and hasn't let up since.

I'll be shielded as much as possible by my brother-in-love, as Candace and I call him, and his team at Quantum.

But they can only do so much to protect me from the bomb that's about to detonate in my life. It's not like I didn't know that would happen if I signed on to do a film with Quantum, especially in a starring role playing my fearless sister who survived a nightmare and ended up married to a superstar. The media has been ravenous in their coverage of the movie about Flynn Godfrey's wife.

I got my first taste of the madness when I was cast to play Natalie.

The flood of attention was unlike anything I've ever experienced. Flynn has done everything he can to prepare me for what's to come with the release, but I'll be walking through the fire alone in many ways.

Candace turns over in our queen-sized bed. "Why are you staring at the ceiling?"

"How do you know I am?"

"After sharing a room with you for most of our lives, I can tell by your breathing that you're not asleep."

"That's weird."

"Stop deflecting. Why aren't you asleep?"

"Why aren't you?"

"That's another deflection. I guess I'm a little stirred up after seeing it come to life on the screen."

"Me, too."

She reaches over for my hand. "You were *so* good, Livvy. So, so good."

"Thank you."

"I don't know how you were able to get through some of it."

"Any time it felt like too much for me, I reminded myself that Nat actually lived it. Her courage gave me the strength to power through the hard stuff."

"That's a really sweet thing to say. You should tell her that."

"I will if I get the chance."

"I don't want you to be scared. No matter what happens, I'll always be right here, and so will Flynn, Natalie and the others. You're surrounded by an incredibly supportive family and so many friends who've been where you're going and know how to help you through it."

"Thank you for the reminder."

"You've got this. *We've* got this. It's going to be so fun and exciting and all the things."

"If you say so."

"I say so, and I'm the big sister, so I'm always right."

I laugh and give her hand a squeeze. I'm so thankful to have her by my side on what promises to be a wild ride. "Hey, Candy Cane?"

"Ugh with that name."

"It's tradition."

"What do ya want now?"

"Teddy texted to say Merry Christmas and he can't wait to see me when I get home."

"I thought that wasn't going to happen?"

"I dunno. Maybe it is."

"You need to make up your mind and put that poor guy out of his misery."

I have to accept that Larkin is going to marry the gorgeous blonde he's engaged to, and that he hasn't given me a thought since we wrapped filming last year. We'll be together again for weeks promoting the film, but that won't change anything.

Candace is right. I've been leading Teddy on since he first hit me up, but after texting nonstop for days now, I need to decide one way or the other about whether I want to meet him in person.

I've got a lot to look forward to in the next few months. The last thing I need is romantic complications. But Teddy... He's persistent. And kind. Not to mention sexy as hell. Plus, if the gossip sites are to be believed, he hasn't been out with anyone else since we started talking. If he had, it would've made news. He's already a pretty big star, and everything he does—and everyone he does it with—makes news.

My head is spinning as everything I dreamed about seems to be coming true at the same time. I hope I can handle what's about to happen.

Watch for Oliva's Quantum Series story MOMENTOUS, coming in 2026!

. . .

WELL, WHAT DO YOU KNOW? QUANTUM IS BACK—AND IN ADDITION TO expanding that universe, we're spinning off to a new series featuring the Remington family, divorce attorneys to the stars! I've been percolating on that idea for ages, and I'm thrilled to be finally getting the chance to move forward with Julian's story, ACRIMONIOUS, followed by CONTENTIOUS, to start with.

This new cast of siblings is determined to AVOID the trappings of true love at all costs after withstanding a protracted custody battle between their parents. Not to mention, they spend their days dismantling happily never afters... But we all know what happens when true love comes a'calling... Even the hardest hearts can't resist destiny. Watch for ACRIMONIOUS, Book 1 in the Remington & Sons Series, coming soon!

While I was writing ILLUSTRIOUS and planning the first Remington family story, also set in Los Angeles, the City of Angels was devastated by massive wildfires that changed so many lives in the course of a few days. My heart broke for everyone who lost their lives, their homes, their businesses and so many other precious things that can never be replaced. I've been donating to fire relief causes and will continue to do so. I urge you to do the same, if you're able. Here are some worthy causes:

- Los Angeles Area Food Bank: *https://secure.lafoodbank.org*
- Emergency Network Los Angeles: *https://enla.org/donate*
- California Community Foundation Wildfire Recovery Fund: *https://www.calfund.org/funds/wildfire-recovery-fund/*
- Los Angeles Fire Department Foundation: *https://support-lafd.kindful.com/?campaign=1040812*
- American Red Cross: *https://www.redcross.org/donate*

Your generosity is so very much appreciated.

Thank you for reading ILLUSTRIOUS and coming along as I reopened a door I thought had been closed for good back in 2019.

Alas, it turns out I had much more to say about the Quantum family! Being back with this group again was such a treat, a visit with dear old friends whom I'd truly missed. And to see their ranks explode with kids and chaos... That was fun to write, as was Max and Stella's story. There they were cruising toward their fiftieth anniversary with hardly a bump in the road. Whoops, not so fast!

I loved every second of writing this book, which was inspired by the photo of my parents' best friends, Bob and Arlene Bouley, the night before their 1958 wedding that's on the cover of this book. Once I saw that amazing photo, all I could think about was using it on a book cover. It's got such an old-time Hollywood vibe to it that it immediately led me to Max and Stella.

Thank you so much to my buddy Arlene, about to be ninety-eight and still going strong, as well as my "Bouley sisters," Linda, Shelley, Rita and Robynne, for their enthusiastic support of my desire to use their parents' iconic photo on the cover of this book. Our families have been friends since the '80s, and we've shared so many good times and laughs. We like to think that Bob is at happy hour in heaven with my parents, whooping it up the way they did when they were here with us. Much love to the Bouleys, friends who've become family.

Join the ILLUSTRIOUS Reader Group at *www.facebook.-com/groups/illustriousreaders/* to talk about this new book with spoilers allowed, and the Quantum Series Group at *www.facebook.-com/groups/QuantumReaders/* to keep up with news about Olivia's story. Finally, make sure you join the Remington & Sons Series Reader Group at *www.facebook.com/groups/remingtonseries/* to hear more about ACRIMONIOUS, CONTENTIOUS and other upcoming books in this exciting new series!

Listen to Jasper read 'Twas The Night Before Christmas right here: *https://geni.us/NePMEsM.*

As always, thank you to the incredible team that supports me every day, beginning right here at home with Dan the man, who does everything he can to keep things running smoothly all around us so I can focus on writing books. No job is too big or too small for him, and he gets it done!

Thank you to Julie Cupp, Lisa Cafferty, Jean Mello, Emily Force, Nikki Haley and Ashley Lopez for being on Team Jack and making it all happen. My incredible editors, Linda Ingmanson and Joyce Lamb, as well as my ace beta readers Anne Woodall, Kara Conrad and Tracey Suppo, are all THE BEST. Thank you to the Quantum Series beta readers for coming out of retirement to read this new book: Gwen, Karina, Sarah, Jennifer, Gina and Amy.

And to you, my devoted readers, thank you for your love of my books and for always supporting me, no matter where the muse leads me next. Much love to all of you!

Marie

ALSO BY MARIE FORCE

Contemporary Romances Available from Marie Force

The Quantum Series

Book 1: Virtuous *(Flynn & Natalie)*

Book 2: Valorous *(Flynn & Natalie)*

Book 3: Victorious *(Flynn & Natalie)*

Book 4: Rapturous *(Addie & Hayden)*

Book 5: Ravenous *(Jasper & Ellie)*

Book 6: Delirious *(Kristian & Aileen)*

Book 7: Outrageous *(Emmett & Leah)*

Book 8: Famous *(Marlowe & Sebastian)*

Book 9: Illustrious *(Max & Stella)*

Book 10: Momentous *(Olivia's story, coming 2026)*

The Gansett Island Series

Book 1: Maid for Love *(Mac & Maddie)*

Book 2: Fool for Love *(Joe & Janey)*

Book 3: Ready for Love *(Luke & Sydney)*

Book 4: Falling for Love *(Grant & Stephanie)*

Book 5: Hoping for Love *(Evan & Grace)*

Book 6: Season for Love *(Owen & Laura)*

Book 7: Longing for Love *(Blaine & Tiffany)*

Book 8: Waiting for Love *(Adam & Abby)*

Book 9: Time for Love *(David & Daisy)*

Book 10: Meant for Love *(Jenny & Alex)*

Book 10.5: Chance for Love, *A Gansett Island Novella (Jared & Lizzie)*

Book 11: Gansett After Dark *(Owen & Laura)*

Book 12: Kisses After Dark *(Shane & Katie)*

Book 13: Love After Dark *(Paul & Hope)*

Book 14: Celebration After Dark *(Big Mac & Linda)*

Book 15: Desire After Dark *(Slim & Erin)*

Book 16: Light After Dark *(Mallory & Quinn)*

Book 17: Victoria & Shannon (Episode 1)

Book 18: Kevin & Chelsea (Episode 2)

A Gansett Island Christmas Novella *(Appears in Mine After Dark)*

Book 19: Mine After Dark *(Riley & Nikki)*

Book 20: Yours After Dark *(Finn & Chloe)*

Book 21: Trouble After Dark *(Deacon & Julia)*

Book 22: Rescue After Dark *(Mason & Jordan)*

Book 23: Blackout After Dark *(Full Cast)*

Book 24: Temptation After Dark *(Gigi & Cooper)*

Book 25: Resilience After Dark *(Jace & Cindy)*

Book 26: Hurricane After Dark *(Full Cast)*

Book 27: Renewal After Dark *(Duke & McKenzie)*

Book 28: Delivery After Dark *(2025)*

Downeast

Dan & Kara: A Downeast Prequel

Homecoming: A Downeast Novel

The Wild Widows Series—a Fatal Series Spin-Off

Book 1: Someone Like You *(Roni & Derek)*

Book 2: Someone to Hold *(Iris & Gage)*

Book 3: Someone to Love *(Winter & Adrian)*

Book 4: Someone to Watch Over Me *(Lexi & Tom)*

Book 5: Someone to Remember *(2025)*

Book 2: How Much I Care *(Maria & Austin)*

Book 3: How Much I Love *(Dee's story)*

Nochebuena, A Miami Nights Novella

Book 4: How Much I Want *(Nico & Sofia)*

Book 5: How Much I Need *(Milo & Gianna)*

Single Titles

In the Air Tonight

Five Years Gone

One Year Home

Sex Machine

Sex God

Georgia on My Mind

True North

The Fall

The Wreck

Love at First Flight

Everyone Loves a Hero

Line of Scrimmage

Romantic Suspense Novels Available from Marie Force

The Fatal Series*

One Night With You, *A Fatal Series Prequel Novella*

Book 1: Fatal Affair

Book 2: Fatal Justice

Book 3: Fatal Consequences

Book 3.5: Fatal Destiny, *the Wedding Novella*

Book 4: Fatal Flaw

Book 5: Fatal Deception

Book 6: Fatal Mistake

Book 7: Fatal Jeopardy

Book 8: Fatal Scandal

Book 9: Fatal Frenzy

Book 10: Fatal Identity

Book 11: Fatal Threat

Book 12: Fatal Chaos

Book 13: Fatal Invasion

Book 14: Fatal Reckoning

Book 15: Fatal Accusation

Book 16: Fatal Fraud

Sam and Nick's story continues...

Book 1: State of Affairs

Book 2: State of Grace

Book 3: State of the Union

Book 4: State of Shock

Book 5: State of Denial

Book 6: State of Bliss

Book 7: State of Suspense

Book 8: State of Alert

Book 9: State of Retribution *(2025)*

Book 10: State of Preservation *(2025)*

Historical Romance Available from Marie Force

The Gilded Series*

Book 1: Duchess by Deception

Book 2: Deceived by Desire

* Completed Series

ABOUT THE AUTHOR

Marie Force is the #1 *Wall Street Journal* best-selling author of more than 100 contemporary romance, romantic suspense and erotic romance novels. Her series include Fatal, First Family, Gansett Island, Butler Vermont, Quantum, Treading Water, Miami Nights and Wild Widows.

    Her books have sold 15 million copies worldwide, have been translated into more than a dozen languages and have appeared on the *New York Times* bestseller list more than 30 times. She is also a *USA Today* bestseller, as well as a Spiegel bestseller in Germany.

    Her goals in life are simple—to spend as much time as she can with her "kids" who are now adults, to keep writing books for as long as she possibly can and to never be on a flight that makes the news.

    Join Marie's mailing list on her website at *marieforce.com* for news about new books and upcoming appearances in your area. Follow her on Facebook, at *www.Facebook.com/MarieForceAuthor*, Instagram *@marieforceauthor* and TikTok *@marieforceauthor*. Contact Marie at *marie@marieforce.com*.

www.ingramcontent.com/pod-product-compliance
Lightning Source LLC
Chambersburg PA
CBHW070438220325
23751CB00004B/10